THE EDGE OF THE SAND

by

P. M. Nugent

Song lyrics/poetry on the following pages are from:

Pictures on the nightstand, TV's on in the den
Your house is waiting, your house is waiting
For you to walk in, for you to walk in
But you're missing, you're missing
You're missing when I shut out the lights
You're missing when I close my eyes
You're missing when I see the sun rise
You're missing

Bruce Springsteen, <u>You're Missing</u> (2002)

One

August 5, 2010

She didn't come back that day. It was a Saturday, right before Memorial Day. May 27, 2000. The day she didn't come back.

That was over ten years ago.

I can still see her strolling away from the little yellow house we were renting that summer in Belmar, the dog at her side, me watching and waving from the open window of our second-floor bedroom, the screen long gone.

The house was on the beach block of 19th Avenue, close to the ocean and not far from the railroad station. It was going to be our first summer, really our first time, living together. As a couple I mean. As in committed to each other. As in for real.

An hour after they left, too long even for their long walks, the dog came back into view. I still feel the soft warm breezes of that blue-sky morning as I leaned out the window. Overhead, the seagulls soared drunkenly in the early heat, laughing at their lame jokes. The drapes framed me, floating back into the room, reaching for the bed, still askew from the night before. The dog dragged the leash connected to her collar. It stretched lifeless on the ground behind her.

Maureen, my Mo, wasn't at the other end of the leash.

The dog lumbered up to the front door. On the stoop directly below me, she raised her head and whined to be let in. I looked back up the street.

Mo wasn't there.

The train whistle punctures this bad dream as the train slows down. From the window, the Belmar station crawls into view. I see them in the small, narrow parking lot bordering the platform. Johnny Bosco resting against his faded green Chevy, his wiry hair reaching for the sky, his arms crossed over his paunch. He has a job for me with his newspaper, as free-lance and off-chance as it might be. Even announced my return on the front page. Louisa, her sharp elbow shooting from the passenger seat, her pale face inside the shade of the car, watches the train roll in, her big eyes wide.

The train crunches gears and screeches and shudders to a stop. The doors won't open at first, and I wait between cars. They open at last with an aching groan. I step down onto the platform into the close heat of a summer day, a beat-up dufflebag hanging from my shoulder, its airline and bus tags flapping.

I can smell the ocean even from here. I inhale long and hard. I hug Johnny, and he grunts his welcome. I squat down at the window and smile in at Louisa.

"Isa …" I say. I say it like she wants it said, *Eesah.* "I …"

She nods and smiles back, reaching out to touch my cheek. "It's alright, Bernie. Get in."

I get in the back behind her and sit next to Maureen's old dog. Bosco had kept her all these years. She licks my face when I grab her jaw and gets close to rub noses. She blinks and sizes me up and then puts her head down with a loud sigh.

I'm back.

But coming back isn't the same as coming home. Maureen was home. And she's not here.

I gaze out the side window as Bosco pulls away from the platform. Standing at a metal bench on our side of the tracks is a stooped, slight figure watching us drive off, the face shrouded under an oversized, gray, hooded sweatshirt, a notebook clutched in a bony hand barely visible from a tattered sleeve. I twist around and watch the solitary figure recede into the distance.

Two

I'm standing on the boardwalk a couple days later. It's Sunday morning. It's 1 a.m.

Saturday night's been chased away by a hard rain. The wet, gleaming wooden road under my feet runs up the shore maybe 3 miles to Bruce Springsteen's Asbury Park, and it heads south another 20 to Seaside Heights, where they filmed that freak show *Jersey Shore*.

But, this place, it's saintly. In his concerts, Springsteen sometimes tells an apocryphal story about a late-night walk on a boardwalk like this. Back on a Friday night, September 3, 1971, the night the music gods ordained that he meet Clarence Clemons.

He and Stevie Van Zandt went out after a gig at one of the bars that used to pack Asbury Park near the ocean those days, the Student Prince on Kingsley. Things weren't going right for the band. It had been a bad night. They hit the boardwalk to air out.

It was as if winter showed up early, Bruce says when he's telling the story from the stage. It was black and cold, with harsh rain and mist blowing. Bruce and Stevie walked these boards toward the north, smoking the cigarettes cupped in their hands as they sucked in the fix, complaining how the band just didn't yet have enough juice to break out.

After walking a while, they looked up. There, where the boardwalk disappeared into gray murk at the horizon, a huge man appeared. They stopped dead in their tracks, nowhere to go. To their left, the boarded-up shops and amusement stands of a fading town and time. To their right, pale, dead sand. Beyond that, a dark roaring, angry ocean they couldn't see.

They panicked. They hustled to an unlit alcove of an abandoned five and dime and hid. They heard the man's steps, and the ground beneath them trembled and shook. The Big Man came closer. He stopped in front of the alcove, the rain crossing sideways behind him, the storm from the heavens raging about them. He was black and badass, as large as beach life and summer, with silver bolts in his ears glistening in the dim light from the boardwalk lamps behind him. He wore a white suit, Bruce says. And in his hand was a saxophone.

The man looked over to the shivering, poor white boys huddled in the dark, his massive hand extended. "I'm Clarence Clemons. I've come to join your band."

Bruce's eventual group of misfits, the E Street Band, was named after E Street, which runs north and south just five blocks from where I'm standing now on Belmar's boardwalk. It occurred to Bruce, that name, when he was sitting one time at the stop sign at 10th and E, before heading to David Sancious's place at 1105 E Street, where Bruce and the boys sometimes rehearsed in the early days before Clarence joined. Sancious played keyboards on the first two breakout E Street albums in the early '70s before Bittan joined.

Rain stings my face like I'm sure it did that night when Bruce and Clarence met. I have to squint to find the ocean waves. They're there, all right, I hear them. I feel their thunder. I can barely see them in the gloom.

I look north, from where Clarence appeared that holy night and see only faded-green boardwalk lamplights soldier one by one into the distance, disappearing into the night. I look south, past the brightly lit Dunkin' Donuts, a few locals and castoffs making it home, past JR's Beach Grill, past EJ's variety store and 3 Brother's Pizza, past D J'ais a couple blocks away, its sign still lit but its electronic dance music now silent, its bars emptied at this stupid hour.

Maybe I came back here, ten years after I left, hoping my magic would walk out of the muddy night and down these boards and join me. Maybe I'm here to find the juice that I'm missing. Maybe I'm here for that that human touch.

I search for the waves out there. Rain bounces off the plastic lid of my coffee cup, making a pitter-patter sound. I inhale slowly, taking it all in.

It's good to breathe that ocean, good to taste that saltwater air, good and right to feel that big and free space beyond the ocean. Behind me, as I gaze out over the sand, 16th Avenue stretches west. To the Garden State Parkway and the Jersey Turnpike that go up north to Newark and New York City a hour and a half away and down south all the way to Cape May at the tip of New Jersey. An hour west behind me, beyond the parkway and the turnpike, is Philly.

Sixteenth, like other Belmar streets, is pockmarked with empty lots, cottages, and bungalows that explode with partiers in the summer and sulk in the winter. Here and there, as some money creeps into a suspect town, new and fixed-up homes pop up, some with grand decks and views, some with windows and doors claiming to be sealed against the elements. Most of those hermitages are occupied in the summer, but more and more have year-round residents.

Behind me I hear rise up the moan of the train that dropped me here two days ago. It's a slow train, leaving New York City's Penn Station almost two hours ago. It stops at Belmar on its way south to Bay Head just above Seaside Heights.

I still find comfort in that train sound. It's a familiar voice telling a sad story you've heard before, one that never gets old. During the summer months, the drunks flop off and stumble back on as the party weekends begin and end. During the winter, that train cries its lonely sob as it begs for company from town to town.

I close my eyes, my chest rising and falling with the waves, the rain hitting my face, the moan aching out loud. I listen to the wind that whines and the waves that choke out on the shoreline. I breathe in. Let it out.

I head back into the Dunkin' Donuts. Isa is inside. She shakes her head at me as I return to the seat across the Day-Glo orange table from her. She's waiting for me. She's always been waiting for me, it seems.

"You all right?" she asks.

I nod.

"Drink some more coffee, then. You need it."

I wipe my face and pull from my poncho one of those shirt-pocket-sized Moleskine lined journals from Italy, the ones Hemingway used, and my sole luxury in life if you don't count my way-too-expensive scotches. I find its sidekick pen and push back my hood. I think for a moment, watch Isa watching me, and then I write:

> *nobody reads my poems*
>
> *my coffee's gone stone cold*
>
> *come on, God, just answer me*
>
> *what's that story I been told*

I page back to check the number and write 673 atop this latest effort. I reread the untitled four lines, shrug, and turn the journal around on the table so Isa can read it. I sit back and watch water hit the window behind her and teardrop down the pane.

"I read your poems, Bernie," she says when finished. "I've always read them." Her eyes are moist. They don't blink.

She has milky-white porcelain skin. Ghostlike. Her thin, straight hair is jet black and pink-streaked, and tonight it's pulled back and falls freely halfway down her back. She has pink lips and has chosen from her wardrobe of crimson, purple, black, and bright pink. Today it's a pink halter top that matches the flames in her hair, a short, fitted black skirt, black stockings. Tomorrow it would be a variation on the same.

"You haven't stopped searching for her," she says.

When she gets intent, her bright blue eyes darken, and a few thin blue veins grow just below the translucent skin on her forehead and on her cheeks near her ears. Sometimes, like now, one long blue vein pulses on either side of her long throat. "You need to stop," she says. "She's not here."

"I know."

"We searched everywhere back then, Bernie. We didn't miss anything."

I shrug.

She looks away, and I glance down at my hands. They're clenched around my closed notebook. Thick knuckles, bulging veins. "Gone," I repeat.

"I need to know … Are you back just for her?"

I pull her hand toward me. She lets it stay a while and then withdraws it in the silence.

"I hope not, Isa. I don't know."

She blinks, and then gets up to leave. "I got to get back to my little girl, Bernie."

"I'm glad you're here, Isa."

She leans down and kisses my head. Like I'm pathetic and lost. Like Mo's dog back then.

My cell phone in my jeans pocket goes off as she heads out the door.

Three

"Bernie boy. You ready to work?"

It's Johnny Bosco. I consider hitting off. But besides being apparently pathetic and lost, I'm 44 and need cash. And Bosco promised me some freelance when I came back.

Bosco's the editor at *The Beach Star*, the local paper that covers the Jersey Shore from Asbury Park to Seaside Heights and a few points inland. It's even got an online edition. It breaks big stories like next year's boardwalk repair budget.

We had been friends in the days before I left Belmar, Bosco and me, together at *The Star*. Over the decade I'd been gone I'd done time at *The Philadelphia Enquirer*. Got laid off. Then the *St. Louis Post Dispatch* for a few years. I took a package, meaning I got fired with maybe a couple months' severance. Then I went coastal and online at *The Huffington Post* in Los Angeles for a year or so. That didn't work out.

"You near a police dispatch, Romeo?" he asks. A few people in Belmar call me Romeo. He's one.

"A police dispatch? No, Johnny. It's after midnight. I'm at the Dunkin' Donuts sobering up from D'Jais. And since when do you cover late-breaking crime?"

"Listen up, douche. We got a young woman dead in Shark River Hills. They just found her in the parking lot of the Beach & Yacht Club on South Riverside. On the other side of Shark River Inlet from the Belmar marina, in case you forgot. Just a few minutes from your coffee klatch. Get over there. Do some fuckin reporting. And brighten your disposition. It's a brand-new day, boy."

"How much?"

A pause. "Fifty bucks. A hundred if it has any juice. I got a feeling about this."

"And how much for me to brighten my disposition?"

Before Bosco could tell me where I could stick my disposition, I ended the call.

I smile at nothing in particular and punch the number for Belmar Taxi. I got numbers for taxis in a dozen cities. Belmar Taxi's hasn't changed in 10 years. I was at the yacht club 15 minutes and $4 later.

Four

I get out of the taxi on South Riverside Road and scan the Beach & Yacht Club. It straddles a narrow stretch of land between South Riverside and the Shark River Inlet. From where I stand, the inlet flows away from me almost due east under a couple of local bridges until it empties into the Atlantic Ocean ten minutes away.

The rain has let up, going from big drops to miserable drizzle. Wisps of mist hang suspended over the ground, giving up some of its summer heat. The sky in the east is thick with heavy, gray clouds squatting on a sunrise trying to claw its way up. Across the inlet from the lot lurk a low apartment building and several houses with lighted windows punching through the night. Mast lines slap softly and steadily in the storm's last gasps.

The Shark River Beach & Yacht Club ain't all that. No Thurston Howell the Thirds running around. Mostly Tonys and Howies. A few Juniors. Definitely no Thirds. To my right are a couple of picnic tables, gas pumps for the members, and a two-story shack, the aforementioned "club," that gives slight cover to a junked-up boat shop with just enough room for a grill that serves light fare during the summer. To the left is a cracked pavement parking lot big enough for maybe 30 jammed-in cars. Beyond the lot are the ramps to the floating docks for 50 hard-bitten power boats and a handful of salted sailboats under 28 feet. And then the undulating inlet.

The lot is usually unlit. There are No Parking signs in effect from 10 p.m. until 5 a.m. Except for tonight. Three cop cars have their light bars raking the landscape. They surround a small, red VW Golf with a couple of dents on the back bumper. The cops and the Golf sit at the far left end of the parking lot, right up against tall sea grass, the farthest from the shack.

I tell the cab to wait at the shack, and I join the action. It's a small-town police force around here, lots of part timers and newbies. Just some local guys rubbing their eyes and their heads. And a body bulging under a yellow police tarp. I can get close.

I nod at the Neptune cop standing guard. Neptune's the town next to Belmar, and Shark River's in Neptune's jurisdiction. "Whaddya have here?"

He gives me a once over. "And you are?"

I tell him. He considers it.

"Her license says she's Allison Formosa. Just turned 30. Work ID says she's a librarian in Belmar. Guys here say they know a bookworm named Allison Formosa. She grew up here in Neptune."

"How'd she get like that?" I nod at the mound under the tarp.

He pauses and takes a deep breath. "Pounded to death with that cinderblock." He points to it on the ground between her body and the passenger side of the car.

"It probably came from over there." He points again, this time down the parking lot to a new boat ramp to the floating docks. On the gravel next to the new ramp, a six-foot pile of cinderblocks broods, giving nothing away.

"She was attacked in the darkest park of the lot," I say as I scan the scene. "Had to happen after hours. And no one up on that hill would have seen what was happening down here." I look behind me up a hill on the other side of South Riverside where some darkened houses try to nestle among trees.

The cop nods back at me. "You got it." His eyes return to the tarp. "Her entire head was crushed in. It couldn't have taken too long with that cinderblock. She was just flattened. Had to be a jilted boyfriend. Someone making a point."

The cop stops. He's young, a better fit for beach traffic than this. He won't forget what he's seen tonight. You can tell. He's dazed in a way that isn't going away anytime soon.

An older cop comes over. "What's up?" He's asking the kid but staring at me.

After explanations, the kid moves away, reluctantly taking up sentry duty next to the Golf, leaving me and the old cop behind in the middle of the parking lot.

The remaining cop glances at the tarp, warbling now in a fresh wind. "Completely crushed her head and face. She's unrecognizable." His lips draw in, and he hisses through clenched teeth. "Damn."

"Any other signs of assault? Rape?"

"First appearances? No. But we'll need to get her back for a physical."

"That's her car I'm guessing."

"Yeah. The VW's registered in her name. No keys though, either on her, anywhere around here, or in the car. We had to pick the lock."

We look at the car, waiting for it to tell us something.

"Who called it in?"

"The officer you were talking to. He was driving his beat. Saw the car. Found the body."

We went silent. He shakes his head. "This seems familiar to me. I dunno why." He squints at me. "You recall anything like it? Looks like you been around the bend a few times."

I shake my head back at him. "I've been gone a while."

"Welcome back." He shrugs and walks away.

I move as close to the tarp as I can without anyone yelling at me. The Belmar emergency medical services vehicle suddenly pulls into the lot, probably on loan to Neptune, its emergency lights ablaze as if someone might be saved. Another Neptune cop car follows right behind.

Several men in plainclothes scramble out of the cramped cop car and huddle. They put on gloves, and one of them barks orders, hurrying the rest to get to work before any more rain or mist fucks up his evidence.

A gust of wet wind slaps my face hard and lifts the tarp to reveal a flat, bloody mash above a pink t-shirt. I don't see anything resembling a face. I don't see any eyes where there should be a couple. I don't see a forehead. Or a nose. Or a chin. It's just thick, dark soup with gleams of floating skull that take turns blinking at me in the flashing lights. I feel my stomach knot up. The alcohol from D'Jais and the coffee from Dunkin' splish-splash down below. I yell to the young cop to cover her the fuck back up. He complies, looking over at the water lapping eagerly against the boat hulls. His cheeks puff out. He's trying not to breathe.

I look around and realize I'm not getting much more than what I got. I walk slowly back to my cab and turn to take in the scene one more time before getting in.

Down beyond where the Golf sits and the cops cluster, a dark car suddenly shoots from a lane running down the hillside. Without stopping it turns left onto South Riverside and pulls away, its lights still off. I shout something to the cops, but they don't hear me. The tall sea grass between them and the road leading away would have blocked their view anyway. I say fuck it and pile in back.

The driver's eyes are glazed with drink or sleep, or both, his baseball cap pulled too low over his eyes. He scratches the scruff on his chin. "Where to?'

"Go back down Riverside. After that car."

"What car?"

"Shit, just go."

We pull away in what seems like slow motion, passing by where the tarp bulges out from the broken pavement, its loose edges waving goodbye in the breeze.

We get to the sharp turn that takes us to the East End Avenue bridge back to the beach area. There are no red lights around the bend. The car's disappeared.

"I don't see no car," says the wakening driver.

"Yeah. Take me to the Honeypot."

"Hey I live there off and on. Never seen you, though."

"Yeah. Small world."

I look back as we cross the bridge to the bonfire of flashing cop lights at the yacht club. It hit me then that I worried it was Mo at first. And now I'm sitting here in this stinking back seat relieved it wasn't Mo. But it's stupid crazy to be thinking it might be Mo. Stupid, desperate crazy.

Isa sees that all over me.

Five

I fall into bed after the cab ride from the yacht club. A car's red backlight eyes stare at me in the night. Allie Formosa's face—or what's left of it—peek-a-boos at me from behind a tarp, fragments of skull glistening freakishly like two bright-yellow eyes in the cops' lights.

I lie there seeing Allie, seeing Mo, seeing Allie again, seeing Mo, until sleep comes. I wake up a few restless hours later. It's Sunday. My t-shirt and shorts are drenched with sweat. I make a pot of coffee, take a long shower, and then write up and file my story for the online edition of *The Beach Star* by early afternoon.

Bosco likes it. It has juice. Good description of the body, he says. Especially that glistening soup where a rounded, firm head should be. It cuts. I have 100 bucks coming my way. I can use it.

My story will go live at five p.m. when it's uploaded to *The Star* website. It won't get into actual physical print until next Thursday's weekly edition hits the stand. Bosco tells me to pimp the story to some local news outlets before the story breaks, and I do.

News 12 New Jersey, the TV channel that tries to be local to the entire state, promises to devote a minute to the murder during several spots that evening. The producer I talk to wants to know why a librarian would be lurking about a private yacht club's parking lot in the middle of a summer night. He's nosing for some jollies I ain't got. The daily *Newark Star-Ledger* and *Asbury Park Press* promise to pick up my story in tomorrow's editions, likely without attribution. *The Ledger* editor can't get enough on the devastation to Formosa's face. Everybody else says they'll read the story when it breaks and call me if they need more info. I'm reminded it's a Sunday, after all.

Nobody probes much into the story beyond the headline and potential of sexual foul play. They missed entirely what happened to a special young woman, Alison Formosa.

The digital photo I scam from the head of the town library confirms that Allie was gorgeous. Wide-eyed, calm, tanned, befreckled, tousled, blond hair, gorgeous. She looked like one of those Jersey Shore surfer girls.

From calls I make and some online research, I learn that Allie's been a star all her life, from her days in grammar school at St. Rose's in Belmar, right through St. Rose's High School, then Monmouth University in West Branch four miles north, and finally a master's from Rutgers Newark in library science.

She's worked with kids. She's donated her time to local reading programs for autistic youth. Started book clubs for the elderly at some of the local old age homes and for the bums who populated the transient hotels you always get in beach towns.

Allie dated around. No one special, so far as I could tell. Why she was in a parking lot in a yacht club, her head smashed in with a hunk of cold concrete, was anyone's guess. And just about everyone I spoke to had a guess, most involving Allie giving head to some Thurston Howell the Third.

I scribble a reminder to talk to the old cop from last night. He said he'd seen something like this before, that it was familiar or some such. I hadn't mentioned it in my piece, nor had I said a word to the local news guys.

I wait for the story to go live in my room at the Honeypot on 12th Avenue in Belmar, just a half block off the boardwalk. I'm pacing the room. It's been a while since I've been published.

The Honeypot is an okay place to spend a night, a weekend, maybe a week or two. If you have no friends, no prospects, and no family in the area, that is. It isn't the Morning Dove Inn a couple of blocks inland, overlooking Silver Lake, which got a rave write-up as the "New Jersey Shore's Best Kept Secret." But then, for that matter, it isn't the Belmar Inn on the beach block up on 10th that has more bedbugs than guests. Bedbugs, I'm told, that pay full summer rates, they have it so good.

I know the Honeypot's owner, Weed Niehoff. We did party time together back in the day. When I showed up a few days ago begging for a room, Weed had just let his resident night manager go. So I stepped into that job, and into #60, the night manager's suite. I could do worse. And have.

The suite is nothing close. It's a big corner room on the third floor, the top floor, with wall-to-wall windows that overlook the air vents and circulating fan hoods of the pizzeria that separates the Honeypot from Ocean Avenue, which runs north and south, and the boardwalk that runs parallel to Ocean on the far side. If you ignore the pizzeria's rooftop machinery, actually if you just look over it, you get a rich man's view up and down a wide span of the wide Jersey Shore and the Atlantic. All for no rent, just my night manager duties. Every night from here on 'til I get lucky.

So I've added Dump Night Manager to my lengthy resume.

Weed's uncle, Henry, covers most days. Because he hasn't got not much else to do, he has promised to help me out, especially on the weekends when I need it. If I've got something to do at night and Henry's not available, like last night when I headed to D'Jais with Isa and then the yacht club, the guests, as I loosely call them, can go eat shit, bark at the moon, and wait until I get back if they need me. Most are passed out anyway.

When you enter my room, the wide ocean view is in front of you. That side of my unit has a low bookcase that stretches wall to wall beneath the windows. It's packed with left-behind books, CDs, DVDs, and VHS videos. The half-full scotch and vodka bottles are mine, but the glasses and mugs from various pubs and eateries along the shoreline have also been bequeathed.

On your right are windows that overlook 12th Avenue, which ends at Ocean. Under my 12th Avenue windows sits a wide desk littered with my laptop, speakers for my iPhone, all my chargers, and piles of news clips, print-outs and notebooks. The clean part of my desk multitasks as my dining room, solitaire and puzzle table, and meeting hall.

On the left wall is a closet and chest of drawers, a decent-sized frig, and a short counter congested with a small sink under a wall clock, a well-used George Foreman grill, an ancient microwave that creaks as it cooks, a fancy toaster, and an ice bucket from some Atlantic City hotel. Over and beneath this counter hang peeling cabinets and drawers jammed with a motley assortment of glasses, beer bottle openers, corkscrews, plastic china, and cutlery. My phone booth of a bathroom is on that wall too, its 6" by 6" mirror perpetually fogged.

My new mattress sits on the floor, no frame. It's between the door into the room and the 12th Avenue wall on the right. My big antique rocker, lifted from the Belmar dump, is mint and always waits patiently for me in the middle of the room.

I'm sitting in it now. Rockin. Waiting 'til the clock says five. How long's it been since a by-line of my own? Maybe a year, maybe more. I'm feeling the buzz.

At five, I move to the low stool at my desk and open my laptop. The fuckin thing is taking forever to load. *The Beach Star's* banner fills out. Then, there it is. The story's live, first headline you scroll to. I read it. I read my name, Bernie Ruane. Right there. I read it again.

I stand and pull my rocker to the front windows and sit. Oyster-hued fog had greeted the new day when I got back from the club, and it was still hanging low out there. Yesterday's winds had slowed to an occasional window-rattling gust that whistled through the loose window frames, and the rain had beat it at last. Low thunder growled at me from a big batch of fresh, black clouds down south, coming closer. I try to figure out where the gray beach stops and the gray sand begins. Now and then a white curl of foam, breaking waves, tells me.

I break open a new bottle of 16-year-old Laphroaig Islay single malt scotch and pour a few inches into a glass half-filled with ice. I let the scotch soak up some water, releasing the subtle smell and taste of peat, pears, peaches, and plums, and sit back and take my first mouthful. I breathe in the bouquet as I await night's fall. To me, I say. To the free press.

I see Allie twisted on the ground as I swirl those earthly tastes in my mouth. I wonder what would make someone turn such a pretty face like hers into the soggy, unrecognizable mess I saw last night. With a cinderblock. I wonder how such people come to be.

I swallow the scotch in my mouth. I take more and swallow it harder. The scotch stretches, trying to soothe me. I look up and down the beach.

Nothing's changed out there since I left. A little erosion, but it's the same beach. It's different water but it's doing the same thing it's always done, in and out, up and down. The same horizon waits for the same sun after one more night.

I'm back doing what I was doing when I left. Writing for Bosco. I'm still looking for Mo. I'm still wondering why I come and go, like the waves, searching for something just beyond my reach.

Home, I guess. As close as it gets.

I get up later and go floor by floor, checking the fire doors and securing the front door and the first-floor windows. I peek behind the registration desk to be sure all is locked up and the money we collected that day isn't scattered about. As, I'm told, has sometimes occurred. Once in a while, Weed tells me, I even will find ol' uncle Henry back there, asleep, his head on his arms atop the scant money he has almost finished counting.

I head back up three flights, chatting with a few boarders on the way. No one mentions Allie. They haven't seen the news in who knows how long.

I microwave an egg and cheese sandwich out of a box. I microwave leftover coffee and pour in the half 'n half. Night strolls up at last and settles in with me. I keep odd hours according to people who are forced to keep regular ones. I like odd hours. So sue me.

I go to bed after a few more scotches. I wait for sleep or for someone to push a buzzer downstairs or at the front door, someone who needs something that had better be really important or who needs to sleep it off for the night in a cheap Honeypot room.

All my electronics on the desk shoot eerie shafts of red, green, and white light into my room. The bright numbers on my bedside clock glow in rigid irritation.

Allie starts playing peek-a-boo with me again. I ask her to stop, but she won't hear me. I don't fall asleep until she finally slips back reluctantly under that tarp.

Six

I'm up early the next morning and take a cab to the Neptune police station looking for Nelson. He's the old cop with the memories that I met at the Yacht club.

The lady at the front desk gives me the hairy eyeball like I'm talking French.

"Nel-son," I repeat. "Old guy. He was on duty very early Sunday morning, when the Allison Formosa call came in."

"And who are you?"

"Bernie Ruane. *Beach Star*."

"*Beach Star*? Oh wait, that little newspaper?" She chuckles.

I wait, trying out my baleful glare.

She stares at me some more through the dirty plexi-glass, clearly not having read my hard-hitting piece from the night before. "Hold on," she says at last. She picks up a phone and talks to someone looking at me the whole time.

A cop shows up and takes his turn squinting at me through the glass. "Detective Nelson is off today."

"Can I get his number? I'm working on a story on Allison Formosa."

"Don't think he can talk to you, boss. This is a criminal investigation."

"He mentioned he'd seen a case like this before. Any idea what he was talking about?"

The cop and the lady exchange a knowing, smirking look. "Holy God," says the cop. "Ya never know what Abnormal Norm's talking about."

I must appear crestfallen because he motions me through the door. It buzzes, and I follow the cop down a badly lit hall. We head into a break room. There's an empty coffeepot on a counter by a sink, a large, round, oak table in the center, and an assortment of down-on-their-luck metal and wood chairs. One out of three bulbs works in the light fixture stuck to the ceiling overhead.

He points to a chair. I sit and pull out my reporter's notebook to look official.

"I'm the officer in charge of the case since it came in this morning," he says. "Nelson works the streets part time. Last night was his bad luck it turned out the way it did. He shoulda been home passed out or watching the SyFy channel, poor guy."

Last night was my bad luck too, I think. I had a nice D'Jais buzz at the Dunkin' Donuts and then, bam, nightmares of Allie's peek-a-boo.

"There's been no case like this in or near Neptune," he continues. "I know every homicide that's within an hour's drive, believe me."

His brow collapses into a deep furrow. "Look, I mean, what happened to Formosa was horrible. She was pounded beyond the point of death. I mean, what kind of shit we got here?"

Some sick shit, I think, that's who. That much I figured out last night.

"Right now we're figuring that it's a one-off case, a spurned lover. Or something like that. But you can't print that yet. I'm being my usual friend of the media here."

"Nelson seemed pretty certain," I say.

"I'll talk to him. I've only been on the force five years, maybe he's going way back."

"Since the murder occurred in Monmouth County, the county folk will prosecute, right?"

"Yup."

"And if she were killed outside the county or outside the state?"

"Then that county or state would take the lead."

"Even if she lived here."

"Yup. Doesn't make a difference where you live, boss. Only where you die. As far as the criminal prosecutors are concerned."

"So I've got to get into the county databases to look for cases similar to Formosa."

He looked at the clock on the wall. "Anything else?"

"Ever hear of a Maureen Logan?"

Furrowed brow. "She get iced too?"

"No. I mean, I hope not."

"Who the fuck is she, then?"

"Missing that's all. Did any of your investigators talk to the neighbors around the yacht club Sunday morning?"

"A few. We knocked on doors all day Sunday for that matter."

"Anyone mention a car parked on the street about the time of the murder or shortly thereafter? An unfamiliar car that was gone by sunrise?"

Eyebrows shoot to the ceiling. "No. You see a car?"

I tell him what I saw. Dark car, no lights, pulled out and away. Not sure what it looked like, what color. Couldn't make out the license plate. Lost it when giving chase.

"You didn't report this?" he asks.

I close my notebook. "It was 3 a.m."

"What, suddenly we're closed at 3 a.m.? We'll take your statement now." He nodded at the closed notebook on the table. "You're not leaving anytime soon."

He stops at the door. "You shoulda said something when it happened. You know that. I'm writing that down too." He looks at me like I'm suddenly stinking the room out and then leaves.

I stare back at the empty doorway and wait.

Seven

I escaped the Neptune cops after a short statement and I'm standing on Main Street in downtown Belmar. The sign over my head says Bongiovanni's Bails and Bonds in black block letters.

It's not bail I need. It's Bongiovanni. I look up and down the street before going in.

Main Street has its few empty stores with optimistic For Rent signs and even more shops announcing endless "Last Chance Clearance" sales in their dusty windows. Bars, liquor stores, and delis line the street, along with a post office that might get shut down, a locally owned hardware store, and the usual CVS. Here and there pop up brave, colorful storefronts with upscale clothes and antiques and beach knickknacks like neighboring Spring Lake has in spades. Even in late summer when it's busiest, like now, Main Street is dull, gray, and a little too revealing of the dank, dark human condition. The new mayor promised to do something to breathe life into the place. But that would bring in fuckwads with upturned noses, clenched jaws, and something stuck up their asses, along with others wearing too much pastel.

Inside Bongiovanni's, I find Louisa Bongiovanni. Isa.

She had called me earlier, saying she had something to show me. She glances up from her desk and gives me a big smile. "Why I still get glad to see you is a mystery to me."

"A mystery you haven't solved? That's a rare thing."

"Not really. I haven't figured your ass out."

Several rows of dented file cabinets rise up behind her. In front of her desk is a modern, uncomfortable waiting room of couches and chairs from a used business furniture store somewhere up Route 35. The walk-ins she has don't hang around much. Most of them prefer to move on before someone catches up with them and serves a subpoena or arrest warrant.

Besides being ghost-like, Isa is as almost as tall as me and thin, maybe a little too thin, with a gawky undeveloped body that never graduated beyond her teenage years. She's a few years younger than Maureen. Her light blue eyes blur at you from under eyelids that ache to close from the weight of her thick, black eyelashes. It gives her a faraway look that she hates, making her seem almost fragile, needing salvation, instead of strong, bailing you out.

We had been dating on and off for almost a year, when, sometime during 1998, Maureen blew into my life. She landed like a tornado without a warning siren, wrenching me suddenly and fully away from everything I needed to leave. My so-called life, my dim prospects, my suffocating family reputation, my strangling home town. Looking back, I know she tore me away from Isa, too.

Then Mo disappeared. She walked down that street with her dog, and she never came back. She blew away.

I had called Mo's flip phone the day the dog came back with just its leash. Called all day. Isa heard the news and walked the streets with me, the same streets Mo and I'd walk the dog. We talked to the people in their front yards, on the sidewalks, at the mailbox. We knocked on doors. We drove the streets at night, the radio playing. Nothing. Isa even checked with her bail buddies in surrounding towns.

Mo had no landline in the family house up in Edison that she shared once in a blue moon with her brother. I had called his cell that night too.

He was a cop with the Edison police back then. Still is, Isa says. He was a prick of the first order back then. Still is, she hears.

So what did I do? I left town. Saying nothing. Left Isa, too.

I like to pretend it's because I was a wreck, because I couldn't think straight after Mo didn't come back. But, in the dark of night, I came to understand that it's because I'm pretty much a shit.

I got the name Romeo Ruane one drunken night for reasons I can't recall. From someone, maybe a bar buddy, probably Weed or Bosco. It's the one thing I'm definitely not. I ain't no Romeo. Except, I guess, for being the one who brings the drinkable poison to the party.

During those years I was gone, Isa gave birth to her sweet Margarita, who's now her world. She hasn't told me who the father is, and I haven't asked. But I see Margarita's a gift to Isa from some kind deity somewhere.

And while I was away, Isa herself was reborn. She inherited the place from her father, who had died. And she grew it. It was more than bail bonds now. Bongiovanni's a mini-conglomerate, for Christ's sake. She started an auto and property insurance agency that was doing pretty well. Ran it out of these same offices. She expanded into part-time debt collection in the back room, where she has 10 people manning the phones at peak times, like after the holidays. She's a realtor and has carved out a niche selling condos and bungalows under $200K. And she's getting her PI license. Private investigator. Yeah, they still have them in places where there's no trust. Like everywhere. Especially my town.

Isa can put you in a house, insure you, find out if your life partner is running around, uncover when your business partner is pocketing your profits, bail your ass out of jail when you violate a restraining order or get a DWI going after one of those partners, and then dun your pathetic ass when you're late on your mortgage payments, credit card bills, or vendor invoices.

She's an A-to-Z provider for the modern age of diminished and diminishing expectations. All she needs is a psychiatry degree to complete the 21st-century survival package. But, now that I think of it, she's got mind-reading down.

She pulls her hair back, her thick mane falling down her neck. "I found something, Bernie. Veronica Landry. That's why I called."

"I know her?"

She rolls an ergonomically correct office chair next to hers and turns her laptop so I can see the screen. She pats the seat. "I remembered something. And I've been doing some research."

I sit and see a *Philadelphia Enquirer* article from late August of 2009 on the screen. I now remember in a flash the woman whose headshot sprawls across two columns on the front page in front of me. I know her, as in I watched late-night TV a bunch when I was in Philly. Veronica Landry, "Ronnie" as the news anchors called her, was an omnipresent beat reporter on the late local news. She did day-to-day homegrown stories like busted water mains, snow-clogged city streets that the municipal department somehow couldn't get to, city hall corruption, street muggings – local mayhem and degradation of any kind. She was pretty good as I recall. I was once introduced to her at some Philly news reporter dinner or awards thing. I remember she had white blond hair then. It was strawberry blond in the photo on the screen. She was Hollywood hot.

"Recognize her from your years in Philly?"

"Sure do."

"She went on to anchor local news, won some Emmys, and became a mini-celebrity on the local social scene. Unmarried by choice, at least according to the records I found in Philly databases, as well as the local society columns and blogs. She put down 50 percent last year on a nice condo overlooking the Schuylkill River from the 23rd floor. And she was murdered in the early hours of August 21, 2009."

"Just last year. I was in LA then, with *Huff Post*. Hadn't heard."

Isa tells me Ronnie Landry was murdered in her underground parking lot after coming home around one in the morning from a late-night local TV talk show where she had been filling in as host. She had been clubbed to death in what Isa calls a blood bath. Her skull had been fractured into pieces. The surveillance camera provided a murky but clear enough video of the brutal assault.

Isa grabs my arm with a thin, pale hand. "I remember this story, Bernie. It hit all the news last summer. Scared the shit out of single working women like me coming home late all the time." She stops, maybe thinking about Ronnie, maybe about her own late nights, and then looks at me funny.

"What?"

"She's from Belmar."

"Ronnie Landry?"

"She lived here through high school. Her parents divorced then. And after high school she went off to college in California, to the USC School of Cinematic Arts, in LA. She would visit her mom and dad now and then during college, mostly during the summers and school breaks. Her father ended up in Philly after the divorce. Her mother stayed in Belmar.

"According to her bio cached on the TV station's website, Veronica worked the summer after her junior year in New York City as an intern at ESPN and after her senior year at NBC.

According to neighbors, she lived with her mom those summers and commuted into the city. Her mother moved away three years ago, right after the old man died. No forwarding address."

She curls her long, thin legs under her. "This case is so similar to Allie Formosa's. I mean the late-night attack. The violence. The hatred for the victim, or whatever Allie or Ronnie represented. I thought of it right away when I heard about Allie Formosa. It felt the same."

I study Veronica Landry's photo on the screen and then scroll through the story. I sit back. "Veronica Landry is, or would have been, around the same age as Allie Formosa."

"Another local girl brutally murdered," Isa says.

"Right, and both around the same age. They could have known each other."

"Like with Allie, it was a blunt instrument. In Ronnie's case, it wasn't a handy cinder block, it was a bat or something like it. ... It's still an open case, Bernie."

She uses her mouse to click through some files. "Watch this video. It's still on YouTube. It's rough, I'm warning you." She sits back as if to move away from the coming carnage on the screen.

The camera is high up, probably on top of a parking column near the concrete ceiling. The attacker suddenly emerges from shadows at the bottom of the screen, wearing dark clothes and a ski mask. We're looking over his shoulder, seeing what he's seeing, and watch Landry get out of the driver side of a low-slung, fancy red sports car. She looks up and freezes. Her features lock as she appears to listen to something being said to her by the dark figure closing in on her. She shakes her head. There's one more exchange. Her mouth opens wide, and she flattens against the closed car door, her eyes wide in fear, a big purse in her left hand now clutched like a shield against her chest, her right arm rising in defense. The attacker swings something lightning fast from right to left across the screen and hits her flush on the side of her head. It actually bounces hard off her opposite shoulder, a contortion showing the brute force of the impact. Black blood syrups in a thick spray against the wall on the left side of the screen. Ronnie crumbles out of sight. The attacker takes another step closer, stands right over her, and then brings the butt end of the weapon straight down maybe another dozen times. It was a blur of motion. You forget to breathe while watching it.

He stares down at her, head cocked, assessing the damage. Then he pounds her with his weapon one last time, the hardest of them all, like he's putting a stake into the ground. And he exits slowly stage right. You catch a flash of face around the eyes, but that's it. It takes less than a minute for Ronnie Landry's life to be pounded away.

I pull Isa gently to me. She puts her head on my shoulder, and I kiss it and then rest mine on top of hers. "Don't worry," I say. "It might be a coincidence."

"I'm not worried. And it's not."

We both stare at the screen now mercifully black.

Two Jersey Shore girls. Brutally killed. And Isa's right. It doesn't feel like a coincidence.

Eight

Abnormal Norm Nelson, part-time Neptune City officer, called *The Beach Star* on Thursday looking for me. That was the day my online story finally cracked into print. Bosco's assistant at *The Star* gave him my cell.

"I'm calling on my own time, Ruane. This ain't an official call, okay?"

"You got it."

He hacks over the phone and gobs something up and into, I hoped, something else. I don't ask though.

"Rosemary something," he says. "Let me see … Pelia, Pelton … Fuck." He listens to what has to be his wife's brittle voice in the background. "Prelia, that's right. Like Ophelia."

"Something happened to her like Allie Formosa?"

"Yeah. It was in your newspaper back in 2002, bud. I dug it up, and so can you. She was a sweetheart from Avon-by-the-Sea. She taught piano and was a real good singer. She would sing at spots around Asbury Park and even played Atlantic City a couple times. She was in some musicals up in Red Bank, you know, the small theaters there. The wife and I saw her there once or twice."

The wife crackles in the background.

"Okay, okay. Four times. Some people thought she was going places. We sure did."

I'm already online as he talks, reading the front page of the archived version of *The Beach Star* from July of 2002. Rosemary Prelia, clubbed to death with a blunt instrument on the night of July 11th, a Saturday. On the back porch of an unrented bungalow in Avon-by-the-Sea two plus blocks from Ocean Avenue and the beach. Not two miles from where I sit now at my desk at the Honeypot. Her face was an unidentifiable mess from repeated bashing. Wood splinters were found deep inside fragments of her brain, and wood shreds were matted in patches of her hair, suggesting either a crude club or a bat. Something swung in murderous rage.

"Was the perpetrator ever caught?"

"Hell if I know. I'm semi-retired. You'll have to check that out yourself. But I don't think so. We'd a heard about it."

Rosemary's photo in *The Beach Star* shows a confident young woman. Punkish, short black hair. Even the black-and-white photo can't hide what had to be a fresh pink complexion and quiet strength. She was 23 at the time.

Alison Formosa and Rosemary Prelia were from neighboring towns, with Avon-on-the-Beach just up the boardwalk from Belmar and lying between Neptune and Shark River Hills on the west and the ocean. Rosemary would have been 31 today. Ronnie Landry, from Belmar originally, would have been around 29. Alison was 30. Bats and bricks used all around.

I ask Nelson if he has anything else he remembers. Anything else to tell me.

He asks the wife and comes back. "No, but if I remember I got your phone."

I end the call and hit 411 to get the prosecutor's number in Freehold. They'd tell me if they had the Rosemary Prelia case. It's public information now.

The young woman who answers is all sugar and spice and I go sour. I want to hear morose from her, maybe somber reserve, something more in line with the criminal prosecutors who handle death and mayhem and society's decline every day. I don't want sweetness right now. I don't like it

But she has what I need. Rosemary Prelia's cold, she chirps. One of seven unsolved cases in Monmouth County. She gives me the name of the investigator-in-charge and puts me through to the Monmouth County prosecutor's office.

When I get to the investigator-in-charge, she offers me no chirp but lots of squat. Yeah, she'll get around to calling Neptune to ask about the Formosa case because, yeah, there do seem to be some similarities. Except for the murder weapon, she smirks over the phone, you know, that big cinderblock. She thanks me with more smirk and takes my number and address. Like I'll hear from her again.

Nine

Francine Waterman's mother calls me late Thursday afternoon. She's read the print story and phoned the offices. She sounds shitfaced. I know shitfaced.

"Francine was hit by a car and run over time and time again," she says. "That's how she died." She pauses between sentences to drink something from what sounds like a glass packed with ice cubes. I know ice cube serenades.

"She was hit August 29, 2003, Mister Ruane." It sounds like Misher Ruane. "Three days from now? It's been seven years. Seven years ago it happened." She lets out a grunt like she'd just been punched in the gut. "Up in Edison."

I know Edison. Mo's hometown. It's almost an hour up the parkway from Belmar and inland some. It's a grimy city west of the Amboys, Perth and South, and the bays off the Atlantic that let you into the waterways around Manhattan. Industrial. Crowded. Lots of urban wasteland and, where there's people, lots of poverty.

"What was she doing in Edison?"

"She was workin up there. God." It's as if she's hearing the same stupid questions she heard seven years earlier. "She'd been outta college maybe a year. She had a hotshot job at the phone company. In the strategy department. She was goin about her business. She was workin. She was goin to be a VP in a couple of years, that's what they told her. A VP. She would have been their youngest. In the whole region."

"Where did you live then?"

"Neptune, same as now."

Neptune. Allie Formosa's hometown. "And Francine? She live there too?"

"She was back home after college. It was nice. She commuted from here every day. Drove a new car too. It was the newest car in the neighborhood."

Rosemary, Francine, Ronnie, Allie. All from neighboring towns. They'd be about the same age had they all lived.

I feel a clutch of anxiety in my lower abdomen. It's grabbing my innards and twisting hard. It happens when time's suddenly up. Like my nightmare about failing my tax course in law school and they're calling me out just as I'm about to get my diploma because the professor handing out the diploma remembers I failed the course and couldn't possibly be graduating.

These women were cut down. And Mo, she had just disappeared. I reach down for a Dewar's scotch bottle and empty what's left into a plastic, insulated mug from a Manasquan beach bar. Neat, no ice. No clinking.

I take a quick hit. "Mrs. Waterman. What did the cops say?"

"Fuckin hit-and-run." I hear another sucker punch grunt. Now I hear clinking.

"That's it? Nothing more?"

"They looked for weeks for a black car that they thought did it because of some witness report. But they got nuthin'. Now you tell me, Misher Reporter. What kind of hit-and-run is it when the car keeps running over the body until it's good and crushed? Francine's face, her head …"

"I … I had to identify her from moles on her legs. I remember her moles. They were like three sisters playing Ring Around the Rosy. That's what her and me called 'em. The three sisters."

What she was trying to drown in a bottle came up in little whelps then, sounding for all the world like a dead-tired, lonely dog wanting to be let in. I say nothing, waiting for it to end.

Finally, "Seven years ago, Mr. Ruane. And now it's this Formosa girl you wrote about. Something isn't right. This isn't how it's s'posed to be for girls like these. These good girls."

"Did the cops say anything about hit 'n run? Did they look into it?"

"Said they couldn't prove it. I'm reading it to you from the papers they sent me. 'Her injuries are consistent with damage accruing from the force of a single impact at high speed along with the automobile's hurried exit from the scene' is what they said. 'Damage.' That's what they called what happened to her, damage. Well, fuck them."

"Did you or Francine know Allie Formosa? Did they go to school together maybe?"

"First I heard of Formosa was today. In yer stirry."

She's slurring everything now or just rushing her memories. She was done. I had no more questions. "Mrs. Waterman, let me get your number ..."

She stops me cold. "And what about that Angliotti girl?" she spits.

"Who?" I type Angliotti into *The Star* database.

"Mary somethin."

"What happened to her? And when?"

"Summer of 2004, a year after my Francine ..." I type in the query.

On August 20, 2004, a year almost to the day after Francine was killed, a Mary Angliotti was run down on Ocean Avenue, the road that runs north and south along the beach and boardwalk. It happened in Bradley Beach. She was 24 at the time. Cop quoted said she was crossing the road late at night to get to her car parked on the ocean side. She had just turned on the air conditioning in an ocean view house that she had up for sale. A retired couple from northern Jersey was coming by early the next morning, a Saturday, to check it out.

I know Ocean Avenue. Drove it since I could drive, even before, with my brother Danny and his friends. It's on the ocean side of the pizzeria right outside my window at the Honeypot. It's two lane and well lit by the streetlights on the west side and the boardwalk lamplights that run just to the east of it. There are no obstacles that would obscure a driver's vision except occasional brick gateways that arch over the avenue and separate each town along the shoreline. The gateways into Belmar are called the Gates of Hell by peace-aspiring denizens of other towns because of all the sinning that goes on here.

Angliotti was from Bradley Beach, a seaside town one up from Rosemary Prelia's Avon, just up and over from Francine's and Allie's Neptune, and two towns up the shore from Ronnie's, and my, Belmar. All these girls would have been about the same age, within a year or so, had they lived.

I summarize aloud to Mrs. Waterman what I found about Mary Angliotti.

"Another hit-and-run, sez the cops," she manages.

And then, "I knew Mary. So did Francine. A real good one. She wuz a real estate agent and all. Made money too. She wuz on the Bradley Beach Town Council. She wuz a real hand grabber and go-getter." She pauses, and I hear ice song. "You 'member that, Mr. Ruane. A real comer."

I end the call and sink into my rocker, exhausted. I'm back exactly only three weeks. A couple days after I return I get called to a broken parking lot where Allie Formosa lies in a heap under a cheap tarp. And now I'm looking at five dead women from the Jersey Shore. Two by brutal hit-and-runs. Three by vicious attacks to the face and head.

It's not right. Something snapped here while I was gone. And it's still out there. Ask Allie.

Ten

I'm still thinking about Francine Waterman's boozy call. The clock over the sink tells me I start the night shift at the Honeypot in a couple of hours. I call Weed who says he's up for a quick dinner. He's already at Surfer's Porch where I wanted to go. Great minds, he says.

I head out from the Honeypot for the boardwalk. I turn off a couple blocks south, at 14th Avenue, go barely a half block inland, and then run up the stairs of one of two of Belmar's ocean-front hotels, The Surf View. I enter the bar on the first floor facing the ocean.

The hotel's bar, called Surfer's Porch, was once the wide front porch of a grand old hotel that looked over Ocean Avenue, the boardwalk, the beach, and then the sea itself. Over the years it became the spot to watch the high waves off Belmar that draw riders from different parts of the globe, especially during the fall hurricane season. The Belmar Pro Surf is coming in a few weeks, in mid-September, and will take place right out front.

In summer the Porch is open air and usually filled every evening to two a.m. with impossibly thin, tanned and squealing young girls in stretchy micro skirts and tops and spiked heels with jet black and bleach-blond hair, accompanied or at least encircled by impossibly muscled, tanned, baritone-voiced guys in t-shirts or striped polos, cargo shorts, and sandals or sneakers, the whole crowd of 'em downing beers, shots of tequila, jello vodka shots, vodka and Red Bull chasers, Long Island Iced Teas, cosmos, lemon drop martinis, you name it. I get a buzz just thinking about it. In the winter, the proprietors lower see-through plastic tarps that cover the porch's open spaces between columns and put in those tall, standing patio heaters that flame under a cap. It gets all nice and cozy.

Old sconces in the shape of seashells glow yellow and low on the walls. Year-round Christmas lights hang from the beams and are strung from the thick columns on the seaside that hold up the three stories of hotel rooms overhead. Beyond those columns tonight, in the blackness, is the wide, wide ocean and ocean liners and then icebergs free-floating from climate change and then Europe and beyond. Photos in sienna shades and in black frames tilt on what wall space is left, reincarnating the souls who had filled these very seats and spaces and who surely ache right this moment to come home again for another round.

The yellowed-pine bar takes up almost the full width of the porch, stretching close to 40 feet. Weed's at his usual spot and waves me over. When I belly up, my back's to the ocean, but I can hear and feel the waves pounding behind me. On the other side of the bar, a magnificent multilayered tabernacle to alcohol in all its many forms elevates up the wall to the ceiling. Dusted bottles glisten in perfect lighting, with mirrors behind enhancing the glow and allure. To the left on the back of the thick door is a flashing Bud Lite sign, the "t" gone dark; to the right down the bar stands Julie, the owner's daughter. A gloomy weather forecast for the next few days has kept away the usual Thursday night crowd. It's pretty empty tonight.

"Romeo," Weed says as I approach.

"Hey, Rome," Julie says. "Whatcha havin?" She purses her big, red lips, waiting.

Julie is all long, black hair, long, black nails, long, tanned legs, and all muscle. Her black nails sport white skulls. Weed tells me she currently dates the Belmar cop with the thickest neck on the force. He likes to thwack his nightstick in his hand when he talks to you. Even when he's out of uniform, like in the bar or at the St. Rose's picnic. Just like his asshole father, someone I grew up with and someone Weed knew well. Eddy was the dad's name. I bet Julie's beau is called Eddy Jr., and I bet they call him Junior and he's compensating.

"Fish and chips," I say, "and a double potato vodka with a drop of cranberry juice."

She flashes a white smile, then goes in back to yell ta her father to get his fat ass out of the chair and cook Romeo some dinner.

"Fuck Romeo" comes out of the TV room that doubles as the hotel lounge.

She comes back and pours me a double and a drop. "He says he's glad you're back. Me too."

Weed eyes my glass. He's drinking beer as always. "Potato vodka. You get all fancy pants out in LA?" Weed is close to 60, no one knows exactly how close, or how far, his skin leathered by years laying or working in the sun down the shore, a thicket of blond hair that's giving way to white on the sides. And always sunglasses except at night or when he's in trouble.

We each take a long draw, smacking them down at the same time on the old oak bar. Like the old days.

Weed puts his hand on my shoulder. "I read that story of yours. Well written, my man."

Julie hears him and comes over. "So did I. So sad and creepy."

"Did you guys know Allie Formosa?"

Weed shakes his head.

"She graduated a year ahead of me from St. Rose's," Julie says, picking up a towel to dry her hands. "Both grammar and high. I think. But I didn't know her. Shit, she was one of the wholesome girls. You know, the ones that were presidents of clubs. Cheerleaders. The ones who worked on the newspaper and the poetry journal. I mean, come on. Me and my crowd, we were like, fuck them."

"Course," I say. "Makes sense. Why would you have any other response?" She sniffs at me and goes off to greet some newcomers. A young couple had just come through the hotel entrance, holding hands.

"Aw, that's sweet," I say to Weed, nodding at the couple.

"Yessir. A romantic weekend in a broken-down hotel on the churning, gray, moody ocean, liberated albeit temporarily from their dismal rat race lives in some grungy half-city up north where they probably live, if you can call it that, on Frosted Flakes, power bars, chardonnay out of a sack, and macaroni and cheese. When one of 'em is getting a paycheck, that is."

We clink glasses again having just marked our Z on the chests of them people and life itself. But I look at em again. It is sweet, them over there. I wish for a half a minute that they don't end up like me and Weed.

Two locals come through the door. "Rome!" they chant in unison. One's an electrician who helps out at the Honeypot in exchange for a room now and then; the other's a homebuilder who gets a nice off-the-books, all-cash side income fixing up the Honeypot's leaks and eroding foundation. Weed had told me once that the Honeypot gave most of the freelance tradesmen around here a little cushion throughout the year, and they had vested interests in keeping the place going. Both are damn drunk, both have on their Yankee shirts, and I'm betting both spend way too much time at the gym and too little time on their personalities and the 100 great books. They take a table behind me, snorting. I stare em down on the way.

Julie's back our way after taking the lovebirds' order. She gives the Yankees the evil eye. "No shit tonight, assholes. You come up to the bar like everyone else. Who the fuck are you?"

The guys elbow each other, giggling as tipsy men in matching sport shirts do. They obediently grab stools to my left, far away enough to suit Weed and me.

Julie serves white wine to the lovebirds and fills the boys up with tap Bud Lite. She freshens up our orders. "On me and my dad, Bernie. Welcome back." She heads off.

I wink at Weed. "The Welcome Wagon's rolling, my friend."

"I'm sure she's right."

"'Bout what?"

"'Bout not hanging with girls like your Allie Formosa. With the Catholic schools back then, if you were in group A, the smart group, you stuck with others in group A. If you were in group D, likely where Julie landed given the way she's got her skirt hitched, you landed in the group D classroom. Only your lunch hours and outdoor breaks allowed for group integration."

"Did you ever know a Francine Waterman? Mary Angliotti? Or Rosemary Prelia?"

Weed's brow wrinkles. "Nope. They go to St. Rose?"

"No but they were local. All Julie's age or thereabouts."

I ask Julie as she leans in to hear what I'm saying about her.

"Wait," she says. She goes over to the open doorway to the back room. "Hey dad, who was that chick that played here and sang Sinatra and Aretha and Carole King and shit a couple of summers ago? She was about my age. From Avon."

A few seconds later Ben, the old man, steps into the well behind the bar, his belly hiding a belt and zipper. "Oh yeah. I remember her. Rosemary something or other. She was the one who got killed in Avon. Yeah, she played here. Who's askin?"

"Me," I say.

He wipes his hands with a towel from below the bar and contemplates me. "You doing that reporter shit again, Bernie?"

"Actually, I been doing it nonstop now for a pretty long time. We call it reporting tho. Not reporter shit."

"Huh. You was gone how long?"

"Ten years."

"Ten fuckin years. Jesus, man. That's right. You split right after your brother got sent up." He puts the towel back on the edge of a sink behind the bar.

"No, I left right before that. Before it all happened actually."

"Huh. And now you're back and writing about that Formosa girl who got killed, and you want to know about that Rosemary girl who got herself killed too. You Ruanes bring the sunshine, all right. You're like Pig-Pen in the Peanuts cartoons. Always got a rain cloud over you."

"That was a dust cloud," I say. "Cuz he was dirty."

"Huh. No way, that was a rain cloud."

Weed nods in agreement.

I change the subject because we're going to get nowhere fast with this.

"So, Rosemary Prelia, the piano woman," I lob. "You know anything about her?"

"Yeah. I mean, no. A sweet girl with a big, strong Dusty Springfield voice." Ben nods at Julie. "A voice like that Nora Ephron's got these days."

"You mean Norah Jones" sniffs Julie, rolling her eyes.

Ben shrugs. "Whogivesafuck," he says. "Anyway, Rosemary always showed up on time. She was always the lady," he adds shooting a glance at Julie. "And she was good to all the patrons. Took suggestions. Kept her nose clean. Collected her tips. Left before the patrons had any ideas about getting lucky. And she never tried to give 'em any ideas either. I mean, always the lady."

"Ever see any boyfriends or guys bothering her?"

He scratches a chin full of whiskers. "Fuck if I remember."

"Yeah," says Julie. "Guys obviously wanting to date her would show up and pull up a stool to the piano, and go gaga over her. Only a couple times would I see em again."

My steaming plate arrives. I look into the mirror behind the bottles as I eat, and Weed drinks in silence. I pity the Yankees as they hit on Julie. I study the lovebirds necking, like I'm taking notes it's been that long for me. Weed signals like a pro for another beer.

In the mirror, I see my thick dark hair is getting long and ragged. Combed straight back from my forehead and behind my ears, it falls over my collar in back. The lighting in here masks the grays coming in, but they're creeping in every day. My LA tan is pretty much gone because I've been working most nights and, when Allie Formosa lets me, sleeping when I can. There are unpacked bags under my dark eyes.

I straighten my back, run my fingers through my hair to put it in place and take a long drink. Within a few months, Isa swears she's gonna get me back to the 180 pounds she remembers. All it's gonna take is a good diet and some exercise. I didn't ask her. But she's right. I need to get a grip. I pull in my gut.

"In case you're wondering, you look like shit," says Weed. He's staring back at me in the mirror. "You getting old, or you just wearing out?"

"Both."

"You done?"

"I always got hope, my man, always. I hope I'm not done."

We hoist glasses and wonder how the earth turns.

"Too young to be done, you fool."

I nod.

"You get over that nut job Maureen? I been wanting to ask since you left town. I figured somewhere along that dark highway you traveled you musta dropped her like luggage that's broke."

"Weed, man, don't start."

Weed looks at me and puts his bottle down. He shakes his head.

"You ain't over her."

"Weed …"

"She was a fuckin lunatic, and it was just a matter of time before she went off. I told you then, and I'm tellin' you now, again. Ruanes by their lonesomes are crazy enough. You don't want to add that crazy chick to the mix."

"Stop. Let me buy the next round."

He shook his head in disgust. "Or maybe crazy needs crazy so they got someone who gets em. Jessus Lord, yes, I'll let you buy the next two rounds, crazy man."

Julie mercifully returns. "Those other girls you asked Weed about …" She takes my empty glass and twirls it slowly between her palms, a bothered look coming over her face.

"Francine Waterman? Mary Angliotti? Did you know them?"

"No, but they're all dead too, right?" Julie leans in with her elbows on the bar.

"Yeah," I say. I pause. And then, "Ever hear of a Ronnie Landry? Veronica Landry?"

Julie nods. "Oh yeah. Her killing was all over TV last summer. Some people were saying back then that she came from around here." She frowns. "But I never saw her in here."

"Also dead," I say.

"What about them?" Weed asks. "Beside all being dead?"

"All three of 'em were around the same age, Julie's age, like the other two. Rosemary and Alison. All were accomplished. All died hard."

Weed regards me. "You know an easy death? Sign me up. I ain't got long."

Julie raises a clenched fist. "I'll lay one on you if you don't shut the hell up." She shakes it at Weed, then turns my way. "What do you mean by 'accomplished?'"

"I don't know. Achievers at a young age. Going places. Getting out of here. Doing something with their lives."

"Just like Rosemary Prelia was 'always the lady,'" Julie says, flipping her head over her shoulder at her father in the back. "But ya know what? She didn't get the fuck out of here, did she? Not all local girls are deadbeats, you know."

She stands tall, hiding in her cloudy brown eyes how desperate she is to get the fuck out of here. I can read the red, black and white of her eyes like an opened roadmap.

"You're right, you're right," offers Weed, pushing his mug Julie's way.

"I don't know if Waterman and Angliotti were murdered," I continue. "They were run down like animals, and no one's been found. It's strange at the very least. Who would do such a thing?"

"Someone who hates women," says Julie. She shrugs. "Or at least someone who hated *those* women," She walks away.

A sudden wind whips through the place, and bar napkins fly. The whole porch groans and creaks. The Porch's door slams loudly against the jukebox.

Ben hustles out from the back and looks. Julie's open mouth falls into a wide grin. She smiles. Ben looks back at me and squints the way he likes to squint at me. He isn't liking how this night is turning out.

I put down my vodka and turn to see who's walked in.

Behind me Weed says "Fuck … all the bozos are climbin aboard the bus tonight."

It's Darby Ruane. She's come back.

Back to this two-bit town at land's end. Where the ocean's waves keep returning despite it all. Always looking for something and finding nothing, retreating only to crawl back. Back, just like me.

Eleven

She slams the bar door behind her. "Fuck *me*. Way too fuckin nasty out there! What is this winter?" She whips off a tight stocking cap, and long brown hair cascades to her shoulders and beyond.

She sees me. Just dead eyes me, her face blank.

Julie screams "Darby!" and runs out from the bar. The two of them embrace and spin in a tight circle making us all dizzy. They pull back, Julie's face now in Darby's hands. The sister soul mates smile at each other and squeal.

"Jules! I just missed you, tramp!" She kisses her a loud, wet one.

Julie's father waves Darby away with the back of one hand and retreats to the back room.

Darby turns back to me and throws her cap at me. She saunters over, sizing me up, as if reluctant to get too close too fast. She stands next to me, twists me around on my barstool and puts her arms around my neck, squeezing just a little too tightly on my carotid.

"Well, look who the fuck is here. Uncle Beat Town Bernie. How long you been back?"

I tell her.

"Three weeks," she repeats. "I see you picked up where you left off. She juts her chin at me. "Drinking."

Before I can say anything she steps back and pulls her sweatshirt over her head, giving the Yankee fans a show. She throws it on the table they had vacated. She's got on a tight t-shirt that says Rocky and Balls and black jeans so tight the pockets probably never got lint. The Yankee fans stare at her, their banter and banality stopped mid-bullshit.

Darby has the rosy, pudgy face of an angel and the red piss temperament of the devil. She got part from her mother, Flamingo, my former sister-in-law. The other part, the anger and menace, is all Danny, my brother.

She stares back at the baseball boys. "You thinking I'm gonna strip down for you?"

They're frozen. Their faces say fight or flight. They slowly stand and put their bar stools between them and Darby.

"Take a photo and go home and jack off with it, wouldya?"

One of them moves carefully back to the bar. He throw down some bills for Julie. "Okay, okay, see ya," he squeaks in as deep a voice as he can muster. "Yeah, we're most definitely out," says the other. They tiptoe a wide arc around Darby for the door.

Darby snarls. "Dipshits." She eyes Weed. "You too, asshole."

Weed shrugs and goes back to his beer, shaking his head. I know what he's thinking. Fucking Ruanes. Crazy as hell. Now there's a whole fuckin gaggle of 'em.

She slides onto the stool next to me. She leans closer and peers into my eyes. "You use to have big, pretty, hazel eyes like my dad's. Now they're just plain dark as shit. Seems you've had a rough decade, Uncle B. Like you lost your soul. Or maybe you have such a hole inside I can't see to the bottom of it. Where's your soul's hiding out down there?"

She cups in two hands the shot of Jack Daniels that Julie puts in front of her.

"I see you're still a Jack girl," I say. "Back then, at 20, and now at 30."

Darby's eyes don't leave my face. She downs the Jack. "You left me behind," she says, her voice barely above a whisper. "I've been meaning to ask why but you never gave me a chance." She bends over to snatch her cap off the floor.

"Let's go somewhere to talk it out," I offer.

"No. You're not going anywhere. Tell me why." She pulls the cap back on.

"I had to get out."

She waits for more. Then, "Philly was it?" She clacks her shot glass on the bar for another. "First stop, Philly, right?"

Julie refills her glass and backs away.

"I lost …"

"Oh, I know, little Maureen walked out of your life. Guess what, Bernie? I don't give a fuck. Happens all the time. You walked outta mine. Without saying a thing. You knew your brother was beatin the shit out of Flamingo and me." She thumps her sternum with a clenched fist. "ME, Bernie!" she now yells, and then she sticks a sharp finger into my ribcage. "He was hitting ME! But you did nothing, you fuck. I see that now. And I hear shit from you all these years."

Weed is standing next to me, a calming hand lifted. "Darby, baby, take it easy …"

"Fuck off, Weed." She turns away from us and downs the second glass in one shot. She looks back, tears in her eyes, and it wasn't the whiskey.

The sweet couple behind me at the bar is repeating "we gotta go," trying to beat it like the Yankee boys, before it's their turn in the ring with Darby.

I put a hand on Darby's shoulder. "I didn't know …"

"Don't!" She slaps my hand away. "Fucking don't!"

"I swear it …"

She signals for one more from Julie. Weed takes his stool. We all sit there in silence, drinking, staring into the mirror, into our cups of fuckitall, avoiding each other's eyes. Feeling the waves pound out our dwindling time on this planet, the Christmas lights in the mirror framing our sad little montage.

"You didn't know, and you didn't care," she says. She retrieves her cap from the floor and her sweatshirt from the table. "Julie, let's talk tomorrow. I need to get out of here right now."

She heads for the door. She turns around before leaving. "Well, we're back now, Bernie. The Ruanes are back in town. Maybe Danny's going to show up. Maybe it's gonna be one big gang bang." She grabs the door handle and flings herself outside.

Julie yanks my glass from my hand before it gets back to my lips.

"She left right after you, Romeo. In case you want to know. Right after her mom's funeral, and her dad, you know, went to Rahway prison. You never fuckin came back for the funeral. You never came back to see how Darby was. You never ever called her all these years." Her face wrinkles with emotion, her eyes blinking a dozen thoughts she wants to swing at me.

"I tried to call a couple of times …"

Julie pushes my dishes and glass to the side, leans over the bar, and puts her face in mine. "You tried to call? Good for you. You kinda suck, you know?" Julie's father's back now and he nods over her shoulder at me. As if he's wholeheartedly agreeing that I do indeed suck, big time.

I catch my face in the mirror again and try to fathom how deep is the hole inside that Darby saw. I see it now too. I couldn't find the bottom either. I missed all that when I was looking before.

"Rome," Weed says in a low voice. He's standing next to me again. "Rome, with Formosa getting whacked and those other girls dead and all, don't ya think ya oughta go after her? I mean, show her you got some kinda feelin for her. Go, man. She needs somethin. She needs her family."

Twelve

I run out of the bar and toward the boardwalk. It's shiny wet from the ocean's spittle rising before a storm. The lamplights sport halos in the mist. Punks and old-timers lounge on the benches before they have to call it a night. I don't see Darby.

I hurry north, past darkened beach mansions fronting the ocean. I hit 12th Avenue where the Honeypot sits a half block inland and stop. I bend over, catching my breath, spinning from my welcome wagon drinks and the sudden hit of oxygen.

I hear foot falls on the boardwalk. She's coming at me full tilt from the north, hard, her eyes locked on me. I crouch, my hands out, ready for her attack.

She pulls up short, just out of reach, breathing heavily, her hair outside her cap whipping wildly in the wind off the ocean. "You fuck!" she screams.

I move close to her and she hammers my chest with clenched fists. She clocks me in the jaw. A couple times, more from missing my chest than anything else.

She's got weight-room strength in those arms and hands, raw anger in her heart. It hurts, the pounding she's giving me. But I'm feeling it. It's sinking in.

All of a sudden she gives up, letting me wrap my arms around her. We sway, and her sobs slowly melt into hard, deep breaths. I'm breathing hard, blinking away tears too.

"You suck so much," she cries softly into my shoulder.

"I know."

A few boardwalkers had stopped to watch us. Some Prince Valiants are ready to pounce on me. She waves them off. I put my arm around her shoulders, and we walk side by side down the steps off the boardwalk across the empty Ocean Avenue to the Honeypot.

We climb the crooked, creaking stairs to the porch and head into the cavernous lobby. Henry's behind the counter, his feet up, all snug and warm under a blanket. His snoring blends with the creaking of the building. A crackling fire bathes the room in a golden glow that moves around the room with the flames. Too crackling, given that it's summer, albeit a blustery night, and given the time of night and Henry's deep slumber.

I drop her into a deep chair in front of the fire. I pull all the curtains closed and turn on a couple of lamps that manage to give off weak light.

"I will make it up to you, Darby."

"Yeah. Sure."

I move over to the counter and squint at the floor above. The hotel rooms all open out onto a hallway with a railing and overlook the lounge where I'm standing. Nobody's hanging out. I check the keys and see the place is a quarter full. Our regular crowd, but we got some space to talk alone for a while.

I drain some hot coffee from the percolator and bring out Henry's Sambuca and schnapps. Gets him through the day and often the night. I rouse him. "Henry, you sleeping here?"

"Yeah," he mumbles, his breath stale and powerful. He stands tall and erect, like New Jersey royalty, the blanket clutched to his shoulders like some potentate. "I called Kitten and blamed you for being late. She gave a fuck. Good night."

He stumbles upstairs to a free room. "I kept the scotch warm for you," he yells from the first-floor balcony. "It's under the counter." Then he's gone.

I bring the coffee and the bottles of Sambuca and schnapps and plunk them down on the table next to Darby. I remember Henry's Jameson's behind the registration desk and grab it. Almost full. Sweet.

She looks at me.

She drinks her laced coffee with her legs up and her arms hugging them. I sit back watching the flames slap each other. Weed stops by, checking in. He doesn't say anything. Just sticks his head in, catches my eye, and nods. He gives me a two-finger salute off his forehead and leaves.

She gets up to lock the front door after him and then grabs a throw from a sofa. She walks around the room with it draped around her like Henry. She takes it in. My new place.

Over a hundred years ago, the place we're sitting now was a parlor for the rich who came to summer in a luxury hotel away from the city. The parlor has ornate standing and table lamps with beaded shades from a long-gone era of gross wealth and conspicuous consumption. Yards of bookcases packed with books, real hardcovers from the 1930s on. Big chairs to sink into for reading and talking. A 10' by 10' platform on the wall opposite the counter where a tight band might perform on a Sunday afternoon for even tighter patrons. A stingy wooden dance floor waits forlornly in front of the bandstand.

We keep pouring coffee and booze and feeding a low fire. The summer storm that was threatening all night lashes out in periodic heaves of rain, whistling through the gaped window frames and rattling the structure's bones. Claps of thunder roll overhead until a big one sounds a climax, with the rain tapering off afterwards. It'll be cooler tomorrow.

We talk. We go at it until dawn. She gets up to slug me only twice in five hours. Three times if you count her kicking my shins. I learn again how inventive Darby can be with a curse and marvel anew at how many sex acts she can suggest one might perform on oneself or with any available orifice, personal, animate, or inanimate.

Darby tells me she left Belmar two weeks after I did. Right after her father killed her mother in their kitchen. Right after Flamingo was buried. She ran.

Running must run in the Ruane family.

She went north to New York City and eventually got into John Jay College of Criminal Justice in Manhattan. Earned a BA over five years in criminology, basically why and how criminals think. She worked for the Freehold, New Jersey police department for almost four years. Where Bruce grew up. Where the Monmouth County prosecutors and all the courts sit.

She's quit that gig to start on Belmar's force next week. She's full time through Labor Day this year, getting an emergency appointment to help with the end of summer crush of crowds and crime. Then she'll go part time until next Memorial Day, which is fine because she's sure to get a ton of part time with only 21 full-time cops during the winter when Belmar's population drops to 6,000. She's planning to take some courses at Monmouth College. She's sure her full-time appointment will come next June as the force ramps up to 45 full timers to handle 30,000 beach goers on a good weekend.

I don't know why she's settling for this small town. She could have gone anywhere.

I ask her.

"It's home," she says. "Right? I mean, where else do I go?"

We finally get around to it. We never spoke about it. About Danny and Flamingo. Not once in all these years. It's hard now.

My older brother Danny beat Darby's mother, Flamingo, to death.

Bang, there it is. The Ruane family's biggest claim to fame.

It was a savage assault, Darby says, flatly staring into the fading fire, her emotion spent. "Did you know that, Bernie?"

I knew. I had read about it way back, but I stopped before I got too far into the story. I knew how it ended.

It happened on the last day of June 2000, a little over a week after I left.

Darby says the police chief, now retired, called it the worst he had seen in his 35 years on the force. Danny was drunker and nastier than the proverbial bar full of muscle-T-shirt-wearing, thickened Jersey Shore knuckleheads on a drunk Friday night. He got voluntary manslaughter and was sent to Rahway for 20 plus years.

Darby left town on the Fourth of July, just before the arraignment, before the trial, just as soon as Flamingo got the burial and sendoff she deserved.

Darby has no one special in her life right now. Never has had anyone special. She's had a boatload of lovers over the years, but no one that stuck. She cruised the bars north and south during the summers, but in all these years she's never come within 20 miles of Belmar.

Last night, Thursday, was her first back in town. When I ask her why, why she's come back now, she says it's time.

"You know, Bernie, we're both back for the same reason."

"What's that?"

"You don't see it?"

I know where she's heading. She knows I know.

I answer her out loud. "We're running away from all our yesterdays?"

"We're back to deal with what blew us out of here. You've come back to find Maureen. Right?"

I take a drink. "It's been ten years …"

"Yeah, for me too. But I'm not back here to replay the past. I'm here to start over."

"How you doing that?"

"This is Flamingo's home. I feel her again, Bernie. I need to feel her again. I'm forgetting
her … I'm forgetting a lot of things."

"You gave up a lot to come back. Big jobs. Big cities."

She shrugged. "They're not home. They're not here, Bernie."

I ask her where she's going to live. She's 30 next April. She'll find a place on her own,
thank you. She knows how to handle things.

We stop and sit in silence. We once met something to each other. We can feel it, dimly,
tonight.

Back then, I'd tell her stories at night time, using a flashlight to bring to life creatures on
her ceiling as she laid in her bed and I on the floor until I'd fall asleep first, snoring loudly. She'd
throw a stuffed animal at me to wake me up and we'd laugh. I was the uncle that once upon a
better time brought her presents in one gargantuan Christmas bag that was big on wrapping and
bows and light, at least to me, on gift. I remember her eyes aglow when I arrived. They were
more luminous than the lights her father threw onto the lopsided tree.

"I need to crash," she says.

I walk her to the third floor and put her in a room on the opposite corner from me and far
enough away from the riff raff. She's asleep by the time she hits the bed. Doesn't even comment
on Weed's décor.

I watch her sleeping from the doorway. This feels good, like this. I'm back somewhere I
belong like she was saying. Someplace I always wanted to escape. A place I needed Maureen to

take me from. Now a place, and people, I maybe need. To see her there, breathing quietly. To know Weed will come by to check up. That Johnny Bosco still goes by Johnny and still gives a shit. And Isa. She still has her big, big heart. And now a little girl.

I lock her door as quietly as I can, slipping the key under it, and head to my corner to sleep. Henry's shift begins in an hour, and until then everybody can just fuck themselves if they need something.

*

Outside, on a boardwalk bench under a lamp that lost its light, someone in a hooded black sweatshirt sits stiffly in the cool wet air after the storm and looks up at Bernie Ruane's apartment lights as they go on and then off. The building is quiet and mostly dark. Only a few lighted windows dot that side of the building.

Allison Formosa. Now people know. Because of Bernie Ruane.

The lone figure heads down the block, pausing at the bottom of the steps to the Honeypot's front porch, then stops at the front entrance and peers through the glass panels in the top third of the large door and into the lounge. A couple lights are left on, and near-empty bottles alongside coffee mugs decorate the big table. A hand emerges from the sweatshirt to twist the door handle, testing it, twisting back and forth.

The figure turns away, walking slowly down the steps to the sidewalk and away from the boardwalk, hands in pockets, down 12th Avenue and into town.

The bench under the overhead broken streetlight sits empty on the boardwalk.

The sun stains the horizon to the east.

Another day.

Thirteen

The rain stops on Sunday. It's almost one p.m. I head out from the Honeypot.

Strollers have stormed the boardwalk. An achingly blue sky has broken out all over, and the sun bounces off the ocean so hard it hurts your eyes. The blustering Atlantic waves like a lunatic at anyone who'll give it a glimpse, feeling the vigor left by the storm.

Balls bounce, umbrellas blossom. Greased muscle boys dart around an obstacle course of blue trashcans on the sand, chasing shimmering, lotion-sprayed girls clad only in patches and string. The heavy chicks with their McDonald's rolls stretch out in beach chairs, legs splayed. They're plopped alongside beef brothers with their Miller guts, all of them craning their thick necks to watch the waves, remembering what it was once like. Rap, trance, and hip hop compete to be the biggest and baddest. Surfboarders bob in the water, waiting stoically for another après-storm, eight-foot wave, careful to avoid the groins, jetty-like rock formations that pop out of the water every 100 yards. They're less careful to avoid the swimmers.

The tanned and the beautiful get more tanned and beautiful. Tonight they'll party, those who don't have to go back to work on Monday and those who do. They'll party at D J'ais and The Surf Porch and a dozen other spots along the shore. Then they'll retire to those tiny beach cottages that get rented out only in the summers, where religiously they'll pursue the rituals passed genetically through the ages – watching Yankee and Mets games on crap TVs, eating pizza and calzones delivered by bike or beat-up car by the latest round of immigrant, getting fucked up, throwing up, fucking and fucking up, and then sleeping it all off until the heat of the next day in the stuffy, little rented shithouse wakes their sorry asses up. All cotton-mouthed, they wonder where that bruise came from, not to mention the stranger asleep in the bed.

I find a free bench on the boardwalk overlooking the bodies on blankets stretched between the ocean and me. I put my arms on the back of the bench and stretch, feeling the sun tingle my skin. I suddenly feel like I've been walking these past ten years.

I think about the last day I remember ten years ago. It was the last day I saw Maureen. I think about that day every day. The day she took a walk and didn't come back.

That morning, she had slipped on a blue jean miniskirt, nothing underneath, and a snug gray t-shirt and flip-flops. She was five foot five on a good day when she didn't slump into a funk. Her lazy, curly brown hair was thrown into a short ponytail that popped right out of the back of her head like a tea handle. When she leaned over the bed to kiss me a quick goodbye, she smelled like the white beach roses along the shore, the ones that lasted most of the year. Her hair was wet from her shower. She smiled as she tapdanced her hair on my face. She brushed it out of my eyes and looked into them.

A big smile came over her. "Your love wants me, right?"

When she smiled like that, her blue eyes glowed and her red lips glistened. She would giggle with smile, and her body would writhe with it. You couldn't help but smile back at that joyful mess. I grinned back like crazy.

"Yes, Mo. I want you."

"No, Bernie. Different question. It's your *love* that wants me, right? Your love?"

"Right, Mo. My love."

She sat next to me, her hand on my chest, her hip joined to mine. The smile vanished. Poof. She reached over to her nightstand and plucked a book from the top.

I still have the book. Her writing's all over it. She'd read a book, and scrawl her reactions, her own poetry, her random thoughts in all the blank space she could find, scribble framing the printed text.

"Listen to this," she said. She read aloud, caressing each word.

> If love wants you,
>
> suddenly your past is obsolete science. Old
>
> maps, disproved theories,
>
> a diorama.

She peered at me. "If *love* wants you, Bernie."

I kept that book. And I've gone back a thousand times to that page she read.

If *love* wants you, you are born anew. You change into someone who simply didn't exist before that love. The big bang theory of love. Bang. You're loved? You're here. That's what she was saying. I realize it now. But why was she saying it? And why then?

After reading those lines, she leaned over me and probed deep. I guess back then I had a soul there, something for her to look into.

She said again, as if repeating an incantation, "Your *love* wants me, Bernie."

I remember answering yes again, pulling her to me.

She pushed back, that smile springing to her lips. "Thank you, Bernie," she said in a whisper. "Thank you."

Then she left to walk the dog.

She became new. With my love. And then she never came back.

It wasn't the first time she had left. She had walked out of my life more than once in the couple years we had been together. She would get pissed and just pick up and leave. Once she left after setting dinner in front of us on the front porch of that house on 19th, not too far from here. She set down the plates and said, "be right back," then called me a week later, sobbing through an apology. She told me she was falling hard for me. Later, she said she was crazy for me.

She was crazy all right. Weed was right about that.

Matt Logan, Mo's big brother, hit her now and then, though I couldn't prove it. Mo never said a word, but I felt it as sure as I knew she felt his blows. She'd never look him in the eye. She'd have bruises in places they shouldn't be. It was darkly quiet when they were together. She'd be beaten down in other ways too, her spirit gone, her hopes slammed, her self worth crushed. I saw it whenever she went back there, to Edison, to her family home.

I think back to what he said, what I heard in his voice the night she left. He wasn't shocked. His voice was flat, measured. He already knew she was gone.

"She had a suitcase, Ruane," he said.

It was like a knuckle punch to the face. I asked him to repeat what he'd said.

"She had a huge fuckin suitcase on her bed for the last week or so. Packed. Ready to go. I thought she was going somewhere with Bernie, the big spender. Guess not, huh?"

I had even less money then than I do now. She had had nothing either. Big spender – what the fuck? "We were going nowhere," I remember telling him.

I remember how I felt right then. As he went on about the suitcase. Pain deep down. Pain that blossomed into pulsing ache of searing loss, of chances blown, of something good gone. I had had everything. And I lost it.

That ache's never given up. It's never left me.

Man, it would've been a different life with Mo. We'd be outta here for good.

On the bench now, in the sunlight I don't feel, I think about the time when she was sitting there in the passenger seat of my car, her legs under her, her smile and her body moving to the music as the radio played, that one hot night, a street lamp lighting her stage. Her eyes wide, blue, glowing, her hair wild, a broad smile lighting her lips. She was alive. She was on fire. I should have leaned in and kissed her. I should have said, shit, I love you, let's just get outta here. You and me. Let's run.

But I didn't. We didn't.

I pound the hot back of the bench. I squint through clogged tears.

That night, her on stage in that blue light, I said nothing. Not a thing. Even though I know in my bones that that night, us together in my car, was a singular moment of clarity in a befogged life, an opened hatch, a blazed path, into a finer world that's now closed off to me forever.

If only I had kissed her, we'd be together now. One "hey, let's blow this place" would've bonded us and moved us forward from that moment to the next and the next. One "I love you, Mo" would have started a chain reaction that would have built a new life.

I look out over the lovers and beaters stretched out to the sea. I wipe my eyes. So here I am. Back to find her? Back to put an end to her? Must be. Darby says so.

That night Mo disappeared I spoke to her brother, Matt. He told me he checked her room when we talked that night. The big suitcase was gone. Her car was gone.

I went up the next day to see for myself. There wasn't much of her left behind in Edison. Her bookcases were empty. Her journals and notebooks were gone. Her closet held a few pieces I'd never seen her wear. I sat on her bed, staring far too long at left-behind clothes on bent hangers, taking in the quiet room, trying to feel her presence.

Like that song goes, it must have been one hell of a suitcase she packed. It looked as if she had long abandoned that soulless house on that empty street. And me.

I went to the Edison police.

"She'll be back." That's what the detective said when I tried to file a missing persons report. "Her brother's in our Accident Investigations Unit and he don't think she disappeared. He thinks she was done wit you. Probably doin some other dude as we speak."

Nobody gave a shit.

I called her cell for weeks afterward until I got a "not in service" message. I couldn't get any information from the phone company without a court order or summons. I walked the streets, with Isa. I stayed in that house we rented on 19th Avenue for as long as I could, hoping she'd show up.

She didn't.

I can say that the great big hole she put in my life was sucking everything else into it. So I edged backward like a sand creature, away from Belmar, away from whatever family I had, everything that was pulling at me, pulling me down, into Maureen's hole.

I ran. I didn't say goodbye to no one.

A week later, the Ruane world continued its grand summer collapse. My brother Danny bludgeoned Darby's mother to death in their dirty kitchen. He used his grubby bare hands and as many greasy appliances off their countertops as he could find to pound her into a bloody mess on their kitchen floor.

Maureen didn't just up and leave me. Something happened. Snapped.

Mo was street smart as shit, so I know she didn't fall for some predator's ruse. She trusted nobody. Barely talked to anybody for that matter. She had run track, sprints and cross-country too, all through high school and the year or two she spent in college. She could outrun any sick shit like whoever killed Allie Formosa. She lifted weights. She had taken self-defense courses. She packed a little nasty pepper spray too.

She was smart and fast, paranoid and wary, strong and tough. And more than a little volatile and ready to act out. She was almost 30 when she went missing. She'll be 40 next year. Ten years older, more or less, than Darby and Julie. And 10 years older than Allie and Ronnie and Rosemary and Francine and Mary, the dead women who have greeted my return to Belmar.

When Isa and I caught up that late night at Dunkin' Donuts, the night Bosco called about Allie Formosa, Isa said something about how love means you don't have to always be the first or the last. Isa was talking about us, about how we have to be open to taking next steps and all that, despite everything before. But maybe she was talking about Mo too. Maybe Mo had stepped out and moved on. Maybe ol' Romeo just didn't have enough to give her. I was never a first or last.

I sit on the bench and breathe in the ocean air and close my eyes. I think about Mo, and Isa, about my brother Danny and how he didn't deserve the phenom that was Flamingo. I think about Flamingo's love of life and her raucous laugh, about her mini-me Darby rumbling around causing outrage and chaos even as a precocious kid. I think again about Matt Logan and open my eyes and lean forward, elbows on knees, hands clasped.

Edison, I think.

Francine Waterman. Francine had been run down repeatedly in Edison. Logan was a cop there. He had to know something about that case.

I had questions for him. About Francine. And maybe a few surprise ones about Mo.

Tomorrow I would head up to Edison.

I get up and go back at the Honeypot. Later in the evening I'm back to sitting, this time in a tilting chair on the porch. I listen to the gentle breezes off the water and the secrets they hold. It's a clear, rare, low-humidity night in August.

Coming back here to find Mo, and maybe me, I find five other local women who have been killed over the last eight years. I wonder where Mo is right now.

I look out at boardwalk's lamplights and its benches filled with night people. I wonder who's out there right now looking out to the sea or even back at me. I wonder what's waiting for these women out there in the dark. I hear muffled conversations in the distance. A sharp gust off the ocean reaches me with a sudden hiss. I write in my notebook.

> *A wind over*
>
> *dry sands*
>
> *off black, hushed streets*
>
> *and nights*
>
>> *harsh*
>>
>> *lifeless*
>>
>> *bitter*
>>
>> *old*
>
> *sounds like*
>
>> *age and the*
>
> *raspy gasps of death.*
>
>
> *Not soft stirrings*
>
> *of spring*

or lush

waves of breath

through the sea grasses

and white roses of summer.

Tonight

I hear and

I feel and

I smell that

ill wind that blows

no good.

I write 674 atop this one and close my journal. I pour another couple inches over a cube of ice and then rock in silence for a long time, straining to hear the words from the dark night, feeling that ill wind wash over me.

Fourteen

The first entry says this.

∞

It began in August of 1999. With Sandy O'Connor.

She was later than usual that night. It was a hot summer Friday night. The beach traffic to Belmar across New Jersey from Trenton had pushed her drive over two hours. It was after three a.m.

She pulled into the dark parking lot behind her parents' two-story condo building. She parked in their open-air spot. She turned off the ignition and lowered the front windows. She took in the night air.

All the surrounding houses and apartments were dark. You could hear a few drunks off in the distance, yelling and laughing on side streets or on their porches. No one was nearby.

Some guy on the beach in front, on the other side of the condo, waited for her. There was no sign of the parents. They had to be away.

She was breathing in that familiar ocean air. She was listening to the waves crashing on the beach close by. They were heavy tonight, and she was bathing in their rhythm and the soft breeze.

At some point she realized I was there. She sat bolt upright and looked through the car window right at me. I was leaning forward with two hands on her hood, staring back at her through the holes of my ski mask. Her lips moved as if she was saying something. That's when I came around and reached through the open window and grabbed her hard by her blouse.

"No," I said, right up close, right in her face. It fell good to say it, finally, to one of them. "No."

Tears filled her eyes. When she squeezed them shut, water fell all the way down her cheeks in a single, heavy, non-stop line. Like a cartoon. She started screaming at last, but my fingers reached around her throat and cracked something, stealing her voice. She made a liquid noise and her head shot forward, hitting my chin, hard. Free for a second, she squirmed into the passenger seat, kicking at me through the open window.

She managed to open the passenger side door and fall partly out. Her larynx had been damaged, and all she could let out was an awful, hoarse whisper.

"Help." Her voice was scratchy, barely audible. "Help."

She was pulling herself onto the pavement. In a second I was there with her. Her head was between my two hands. I gripped her hard, wouldn't let her move that pretty head. I pulled her out and shut the car door with a kick, putting out what little light shone on what she and I both knew were her last moments.

Sandy looked up to the night sky. She surely marveled at how many stars there were. She must have seen bright Venus, which her father had pointed out since she was a child. Nights, this night, that would no longer blossom into glorious days. No more, Sandy.

The first hard thud of her skull on the asphalt sounded so far away. The others blurred with the sound of the pounding waves she said she loved so much and shook her world.

If she had lived, she would have remembered my eyes through those holes. She would have remembered my voice. But she didn't. Live, that is. Sandy went away.

∞

Fifteen

Matt Logan agreed to see me right after Labor Day. I'm not sure why. His sneering voice said he still hated my guts. But when I said I wanted to talk about the seven-year-old Francine Waterman hit-and-run, he paused, he said okay, come on up. Maybe he wanted to know what I knew. Maybe he wanted to defend the Edison police. Maybe he had his own reasons.

Isa lent me her Volvo to make the drive to Edison. Darby had the day off and joined me. I figured she might come in handy talking to Logan. If only for protection. Which is probably the reason I also put a bat in the backseat, a signed Ozzie Smith Hall of Fame bat I had picked up in St. Louis.

En route, Darby has her feet on the dashboard. She's doing her nails and filling the car with fumes, listening as I fill her in on the Rosemary Prelia and Ronnie Landry assaults and the two hit-and-runs. "I'm not seeing a connection," she sniffs when I finish.

"Other than that they're all female, the same age, from the same neighborhood, and every one of them going places?"

"Not enough. Any number of such females are assaulted or murdered all across America. What you've got, Bernie, are three murders with similar overall MO, one that's common in other crimes. You have two hit-and-runs that can't be presumed to be murder, meaning that we don't have evidence of homicide – unlawful killing with malice aforethought."

"I got five dead women, that's what I got. Five dead women with a lot in common. The hit-and-runs knew each other. And I've got a gut feeling, Darby."

She grabs the bat from the back and points the head at me. "A gut feeling's not enough to connect the dots. You need to look for someone who hated the two hit-and-run victims. Someone who would never, ever forgive them for whatever it is they did. Someone batshit crazy. Connect those dots and build a path you can actually follow."

I push the bat away. "I know there's some place, some event, some person that connects all five of them. I can feel it. We haven't found it yet."

"Hey, listen. I have an idea." She turns a pseudo-eager face to me. "The motto for *The Beach Star* should be 'All the Guesswork That Fits We Print.' You'll be a fuckin cinch for that Pulitzer Bosco's creamin' in his pants for."

She pops the bat head into my rib cage with a quick slap to the handle and then pulls it away, ready to repeat. It all happens so fast that I can't stop her in time.

"Ow! You suck."

"That's what happens when you're guessing, Uncle Bernie, you leave yourself open to attack. Your enemies will take that opening and they will attack."

"You learn that at John Jay?"

"Life, Uncle B, life." She fishes a CD from the road trip pile I brought and pouts at the cover. It's Bruce Springsteen's "The Rising."

"Play track 12," I say.

She pushes the CD into the Volvo's player and advances to 12. It's "You're Missing."

"God, no!" She reaches over to pop the CD out.

"Wait. Just once. I won't fall apart. Promise."

She shakes her head and looks me over. We listen, and I don't. Fall apart, that is. I sing it out loud, only once, to "You're missing when I see the sun rise / you're missing." I sing it serious and with heartbreak.

She sighs when I finish. "Enough, Unc. Let's just call it Mo's Song."

She pops the CD out. "My turn. You want Bruce? Let's do 'Pretty Flamingo.'" She's flipping through the plastic cases.

"That's not on any album. And it's a Manfred Mann song anyway. 1966. Although Bruce would do a mean version in concert, with piano and sax. He'd intro it with a story about him and Stevie sitting on his porch at night in Freehold, next to the Sinclair gas station, watching this classy girl go by every evening, ignoring them …"

"Whatever. It's my momma's song." She waves me off, and then sits straight in the seat. Channeling. She waits, catches her muse, and then lifts her index fingers into the air, her eyes closed, rocking to the slow, rolling tune in her head. She shouts to the rooftop:

On our block

all of the guys

they call her flamingo

Cause her hair

glows like the sun

And her eyes

can light the skies

When she walks she …

Yes, when she walks she …

moves so fine

like a flamingo.

She shouts "yes" at the end and then does an encore, and I'm there with her, really working the "like a flamingo" part. We laugh at our production and find a few more songs to mangle together as we tool up the road. Mostly Bruce. Southside Johnny's "I Don't Wanna Go

Home." Some Patti Scialfa – "Rumble Doll" for Darby, "Romeo" for me, me belting out that "ohhh, Romeo" line. Darby did "Because the Night" so down and dirty it made you wonder if Bruce would have still given it to Patti Smith.

It feels good, Darby and me doing what, I guess, family does. Or maybe it's her starting to forgive me, and I need that. Or maybe she reminds me of Flamingo, and even Danny when he was good, or at least under control, and the crazy-happy times we all had a lifetime ago dancing and singing on summer nights at their impromptu parties. Or maybe it's just down-the-shore music on some good speakers, heading up the highway, a little too heavy on the bass and the gas. Just like I like it.

Sixteen

The next hour breezes by along with the exit signs and the easy songs. We pull off the turnpike. I drive down a few bombed-out streets and pick an empty space in front of the Edison Police Department. The sprawling building takes up a full block wide and deep. The barred windows and red brick structure loom over us like a bunker in a hostile town. It breaks our mood.

We brace ourselves and get out of the car. We cross the cracked sidewalk and enter the lobby through a glass door with its lower pane taped in an x to hold it in. We get scanned by tired cops with slits for eyes and take the cramped elevator to the third floor where Sergeant Matt Logan has his office. He's down a long hall under a yellowed, suspended ceiling with florescent lights that glow harshly through filmy, barely see-through plastic panels. Each of the doors we pass has a name plaque stuck to the drywall to the right of the doorway.

We find Logan with his door wide open. The nameplate says "Chief – Community Relations Unit." He's at his desk yelling something into a black phone mashed against his fleshy cheek as he glares red-faced into a monitor.

He has gotten huge in the 10 years since I saw him last. Thick, muscular, a belly plopped atop the small desk he's somehow wedged behind. His hair is military short as always, his thick ears thicker than before, his face florid like only the Irish can pull off, with scary purple veins traversing his bulbous nose. He's stuffed into Edison's black police uniform and has a couple bars of meaningless ribbons over where his heart should be.

He keeps talking, but his eyes come to life and go straight to Darby, who stands by my side. She's chewing gum with her lips closed, her hands on her hips.

His eyes spend too long on her.

"Logan, yo, over here," I say.

His eyes stagger over to meet mine.

"Later," he spits into the phone and slams it back into its holder. He waves us forward then points us to the two straight-backed aluminum chairs on our side of the desk. He watches Darby drape her jacket on the back of her chair and settle in front of him.

He shakes his head and wipes his lips with the back of his right hand. "Bernie Ruane. What the fuck. Where you been, asswipe?" His eyes flit between me and Darby. "Who's this?" He jerks his head toward Darby.

"Darby Ruane. Belmar Police's newest member. And my niece."

He goes blank for a moment as his brain does some heavy lifting. He sizes her up. "Danny and Flamingo's kid? My, oh my. Seen your daddy lately?"

Darby cocks her head to one side, blinks fuck you back to him and then looks around. As if hunting for something sharp and rusted. Or blunt. Just for Matty.

In the small room, we let awkward cram in with us and find its own space. Logan wipes his upper lip again. Our chairs are two feet from metal file cabinets that rise high behind us. The wall to our left is within my reach; the one to the right props up a jammed set of metal shelves. The wall behind Logan has a small, barred window that doesn't need a shade it's so dirty and clouded with cobwebs. Overhead, a single bulb burns like the punishing sun over a barren desert.

Darby shifts in her seat oh so slightly, not yet breaking a sweat like Logan and me. Logan creaks loudly in his protesting chair. He returns his attention to me.

"She's here why?"

"Day off," Darby replies through gum chews.

He shoots his chin at me. "Let's do this, my man. Get it over with."

78

I'm ready. "Did the Edison police ever end up investigating Maureen's disappearance?"

His eyebrows raise, and he creaks again loudly in his chair. "What the fuck, Ruane? I thought you were here to talk Francine Waterman. The hit-and-run."

"I'll get there. You haven't heard from Maureen in, what, 10 years? And all that time you haven't pushed for any kind of investigation into where she is?"

"That ain't an open case, Ruane. It ain't even a closed case. Excuse me, dipshit, but it ain't no case at all. If that's why you're here, then get the fuck out." He nods at Darby. "You can leave your sweet niece though."

"Can't believe she's been gone all these years with you doing squat."

His head jerks back in my direction. "Look, Ruane, Maureen wised up. She dumped your ass, and got the fuck out. Long ago. Nothin else to know."

"I'm not buying that."

"What can I say."

"She didn't leave me. The only thing she ran from back then was her family. From her father who hit her. Her mother so cold she frosted your breath. And, most definitely, she tried to escape you. Those fists."

He stares back over the small desktop. His hands surface and go palm down in front of him like he's trying to steady himself on a rocky sea.

"We were out of her life by the time she disappeared. You were the only one she had then. You were the only one she could leave. And her being her, she fuckin left. Deal with it, Romeo."

"So, where did she go? You don't care?"

He sits back, brings his knuckles to his chest, his face now crispy red. He cracks his knuckles with a volley of pops that echo off the blank walls and cold metal. He looks from Darby to me and back again. Finally he settles on me.

"Don't care. The only hole in her body that got more action than her nose and the ones she opened up with needles was the one between her legs. Ya know what I mean? At the end of the day, Ruane, she was done and gone long before she left."

Darby grabs my arm as if to say, I got this. She leans toward Logan, her hair framing her face. "I don't like you talking about your sister like that."

Logan looks at her. "She speaks."

"You just disrespected her. Yet she had problems. She was probably mental. Have some sympathy for your family. For the little sister you were supposed to care for." She points a finger half-way across Logan's desk. "I don't wanna hear your shit mouth goin off like that again."

Logan's eyes widen, his tongue punching out a cheek as he crawls all over her face. "Damn! A little Flamingo!"

Darby straightens, her hands grabbing her seat bottom to keep her from springing up over the desktop. Logan pushes back from the desk, as much as his girth allows, instinctively sensing the very real possibility of physical assault.

It gets quiet except for creaking chairs.

"Logan," I say.

He glances over, his eyes flicking back to Darby a couple times. Just in case.

"Let's start over," I begin, trying a soft touch. "Your sister's gone all these years. You never even declared her dead. I checked. Why'd you let her go like that? When she's missing."

He hears my question but he's somewhere a million miles away. Even Darby's dropped out of his mind. And, then, he squares his jaw and shoulders. He's back and squints at me, stabbing a thick finger into his desktop as he spits his words.

"You know it just fuckin occurred to me, Bernie. You're right. I shoulda looked into this more. I mean, you were the last to see her. And you got some violence in your genes." He eyes Darby, his eyebrows arched. He pauses. "Ain't that right, sweetness? You know, your Daddy and all?"

He doesn't wait for her answer. He's back at me.

"You take off, what, right after she disappears, Bernie? I mean you just run? That's odd, man. Somethin's off, you know? And then, what, you come back to town and, bang," his pale, fat, hairless arm pushes a bulbous hand into a catching mitt of a palm, "bang, bang, bang, a whole bunch of chicks are dead and gone. Bang. Bang. Bang."

"So, tell me about Francine Waterman," I say.

"What the fuck?" he blurts out. "Why you changing the subject all the sudden? What's she got to do with Maureen?"

"Nothing, so far as I know."

Logan starts shaking his head. He looks at Darby and shrugs.

"Francine was killed in Edison," I start. "But she grew up in Neptune. Had she lived, she'd be around the same age as Allie Formosa. Allie's the one we found at the yacht club. She was from Neptune. And something else. Francine Waterman was the same age as that reporter Ronnie Landry whose murder was splashed all over the paper last summer. Ronnie Landry's from Belmar. You see where I'm going with this, Logan?"

He blinks at me, saying nothing.

"Mo disappeared in Belmar," I continue. "And with all these murders of young, local women over the years since Mo's been gone, you do nothing to look into Mo's disappearance. Your sister, for Christ sake."

"I'm not following you," says Logan.

"I don't see your name on any of the Francine Waterman police reports," I say. "You didn't work the investigation. I checked. How come? A hit-and-run's got no connection to Accident Investigations where you were in 2003?"

"I was out of Accidents when Waterman went down. Besides, dickweed, the Criminal Investigations Bureau would have looked into the Waterman case if anything was there."

"So you know nothing about the case?"

"No, señor. Not my yob, amigo."

"I'd like to talk to the cops on Francine's case."

"Knock yourself out." He types something, pulls a printout, and slides it across the desktop. It's contact info for two Edison cops in the Criminal Investigations Bureau. "These the guys. These the numbers to call. Now I'd like you to get fuck out of my office."

I fold the sheet and put it in my shirt pocket. Darby and I do not get the fuck out.

Logan's shaking his head again. "Your askin about Maureen, is it just personal, or is it part of the story you're writing?"

"You think they're part of the same story? Maureen and the dead Jersey Shore girls?"

Logan's armpits are showing stain. "Lemme ask you something, Ruane. Where were you when Waterman's face met the front grill of that car what hit her?" Any chance you mighta been in Edison that night? Seems I'm also recalling something about that. You remember anything?"

He grinds his jaw back and forth. Darby's head goes from Logan to me and back to Logan. A good cop, she's keeping her mouth shut, stifling the questions crowding her mind.

"Come on, Ruane, tell me, where were you that night?" A thin smile cracks wide open around yellowed teeth. He's on a roll.

"And speaking about the Ruanes, going back to your and Darby's genes and predisposition, and all that. Wasn't your fuckin daddy pretty violent too, Bernie? Like schitzo violent? Like bubba Danny?"

"You know, Matt, my father never hurt my mother. Never hit my brother. Never touched me. Unlike some other fathers I've heard about."

"I seem to recall he tried to run Danny the fuck down with his car. No?"

"Danny wasn't allowed on the property. He was seeing him off."

"Maybe your saintly father saw Danny for the sick fuck he was. Maybe he knew what Danny could be capable of, like killing his wife, the mother of his grandchild." Logan looks at Darby, then back at me. "Maybe he knew about the family predilection for violence and you just missed it. I heard some of the old timers talk about your father when Danny got convicted and sent up. Something about apples not falling far out of the orchard."

"You mean not far from the tree. Not 'not far out of the orchard,' you stupid fuck."

"Huh?" He eyes me, lost. "What the fuck ever, Ruane. You're the man of words. Why don't you find some of those words to tell me how you're the last one to see my baby sister? When Maureen and you started hooking up, she was too damn old to have her daddy or brother check you out. Far as we were concerned, you were just another bad drug." He shrugs at his memory. "Maybe we shoulda paid more attention to who Maureen was fucking."

He shuts up long enough to see how his words are hitting Darby and me. We show zero. He laughs anyway.

"Well, I'm on it now, Ruane. I'm on the case, just like you were asking about. You can expect some questions from Edison now. So, keep us up to speed on where yer headin if yer thinkin of traveling anyplace, you know what I mean?"

"Go fuck yourself, Logan. You're in Community Relations. And I ain't in your community. Ain't nowhere close."

He pushes himself to his feet. No small task, a man of his size. He dwarfs his kid desk down below. "I'm done for now with both of you Ruanes. But I'm not done for good."

Darby's flushed. She shoots up and presses against the front of the desk. She starts speaking in a low, controlled voice. It's a voice she surely uses to take charge in an emotional, hostile environment.

"Listen," she begins. "Slow down. I'm on the Belmar police force, and not Community Pussy Relations. I'm telling you to watch how you play it here. Cause I play hard. You fuck with Bernie, you fuck with me. And you don't want to fuck with me."

I put my arm out in front of her. I don't want her fighting my fights. She pushes it away.

"Sounds like a date," Logan manages. "I'll look you up, babe."

I push Darby gently to the door.

Logan watches us, moving slowly around the desk.

We stop in the doorway. "And, Logan," I say, "one last thing. The brother of a long-time missing woman might think twice before launching an investigation into an enterprising journalist who's trying to solve the murders of young women on the Jersey Shore."

He snorts. "And I'd say the jilted boyfriend who last saw her alive might think twice about pissing me off."

Darby flashes a middle finger back into the room as we exit the sweatbox. We move quickly back down the long hall without looking back.

"Fuck you, assholes!" roars from Logan's office as we keep walking.

Seventeen

We pile back into the car. Darby grabs Ozzie again from the backseat. She puts the handle at the bottom between her feet and grips the huge bat head in her hands as she speaks.

"What the fuck was going on in there? Between you two"

I pull away from the curb. "Nothing. He knows I kept looking for Maureen. He knows I searched everywhere."

"That's it," she says to the glass. "Although he was nosing around especially about you and Francine Waterman. Why?"

I shrug as I drive down bleak streets. Here and there life squats on the stoops and the curbs, watching us with suspicious eyes. Joining Darby in the passenger seat who's giving me the evil eye.

"Maybe Logan thinks I knew Waterman. I was up in Edison enough back when Maureen and I were together. Maybe he's thinking something like that."

I look over at her and she's pursing her lips into a solid rejection of my guesswork. "Okay, whatever," she says, looking out her window. "But one thing is certain. His disdain for his missing sister is disgusting."

I pull onto the turnpike. The traffic slows to a bump and grind.

"And he's the one who's lying," I say. "He knows something about Francine Waterman's hit-and-run."

"Other than his sweating profusely, how'd ya guess?"

"I looked into it some. The phone company where she worked bitched publicly about the lack of police security for its late-working employees and complained about how there were no arrests in Waterman's case. Employee work groups petitioned management and the town. There were small protest marches, mostly union stiffs. It was a big deal for a while."

"Some cops just keep their noses in their own case files. Let's them hang around long enough to collect their pensions. Twenty and out. Who cares about justice in between? It's about getting by. I mean, he's in Community Relations now? Jesus God."

She grows silent and then, "Bernie, he's going to make sure the cops come after you. You got an alibi?"

I start to say something but I don't know. So I shrug again.

"I'm talking to Rizzo," she says after another exit passes by. She means her police chief in Belmar. "Mo's name was on a lease in Belmar when she disappeared, right?"

"Yeah. Right next to mine."

"I'll see if he'll open Maureen's case based on residence."

"You want to find her? Really?"

"I want to stick it to Fat Logan back there. And maybe the police who are interested in helping can find out something. Something to put an end to your not-romantic-actually-sad quest to find her."

I don't take her bait. I grip the wheel and plow through.

She punches my arm. "Poor Uncle Bernie. Poor Romeo!"

I look over at her. "Thanks for having my back back there. You're a fighter. I felt a pang of pride back there."

"I think you're getting old. Acid reflux is probably the pang you're feelin."

"You got the best of Danny and Flamingo in you. A little bit of their worst too, but mostly their best. Net-net, you're alright."

She arches her back, thrusts out her chest and puts her hands on her knees, her chin lifted high. She licks her index fingertip and puts it on her right knee, gives a sizzling sound.

"HOT! Ouch! Watch out!"

I shake my head and watch the road ahead. The traffic breaks, and we sail. I flip on the radio, and Darby dives into her biting commentary about the radio news on 880. Nothing escapes her jabs. The banks that rip us off. The prosecutors who let Wall Street plunder the people but who can't stop busting punks selling marijuana on the street. The corporations that pocket huge profits but can't be bothered to hire. The pukes that give up looking for work, who just drop out. The Pope. Pedophile priests. The President. Parliament. Prince Charles. Prince. Pink. Justin Bieber. Mariah Carey. And Disney too. Don't ever get her going about the hidden menace of theme parks. Please, not when I'm around.

We make it back by mid-afternoon. We grab some pork rolls from Bing's in Avon just up Main Street from Belmar and eat 'em at a table in the window there before I drop her off at her bungalow fuck palace. She had rented the place for the off-season. It's in the ocean block on 5th in Belmar. It has no insulation, she complains. I promise to bring her a spare electric blanket for the coming fall, and she tells me not to bother. She always manages to keep warm.

She walks to her door and goes inside. Before the door closes a hand shoots out, flashing the finger at me and then a big wave. The door shuts.

I head to the Honeypot and stand on the front porch, watching the ocean sparkle like a wide net of diamonds under a blue sky without clouds or gulls. I fall into one of the tattered wicker chairs near the railing and wonder how Mo grew up in that house in Edison yet emerged intact. I think about how twisted her family had been. How fucked up her brother might be. He just wasn't right. Never was.

I think about Danny and Flamingo and Darby, about what happened to them and what I missed. When did Danny start his downward spiral that ended in murder? Why hadn't Flamingo said something? Why hadn't Darby? And where the fuck was I? I missed it all. How can you miss it all?

I think about the hole Darby saw in me her first night back. I think about how long it has been there. And how it got dug.

I wonder how Isa and I found nothing after Maureen left. How I just up and left. I shed this town and said goodbye to no one. Afterward, I left all those other towns – Philly, St. Louis, LA – with no goodbyes, no bon voyages, no gonna miss yous. This Romeo leaves no traces.

I say thank you to Isa. I say it out loud, right there on the porch in the glistening, quiet sun. I feel a swell of happiness that no man stayed in her life while I was gone. I am glad she's so imperfect that she still needs me. And I'm grateful.

Instantly I regret these thoughts. Instantly I hear my own thoughts replay. What a shit.

I watch the resilient waves as they roll hard ashore and as they scramble away almost as quickly. They try again and again, over and over, and then I pull out the Hemingway and pen. #675.

The tide

flows,

grasping for

something

that

is

nothing,

then

   ebbs,

               retreating

          from

        the reality

     it

  finds.

"Fuck me," I say aloud back to the judgmental sea. It roars back. I close up and head into the dark hotel.

Eighteen

Darby's at her desk at the Belmar PD with a jumbo coffee cup letting off steam. It's dark out now, the end of a long day. Outside the windows is the lighted police parking lot. Beyond that hovers the short bridge to Avon, its lights sparkling in an arc across the blackness.

She had gotten most of what she wanted out of Rizzo today. Although it didn't start out that way.

Rizzo was all business. His office door stayed open. He'd been watching her, he said. And then he complimented her on her work to date. She kept long hours. She showed up early. She filed concise, clear reports chock full of insight. He had read her file and congratulated her on her John Jay transcript. First in her class. A large, hard-ass class, according to his contacts in other jurisdictions. A class of achievers. She had received commendations from Freehold. A tough beat filled by tough guys and assholes. She out-assholed all of 'em.

She told Rizzo she was interested in criminal investigation work. She'd like to head a criminal bureau one day. Here in Belmar, or maybe Atlantic City or Asbury Park, which had bigger departments. He said he'd make a note of it, and he did, right then and there in her personnel folder.

She sprung it on him right about then. Said she wanted a special investigation into Maureen Logan's disappearance. No way, he said. She had no new evidence, nothing to justify an expensive and manpower-intensive inquiry into her 10-year old disappearance. His face showed disappointment that she brought it up, as if he was going to take back everything good he had just said about her. So she eased into Plan B.

She told him about her and Bernie's visit with Matt Logan in Edison. About Francine Waterman. And about how Maureen Logan had simply vanished into thin air 10 years earlier. One dead. The other gone. Both Edison girls.

She then turned the conversation to the recently killed Formosa, and though they shook their heads over it, he was still a no-go. And so she spilled. And in doing so she violated Bernie's trust. She told Rizzo about the other victims that Bernie had mentioned. Angliotti and Prelia and Ronnie Landry.

Rizzo's permanently tanned and deeply creased face ended in a sharp V of a beardless chin that he often stroked when he was thinking. He finally left his chin alone and began pulling a flabby left earlobe. She wondered if the earlobe had been tight once and if his pulling on it all these years made it hang lower than the right.

Rizzo listened to what she had to say about the cold cases. He asked her how they might be related, and she replayed Bernie's theories, saying essentially that they had to be related – there was too much coincidence with five dead women of common age all from the area. He frowned, studied her, stroked the V.

She made the big ask. She asked for permission to work after hours on what happened to Maureen Logan here in Belmar ten years ago. She said she wanted, eventually, to present a case that her disappearance was criminal, or merely a case of an unstable woman skipping town. Darby reminded Rizzo that she had had a shitload of training at John Jay into how to research public and private databases to find people and track down their activity. Belmar had it all at its fingertips, and, tell the truth, she argued, nobody else really knew how to work it and, so, it was going to waste anyway. No sense in wasting her skills and talent here, she concluded.

He nodded when she finished her pitch and approved the extra paid hours. But only if she didn't interfere with others working specific cases, logged her research, and put together a class instructing the rest of the officers on how to use online resources in their investigations.

Good enough. She took the deal and left Rizzo's office quickly before he could reconsider.

She leaned over to flip on her desk lamp. The rest of the cops' pen is dark with only the emergency signs over the doors and computer lights aglow. She takes a long sip of coffee and closed a few windows on her bright screen.

She opened a spreadsheet. Every open case that involved the murder or violent death of a young woman from New Jersey who would now be 29 or 30, Darby's own age, had they lived. Each name had a field populated with embedded documents of various kind capturing everything she had been able to collect to date, everything officially known or alleged about the victim and her possible assailants where identified. She was going jurisdiction by jurisdiction and victim by victim.

She'd have to make some phone calls to fill in a lot of missing details. She might not be able to pull it all together, but when she was done, or got as close as she could, she'd know pretty much what any cop could put together about unsolved cases involving dead girls from New Jersey over the past ten years.

But only she would have taken the time to do all of this work now, in advance of all the other cops. You take a little time to get ready, and you'll be way ahead of everyone when the time comes.

Make no mistake. She'd be ready.

She downed her coffee and chucked the crumpled cup into a waste basket. Two points.

Nineteen

The second entry says this.

∞

Sandy was first. But not the last. There were others. Like in July of 2008, it was Grace Giuliani. It was supposed to be Jennifer Botta. But things got mixed up. So what. Grace was one more perfect girl.

And Grace died like this.

She came out of Newark Symphony Hall about an hour after the concert. She was principal oboe, she was that good. And not even 30 yet. She was late because she always stayed to chat with all the other performers and help the older members of the audience call for their cabs. She was just like Jennifer. A real sweetie.

Maybe 100 people, mostly black, came out of the concert when it was over. It was a hot summer night, and few whites ventured downtown from the suburbs. The hall rose up like a Greek temple from the wide expanse of Broad Street, pissing on the low storefronts scattered on either side of the street. The place had marble columns, garland-draped cornices, two-story-tall windows, heavy brass doors, like from another era. From someone else's world.

Grace paused under the brightly lit canopy. The billboard above proclaimed that this was Newark Symphony Hall. The canopy was too modern for the tradition sought by the building, its billboards too crass, for the Doric architecture behind it. But no one really noticed, or cared. On either side of the canopy, billboards facing the sidewalks shouted TONIGHT, JULY 6, THE NEW JERSEY SYMPHONY ORCHESTRA PLAYS MOZART'S OBOE CONCERTO.

Grace's dark hair was cut short and swept back with a yellow flower on one side, allowing all to see her fine bone structure. She had a striking face. Her diamond earrings gleamed in the lights overhead.

She paused at the curb before she ran across Broad Street's six wide lanes to the parking lot across the street. Next to the lot, on the right, was the dark Newark Teacher's Union building. The building was black. The lot wasn't well lit.

She walked past the empty parking attendant's hut to her Toyota Camry in the back, farthest from the street, against the rear, barbed wire fence. In the dark because the overhead pole light was out. She set her oboe case next to the car and unlocked the driver-side door. She didn't notice the broken window on the passenger side. She didn't notice a dark shape in the front passenger seat when she put the oboe in the backseat. She didn't notice the dark presence in front when she hiked up her skirt, revealed her long, lean, tan legs, backed into the low front seat.

She finally turned her head to the right, aware of something there. But, musically brilliant as she was, she was so, so slow on the uptake.

The top of the thick pipe went straight and hard into her right eye socket, making first a crunching and then a sucking sound. It fit almost like one of those corers you use to pluck out the center of an apple or a tomato. Blood sprayed out like a popped pimple and gushed out and down her cheek. Two more hard shoves, and Grace slumped back against the door.

Grace was of course dazed, the lights inside going dim. The third shot did the trick. You couldn't see any part of her eyeball on that side of her face. It must have been pushed all the way in. Or maybe it was stuck in the pipe. The earring on that lobe, covered with muck, stopped gleaming. Finally.

I whispered her name, Jennifer, my face close to hers. She smelled of blood and her ooze, and it felt good to be doing this to one more of them. It felt right. I breathed it in. It was sour and sweet and, what? Earthy. Natural.

Grace looked stupidly at me with her one good eye. The blood now drenched her pretty white silk blouse and pearl necklace. She didn't make a sound.

I asked her if the music tonight had lifted her soul. If it had lifted the soul of the audience. If she had ascended with them to the heavens on the stairway of her music.

She blinked that one eye.

I said her name again. Jennifer.

That's when she said it. She said it low, her mouth bubbling with dark red slush that spilled through her teeth and down her chin.

She said "Not Jennifer." "Not Jenifuh" was all she could manage. Jenifuh. So funny.

I plunged the pipe into her other eye, my right hand driving it and my left hand placing it just right. Twice. Quickly. The next thrust put the pipe into her mouth, cracking teeth, chips popping onto her blood-soaked blouse.

I pulled her out of the car and onto the ground. Her skirt rode up above her waist. I stood above her and swung the pipe down across her face like a bat. Eventually I stopped.

That's where I left her. Later on that night she was raped, or so the papers said. Some sick piece of shit from the street found that poor girl with her skirt up, waiting for him. Guess he had to use a bag for the face, right?

The news said it was Grace Giuliani who died that night. Not Jennifer. Same difference.

Now I have to find Jenifuh. So funny.

∞

Twenty

I'm at the Honeypot, thinking about that Ronnie Landry video Isa showed me. We saw something else besides sheer, raw hate in the images. Ronnie was hunted down and then put down. You could see it in the exchange of words, the sudden fury of the blows, the final pounding. The slow, satisfied walk off at the end.

"What was it?" I had asked Isa at the time. "Revenge?"

Isa shook her head. I remember those veins of hers laying out a light blue ghostly grid near her temples. Her answer? "Vengeance."

"What's the difference?" I had asked.

"Revenge is payback for a wrong, tit for tat. Vengeance is self-righteous visitation of justice. Vengeance is loftier. The avenger feels the victim has it coming, believes they're getting their due. The avenger rises above the victim to a position of power or control." She punctuated her thoughts with her right hand jabbing at the air. She was so emphatic. I felt a chill then as she said it and I feel it again now.

Three of the five deaths that haunted me were by attack with a blunt instrument. All aimed at the face and head. Alison. Ronnie. Rosemary. Two were hit-and-runs. Francine and Mary, with an emphasis on crushing the skull. All vicious. Each purposeful. The two cops I reached in Edison, the ones Logan reluctantly gave me numbers for, agreed that Francine's rundown showed some signs of intention.

Francine was struck down on the fourth night of a late-night work binge. She left her office building alone after midnight each night, according to the security guard at the inside post who had been interviewed by the Edison cops. You have to cross the street at an intersection to get to the lot. Phone company employees have key card access. Anyone watching Francine would know the route and her time of exit.

It was raining the night she was killed, so she must have been moving quickly because she had no umbrella. She complained about that to the security guard. The car that hit her had to be going more than 40 miles an hour. Even though rain obscured tire tracks and evidence, a pool of watery blood on the sidewalk right in front of the parking lot entry gate suggested that was where she likely landed after the first impact. The cops said she was found in the street, however, further suggesting she had been dragged back off the sidewalk so she could be run over several times more. Her head had been crushed flat.

Francine Waterman had been murdered, one of the cops told me, brutalized with a brunt instrument that happened to be automotive in nature. They never found the car, although someone a block away saw a black car speeding away from the phone company about the time Waterman left. The cop with the little girls said he still checked every month to see if anything came up that related to her case. He himself had three girls. He wasn't about to let it go.

Vengeance. The attacker knew Francine. It was the same story with her friend Mary Angliotti. I knew that because I found out from the Bradley Beach cops that they had checked on the couple from north Jersey who were supposed to show the next morning. Except there was no retired couple. And the phone number was for a payday loan shop in Edison. The cops checked Angliotti's office. She had received a call, and her calendar showed the Saturday appointment. And the Friday night before a notation read "turn on AC for Sat. morning showing." Mary Angliotti had been lured out into the open.

I open my laptop and take a mouthful of cheap scotch, a gift from a former tenant to make up for the fist holes he left behind in his walls. I peer at a blank screen that will become my second story on Allie Formosa's death. And maybe a hundred bucks.

My story line? Formosa's was no isolated case. It was the latest in a series.

I think of something and call Isa. "How far back did you go?" I begin.

"Long time no hear. You're welcome for my car. How was Edison?"

I tell her what Darby and I learned. I leave out the part about Matt Logan nosing around about Francine Waterman like he did.

I change the topic. "Isa, are there earlier cases like Veronica Landry's or Alison's?"

"Well, I researched Veronica because of the similarities I saw with Formosa. I really didn't look anywhere else. I probably should have thought of Rosemary Prelia who got killed way back, the one that old, part-time cop told you about. But 2002 is a long time ago. "

She paused. "Bernie, one thing. Ronnie was from Belmar, remember? I just happened to stumble on that fact when Formosa's murder got me thinking, and I went back and researched Ronnie Landry's death."

"It wasn't mentioned in the papers or the media coverage you saw?"

"Nothing I looked at. And I never heard it back then. It would have spooked me even more. The police reports, the news stories, had nothing on Ronnie's background. I poked around some, and there it was. Belmar."

"So Landry's connection to Belmar, through her mother, is new news."

"I'm thinking yes."

"Yet Matt Logan didn't seem surprised when I mentioned it to him a few days ago."

"Maybe word had gotten around the stations. That happens all the time."

"Maybe. Listen, Isa, can you check obituaries easily enough?"

"It depends on how much the local newspaper has online and where their paper files are."

"Can you look for murders of women the age of our five. From say Asbury Park down to Seaside Heights to start. That's Bosco's readership."

"What time period?"

I take a sip from my glass and think some more. "Can you go back to 2000?"

"That's a lifetime ago."

I know she's conveying multiple messages here. Like, I been gone a lifetime. "I'm payin," I said.

Isa says the work would take a couple days, and she'll start tomorrow morning. Ten years of obits from dozens of newspapers, not all of which were online. She'd do what she could. She reminds me that she already has several full-time jobs and she doesn't want my money. And right then she had to head across the street to fetch her daughter, Margarita, from St. Rose's Elementary on Main.

Now it's my turn to pause. "And Isa ... be careful. Keep your eyes open."

"You worried 'bout me?"

"A little."

"You must be fallin for me at last." She laughs.

"It means I really need that obit research."

"Asshole." She hangs up.

Two hours of waiting, callbacks, voicemail, and the best gravel-throated threats I could muster get me through to a Detective Pat Ainsworth in Philly. He remembers me from a series I did on Philly police dogs, one of my more popular pieces. I remember him too. He was in charge of the canine unit back then and made it into a nice photo in the features section in one of my stories. He met his wife, a vet at an animal shelter, through me. Through that photo, I mean. He remembers Veronica Landry too.

"Look, Ruane," he says, "what we didn't tell anyone back then was that Landry thought she was being stalked."

"By who?"

"*Whom-ma*? Jesus, such grammar, Ruane. No, she didn't fuckin know who, which is why she came to us, or fuck sake. You been 'mokin' too much of that Cali wacky weed?" He snorts at his biting sarcasm and wit, as was his wont. Some things never change.

No, I've never smoked too much of that wacky weed, I think to myself. It's kinda like that song says. There's a whole lotta things I ain't never done, but I ain't never had too much fun.

"Landry said she got some voicemails from someone who said he'd 'found' her,'" Ainsworth continues. "That's the word she used. 'Found.' She said she deleted the voicemails because they scared her. Frankly, she was so full of herself we weren't sure if she was playing the celebrity game, if you know what I mean. Like, you ain't nothing unless you're being stalked somewhere."

I remind him I had been in LA for three years. I had seen stalking in spades. In fact, I tell him, there are companies in LA that hire out stalkers by the hour.

"No shit?"

Yes, complete shit, Ainsworth. Jesus. "Sex?"

"No thanks, Romeo. … Wow, I guess you really did change in Cali." He laughs. He's on a roll. Don't hold him back. "She said the voice sounded like a guy. But she also said the voice was muffled. Likely disguised."

"Like maybe whoever it was knew her and was hiding it."

I could almost see him shrug on the other end. "Got me. Wouldn't bet on anything she told us."

I tell him to explain the back and forth between Landry and the attacker. They seemed to know each other. They were familiar on some level.

"Could be anything. These psychos. I mean, he could have asked whether she liked baseball. Or if she was a Philly fan. With that bat and all."

I tell him Isa's theory about vengeance versus revenge. He agrees. "Oh yeah, this was a message. The assailant made a point."

"Made a point to who?"

"To *whom-ma*? To the fuckin victim, Bernie. That's to whom-ma."

"And the point is … 'Don't fuck with me'?"

"It's 'You did me wrong. You hurt me, and it's time you learned a lesson. And by God you will learn it.' And then bang."

I hang up and go through everything I had on the five dead women to see what might fit into a pattern beyond hometown, mode of death, and early success bespeaking a life of promise. I type out a grid and print it out.

Allie Formosa	Neptune	Shark River Hills	8.07.10	Cinderblock, open parking lot	Librarian, reading activist
Veronica Landry	Belmar	Philly	8.21.09, video	Bat/pipe, parking lot, "found you" on voicemail	Local TV anchor
Mary Angliotti (knew Waterman)	Bradley Beach	Bradley Beach	8.20.04	Hit & Run on Ocean Ave, fake phone call/set up	SSVP – realt estate, town council
Francine Waterman (knew Angliotti)	Neptune	Edison	8.29.03	Hit-and-run, dragged to street, repeat hits	Strategy Planning, to be ATT VP
Rosemary Prelia	Avon-by-the-Sea	Avon-by-the-Sea	7.11.02	Blunt/bat, back porch, vacant house	Piano player, singer, local performer

I think about the young women's ages, their early career success, their dates of death, all packed close in late summer, their hometowns all clustered on the Jersey Shore. Taken together, it suggests a pattern. The gap between '04 and '09 makes those dots hard to connect. Unless the killer left in 2004 and then returned last year. Or took some time off.

Or maybe others were killed during that time. Others unknown.

I wonder if I have a story at all. A hook that will grab Bosco.

I stare at the column of names. Who did you all piss off?

I think about adding Mo's name, but she doesn't fit here. Darby was right. She didn't have that promising profile, she hadn't been a rising star. She was older by 10 years. And there was no bloodied, lifeless body left behind, its face and skull flattened.

I think some more, drink some more. I find my hook. I pour another drink and start writing.

Twenty-One

Bosco hates the story. Too many gaps.

So we cut it back to the one storyline we can muster – five unsolved, brutal cases going back eight years involving young women of roughly the same age from neighboring towns on the Jersey Shore. It would have to do. It is indeed new news.

"It's good headline, Rome," Bosco said over the phone. "Whether their deaths are linked, whether it was the same guy what did it, is a reach right now. That's your next story."

We're breaking the story in tomorrow's Thursday print edition of *The Beach Star*. We're foregoing the web edition until Thursday night to let the paid print edition get the scoop. Rake it a little cash. And Bosco's going to send the story out to *The New York Times* after it breaks in *The Beach Star*, and then on to AP, UPI, *The Asbury Park Press*, *The Press* in Atlantic City, *The Philadelphia Enquirer*, and the *Newark Star-Ledger*, as well as all the local cable, TV, and media outlets.

I start celebrating too early. Isa's at some PTA thing for Margarita, and Darby has a date. I head out to Jack's on 10th, about a half block from the train station, to find some of my former beach buddies. After you plow through the smokers on the sidewalk, you can head into the circa 1970 dining area, which is either charming or a smoke-stained disgrace depending on whether your beer mug is half empty or half full. Or you can head into the boisterous taproom with its square bar, 20 feet on each side, locking in the barmaids.

The taproom is dark, cool, and packed. The TVs on the wall are showing an early Yankees-Rays game, and the bar is filled with the same people I left here 10 years ago. In fact, some may not have moved.

I get a lot of, "Hey, where you been? Didja go away or what? You gain some weight?" Like I never left. Mind-numbing.

I order standing up, and the cheap vodka with a splash of cranberry is in front of me already as I slide onto a retro barstool. Correction. Make that yet another unstable remnant from the '70s.

I'm between a guy who just broke ground on the new condo going up a half block away, covered in flannel, jeans and dried sweat, and a red-faced guy in a blue jacket, blue shirt and loosened red tie who's probably been knocking them back since he got off the train. A gaggle of local women, some of whom I'm sure I dated long ago, are hugging the bar, facing me. Beefy now, bottoming-up same as ever, their hair tousled from long days, bothersome kids, husbands never home, drinking with their mates. Two of them toast me, and I toast right back.

"Romeo!"

"My Juliets!"

They like that, laugh in unison, and blow me kisses off the backs of their hands.

I'm killing it, and it's only 7:25 p.m.

A guy I went to grammar school with perches in his favorite stool down the bar on the left. I'm sure his cheek impressions are planted in that seat cushion like those Hollywood stars in front of that Chinese Theater on Sunset Boulevard in Hollywood. We nod in each other's direction and then turn away. What looks like a gay couple sits on the opposite side, drinking highballs. The first she is blond, gaunt, tanned. Age marks around her eyes and lining her cheeks track the many roads of her decline. The other she is big, muscular, with short-cropped hair, and big tits in a flowered shirt off a Goodwill rack. I applauded Belmar for its progress. Opening up a bit. An hour later, I hear a deep belly laugh and realize the one with big tits is actually the husband of the bronzed blond sitting next to him. I also realize the bronzed blonde is Beverly, who had worked at *The Beach Star* as a receptionist 20 years ago. Back when offices had receptionists. Back when we didn't all work from home to save rent. Back when people bought newspapers. And read them. I barely recognize her now through her hardened skin and eyes. Or her husband with the belly laugh. God knows what roads of ruin he's run. We air-clink upraised glasses. Peace, love, dove.

I'm into my third big double by then, and the warning flare shoots across the night sky: stop now and salvage whatever reputation and dignity you brought with you and still have. One more and I'll enter the trouble zone.

I throttle back and order a goblet of Chablis and get the single lobster tail with mashed potatoes. Jack's classic. I watch Tampa go on to win and share with my brothers and sisters at Jack's the nostalgic remorse that descends communally on us all with the last out on a bad night at the ballpark in the glory days of summer, a remorse that lasts as long as the next commercial for the fall TV lineup and the next round. I wave off another round and settle up. I move from my stool slowly and carefully.

I pull with me my neighbor in the jacket and tie. I pour him into one of the cabs that waits every night at the curb for Jack's to disgorge fares starting around 10. He'll find his car at the train station in the morning. They drop me off first at the Honeypot. I pay for the two of us. The guy in the tie doesn't have far to go.

Henry takes one glance at me and pushes me up the stairs. "You owe me about a week of nights already," he flat tones. "Kitty …"

"Fuck Kitty."

"No, thank you." He shoves me into my rocking chair and locks the door behind me, the key slipped back under the door.

After a night of drinking like tonight, I'd often go back to my apartment and search Google, reverse lookup, mylife.com, Instagram, Facebook, LinkedIn, and any sites yielding even scant hope, including the paid search services available through my employers. Then I start making calls.

I would look up every Maureen Logan I could find in the mid-Atlantic and northeast states. I once tried Florida a few times on a whim, recalling one time she mentioned heading there and hiding out. A few times someone would pick up, but none of them sounded right. I'd slur desperate voicemail messages. Once I thought I found her working in some New Jersey state office. I must have left 10 messages. One day I got a return call from a male calling on behalf of Deputy Assistant Secretary Maureen Logan. He informed me I had the wrong number and that the next call I'd get would be from the New Jersey state police.

Every once in a while I'd dial the deputy assistant secretary anyway. Just to hear her voice. I do that now after Henry leaves me. A few times.

I down a couple glasses filled with ice and vodka while listening to Maureen Logan. She's added "deputy assistant secretary" to her message, probably to remind me she wasn't my Maureen. The last time I listen, I clutch my cell, staring blankly at my lap.

I get the beep.

"Iz that you," I manage. "Hey, iz that you?" How many times had she heard this pathetic sadness? How many Maureen Logans had I spooked to death? I shrug. Fuck 'em.

I hang up on the good deputy assistant secretary. No number this time. And I rock back and forth. No, of course it wasn't her. Never had been. But her voice ... so close. Just like she sounded the last time I heard it.

That last morning. "Thank you," she said. For bringing her to life with my love. Bernie "Romeo" Ruane, lover, life giver.

I wonder one more time if there was any finality I should have heard in those words. It didn't feel as if she was leaving me. Something took her away. Something grabbed her.

I pour one more. I'm out of ice. I down a long swallow.

I fall back on the bed, glass in hand, cheap, stinking vodka sloshing out and onto my hand and the blanket. I sit up and drain what's left and then throw the glass hard, like the Tampa pitcher tonight, David Price. It slams into the wall over the sink. The clock crashes onto the dirty pots left there. Glass showers onto the counter and floor. Cheap shit, thin glass from some lowlife bar. Shards everywhere. Gotta remember to go with plastic from now on. Although it makes for a less impressive show.

I take off my shoes and socks and let them fall to the floor amidst the glass that will await me in the morning. I hope I remember.

I turn off the lights. The glass on the floor glows in the red, green, and white lights from all my electronics. Pretty, I think. I lay back again. Sparkly.

I think ugly thoughts between nods of darkness. Each time my lids drop, I see Allie winking eyelessly and grinning toothlessly at me.

Sometimes I think a big reason I kept moving on over the past 10 years was to escape these blackouts. I wasn't sure if the distance I sometimes felt from new coworkers, new women, bosses, was Philly nonchalance, Midwest aloofness, LA haughtiness, or something I said or did or phoned or texted when I was drinking. But you move on. You don't have to carry about all that jettison with you. Leave it in your wake, baby. Bubye. Jettison that jetsam.

I suddenly want to punch something. Hit it. Hard. I try to sit up but I can't without spinning. And there's nothing but air to hit within reach, and then there's all that glass. I fall back again and look down my body at my pale feet glowing in the colored lights, naked, pointed alertly to the ceiling, anxious about their fate tomorrow. Join the club.

I pass out in my clothes on top of the sheets and blanket. Allison, disgusted, pulls the tarp over her slushy face.

Twenty-Two

The Beach Star banner headline screams the next day. It's not my head. It's the 45-point font.

"FIVE LOCAL WOMEN ARE COLD CASES."

The byline says Bernard Ruane. I have to admit, reading the headline, my byline, the story, it felt good. Back in the ol' saddle good.

The day started with Darby letting herself in my room around seven. She had a copy of *The Star*, and she was beaming at me. Her smile fell hard as she took me in sitting there in my rocking chair in the center of the room, pale, barefoot, hair rumpled, clothes matted. Glass on the floor.

She threw the paper into the air. The three slim sections separated and floated lazily to the floor atop the glass.

She called me an asshole and left. She came back with Henry, and together they helped me clean up. A mercy cleaning. Not a word spoken. Just the clatter and fuss of removing last night's carnage, the glass tinkling as it fell from dustpan into metal wastebasket.

Now we all sit there at my excuse of a table. Darby, Henry and me, along with a second pot of coffee, a front page, and a boatload of silence.

She breaks the ice after draining a second cup and landing it with a thud. "Listen, Bernie, Louisa's makes me sick. She's too dependent on you. She is too lost in love for you for her own good. Always has been. That's her problem."

"So?" I am trying to figure out where she's going with this but it hurts.

"I don't want her to see you like this, okay? Isa may walk. She may finally drop you like she should. You'd deserve it, but, damn it, you need her. You fuckin need something like her in your life to protect you from yourself. To make you not do what you always want to do."

With that, she gets and storms out, slamming the door. Henry finishes his coffee, nods in agreement with something he heard, rinses his cup and leaves, softly shutting the door behind him. Probably because he knows my head and maybe my pride hurt enough already.

I shower, forget to shave, dress in a black t-shirt and jeans and slip on a black sweatshirt. And then three things happen, despite my ass dragging all day and my head pile-driving.

First, I get hired. Bosco calls and gives me a full-time job. At last I'm gonna get some business cards. He wants to make it official now that the story broke. The guy absolutely shit himself over the prospect that he had a real story in his paper.

It's not much. I'll get $2,100 a month and all the coffee I can drink so long as I make it into the office. With real half and half. I don't have to do school board and city council meetings until the story winds up, but after that all bets are off because at my salary I'll have to handle most of the reporting.

Second, my cell phone won't stop ringing. Bosco had succeeded big time in stirring up the media. They clamor to follow us up with their own storylines. Papers in Newark, New York, Philly, and up and down the shore are running something online and in their Friday print editions. *The Beach Star* and Bernard Ruane are going to get a lot of mention. By three o'clock I speak to CNN, News12 NJ, the networks out of New York and Philly, and a few of their counterparts in Wilmington, Baltimore, and Washington, DC. *The Today Show* wants to interview me on Monday. The Jersey Shore is the angle – meaning decadence, decay, and depravity.

Dead girls, dead girls, what you gonna do. What you gonna do when they come for you.

I stop answering the phone around noon. Mid-afternoon, Henry brings me a fat burger and crisp fries from the beach grill on the boardwalk, some iced beers, and a stiff shot of warm Sambuca shots from downstairs. He tells me the Honeypot is breaking September records for room rentals. At this rate, he says, we'll be renting out all 40 rooms to reporters and camera crew.

Third, something's coming. It's in the air. It's like a dense fog off the ocean in the morning. It's there waiting when you go outside, surrounding you, closing you off from what was there yesterday. Heavy, but it steals in so quietly, imperceptibly, that its grasp, its tenacity, its depth surprise you.

I'm saying that Belmar's scared. Fear has come ashore.

Same with the other beach towns. Isa stops by after work and gives me the lowdown. The local radio station, Belmar's WRAT, became all talk during the day as people called in nonstop. Seems like everybody has seen somebody lurking somewhere, here, there, somebody with a pipe or a bat. Someone saw some freak on Main Street with a club whittled from a log. The story's on people's lips in every corner, from downtown Belmar and the post office on Main, to Jody's Fishery and Kelly's Korner Tavern over the bridge in Neptune, to the Who's On Third Diner in Spring Lake. They see darkness at the edge of town, and it's creeping in. It's always been out there, evil waiting for its moment.

Darby calls at day's end to tell me tips and prowler calls were coming in like crazy. She didn't ask how I was feeling. She hung up too fast.

Later I turn on the tube. Local TV on cable is running with whatever photos they can find. They start with the still shots published this morning in *The Star*. They're mostly headshots, beauty shots, showing five happy, clean, vibrant women peering back at you with all the hope and dreams in their starry brown, hazel, and blue eyes. Then come the live action/eyewitness/on the scene/breaking news spots filmed throughout the day by TV reporters along the Belmar boardwalk. All of them regurgitate the *Star* facts, local cops at their side, the ocean behind them blinking, innocent and full of expectation, in the sterile, cold sun trolling above.

The cameras uniformly pan either up or down the boardwalk as the stories wind up, and the talking heads ask viewers to think where might the murderer be, where might he next strike. And then comes the intoning plea, as the reporters get all close and intimate with the camera, with you, their hair blowing in the ocean breeze. With imploring eyes, they remind viewers to stay safe, look before crossing the street, stay away from unlit places, from empty parking lots and dark corners. Don't go out alone. Anywhere.

Later in the evening, the news moves on to more intimate photos that family and friends had emailed and texted in over the day. Childhood party, prom date, beach fun, graduation. Pain crawls through the lines of the reporters' stiff faces as they ask viewers to watch these five women grow up on TV. "If there are children in the room," becomes the intro chant, "this might be a good time for them to leave." Images flash across the screen of the grisly murder scenes and of the ashen faces of police officers and neighbors, grief-stricken mothers and fathers, sisters and brothers, boyfriends and hangers-on. Born-agains preach the end is nigh. NJ12 promises a two-hour special Friday night – Cold Cases on the Hot Jersey Shore. We'll tell the whole story, they promise. Every last damn thing.

You'll see and hear it all play out on the tube and the radio again and again until the next horrible tragedy involving a pretty young thing.

The reporters eat up the cold case storyline, cases unsolved, young girls in their prime. Forgotten. Until now. The local cops surely would be feeling the heat tomorrow and for days to come.

Bosco's all over me when we get together at a back table of the Dunkin' Donuts on 16th close to midnight, our eyes on the door. He dumps extra sugar in his coffee and stirs it slowly. When he's done with the sugar and his stirring, he wags a finger at me.

"You know what's happened?"

"What?"

"This story's already bigger than us. It's gonna hit the *Today Show*. But someone else will be talking about it, guaranteed. You'll get your ass bumped by some talking head. Some big professor or prosecutor. Some women's rights chick. Not me. Not you. You'll be lucky if you're the one doing the local radio interview with WRAT, maybe that hot chick that does the heavy metal show, the one that hangs out at Surfer's Porch."

"Joanie."

"Yeah, her. I hope someone remembers we broke this story."

"Someone like Mr. and Mrs. Pulitzer."

He smiles and toasts his steaming coffee at me. "That'll do."

He can't stop talking. "I'm hearing the Monmouth County chief prosecutor's got interviews with local and national press all day tomorrow. I'm hearing that every area police department has interviews all fuckin day. Their asses are on the firing line."

"That's good, right?"

"I'm warning ya, don't get stupid, Bernie. Don't cross any fuckin line in any fuckin bar or hangout of yours. No speeding. No reefer in the goddamned glove compartment. No blow in a folded-up paper in your shirt pocket. Cops ain't gonna be liking your ass one bit. It's looking like they all fucked up big time. And now they'll fuck you up as soon as look at you. And me."

I nod solemnly. "No reefer in the glove compartment. No blow in the pocket. Sage advice."

"No shitting around, Bernie. And by Monday, my man, if not sooner, our fellow travelers of the Fourth Estate will be hitting up the New Jersey governor. Why no task force? Why no attention? Where you been, tough guy? You too busy handing out speeding tickets to care about all these Jersey Shore girls dying right and left?"

Bosco's rubbing his hands. "Our focus, our angle, has to be investigatory. We don't blame. Let others do that using the facts we bring to the light of day. We take the high road, dude. Relentless pursuit of justice. We want to find the perpetrator and help bring him in. No muckraking, no name-calling, no self-serving TV shit. We're going for the Pulitzer."

"Wow, Bosco. Take a breath."

"I haven't been in this business for two decades pullin my dick, dude. Finally, my time, our time, has come." His hands are red from his rubbing them together greedily. His beady eyes glow and widen. He's a sight on a late night at a table in a boardwalk Dunkin' Donuts at the Jersey Shore. And that's saying something.

Darby pushes through the door. She had called me earlier saying she had something to say privately to Bosco and me. She's wearing a crisp uniform, all business. She gets a cup of coffee and joins us. She flips the lid and sips it black through a haze of steam.

She takes off her cap. She's cut her hair so it comes just below her ears and is a tad longer on the right and cut short in back.

"Nice 'do," I offer.

"Hot," blinks Bosco, his palms red and his eyes still wide.

"Thanks, fashion and lifestyle experts. You got a glamour section at the paper now? Jesus fuck, let's get on with it, okay, dickheads?"

The assembled dickheads shut up to listen. We slurp our coffees. All ears.

"You missed one."

"One what?" I asked.

"One victim."

My phone vibrates, and I lower my gaze. It's Isa. I raise an index finger back at Darby and pick up. Darby sighs and sits back, punching her cell to catch the time.

"Bernie, I finished the obituaries," she says. "Turns out there's one more dead girl."

I scan the premises. The place is empty except for the space cadet behind the counter with the glazed eyes. I put her on low speaker. I tell Bosco and Darby that Isa's found another victim. I pump down the volume, and we all lean in to listen.

Isa starts, but Darby cuts her off. "Sandy O'Conner," she says.

"Right," says Isa.

"I've been looking into cold files," Darby says. "Rizzo said I could look at priors involving, well, female assault and murder victims in New Jersey who are roughly the same age as the victims we know about." She almost said Maureen Logan.

"Why didn't you mention this?" I ask.

She shrugs. Bosco looks at Darby, waiting. "And?"

"And, I found something," she says. "Something that happened right here in Belmar. But you have to find another source than me about this. You run with it without another source, and I'm truly fucked. Rizzo will chew my ass out. Credit Isa, got it?"

"I don't need your freebie, Darby," says Isa.

Darby leans in closer to the phone on the table, whispering now. "Sandy O'Conner was killed in August of '99. She was 19 then, a year plus out of high school. Same age as your other girls, Bernie, if they had all lived."

"Your age at the time, too" I say. "You were 19 then."

"I remember this. Sandy got her head beat into the pavement until she died, and then some. Her brain was leaking out, that's how violent it was. Happened a couple blocks over from here, in the parking lot behind her parent's two-bedroom condo."

"The two-story condo on Ocean? Between 13th and 14th?" Bosco asks. Darby nods. A block north of the Surfer's Porch and a block south of the Honeypot.

"Sandy O'Connor," I say. "I remember I had been back a couple of weeks from Woodstock '99 when she was killed. Mid-August it happened. But Sandy's case was different. It was love gone bad, wasn't it? And I thought they put someone away for it." Bosco's nodding his head while I speak.

"Her boyfriend, Timothy Darnall," Darby continues, "black dude from Asbury Park she met in high school. She was running late from her summer job. She was interning at *The Trenton Times*. It was her last week before heading back to college."

"Darnall claimed she told him to wait for her on the beach. She was going to bring him a joint and some soda and munchies so they could stay up and watch the stars. That's where he was, he said, when it all went down in the parking lot. That was his fucking alibi. When she didn't come down, he said he left the beach and checked out the apartment and it was locked. He went into the back parking lot and saw her car. He found her on the ground next to it. Said he lifted her head in his hands and felt something thick and wet drip between his freakin' fingers, and he dropped her head back to the ground. He called 911 from a payphone on the boardwalk. There was blood and brains all over him. All over the phone."

Isa's voice squawks over the phone, "I was going to tell you I found Sandy's obituary. I also went through the Darnall trial transcript."

"Prosecution said Sandy and Darnall had a huge fight that summer. Seems Sandy told Darnall she was going places and was buying herself a one-way ticket outta here. She wanted to be at *The New York Times* or *Washington Post*, and she already had a ton of credentials for a kid her age. This was going to be her last summer in Jersey, certainly Trenton, and for sure Belmar."

"So he killed her? Like that?" Bosco and I shake our heads in syncopated style. "No," we say as one.

"Prosecution claimed it was a trap," says Isa. "That he called her down to the shore to beg her not to leave. Or keep her there forever. So believed the jury apparently. He had motive. He was fuzzy about when and how he found her. They tripped him up on the stand and got him showing his fangs. He got into fights a lot. Had a couple misdemeanor disorderly conduct convictions. One assault charge that was dropped. And he had her damn blood all over him, even on the payphone. There was no other plausible story. I mean, no one else knew she was headed to Belmar that weekend. Defense produced NO one. ... Snap. Life up in Rahway prison."

Darby and I look at each other. With Danny Ruane.

"Is Darnall still in prison?"

Darby shakes her head at Bosco. "Dead, Johnny," she answers flatly. "Shanked, after being raped a bunch of times by the welcome wagon. Seemed he was resisting his new bottom role too much."

"Jesus, stop." I wave my hand in the air.

"Bernie," Isa says, "I found nothing else in the obits for the time period you asked me to search. Only Sandy. And listen to this. Her obit in *The Beach Star* and a longer one in the *Newark Star-Ledger* said she'd been an A+ student all her life. She went to Benedictine Academy for high school up north in Elizabeth and some grammar school up there. Was in her first year at Princeton, majoring in English."

"And?" Darby's frowning, wondering what this means.

"And so I called the guidance counselor at Benedictine and asked about Sandy. I got some nun. She couldn't stop talking about her."

"She still remembers her all these years later? What'd she say?" Darby looks at me with arched brows.

"She went on and on with a ton of superlatives. Sandy this, Sandy that. She said Sandy won some young women's award just after Christmas one year. The Christmas before the summer she got murdered."

"The Christmas before the summer … so very late 1998 or early 1999?"

"I think so. But that's all I got for now."

We sit back and take it in. Some unfamiliar faces enter, several of them with cables in their hands, one in a white shirt and red tie with a mike popping out of the breast pocket of his dark blue sports jacket. Cameramen. And a talking head, probably a Sterling or a Lance. They notice us and are stopped cold by the vision of newly coiffed Darby in a tight cop uniform chatting with me and Bosco sporting our stone-washed, unemployed bum looks, all clustered conspiratorially around a cell phone on a tabletop late at night in a Dunkin's in the newly named murder capital of the western world.

"Good stuff, Isa," I say over the phone. "But we gotta go. We just lost our privacy."

We all head out past the TV crew and into the night.

Darby slides into the driver seat of her squad car and squeals out north onto Ocean Avenue. I walk back to the Honeypot, while Bosco crosses Ocean and shuffles south on the boardwalk.

Henry pulls out the scotch bottle when I enter the lobby and sets it on the registry counter with a couple of sentry glasses on either side. The place is lousy with the free press, some asleep in their rooms upstairs, most getting hammered in the lounge where Darby and I first talked the night she got back into town. A few industrious sorts are heading to the boardwalk to stake out positions for the morning interviews.

Henry and I down a couple behind the desk. I tell Henry I got it tonight, and he sulks out the front door to pet Kitty. I nurse one more in the lounge with some of the boys and then tidy up and climb the stairs to bed. I only had to bang on three doors to tell them to turn down the non-stop coverage of the Jersey Shore Murders.

I find two Jersey reporters waiting for me outside my door, one from Cape May down south and one from Atlantic City. I bring them up to speed. Professional courtesy. We kick the cases around for another half hour over some India pale ales from a stocked ice chest in one of the reporters' rooms.

I fall into bed. I think about Sandy O'Connor and nuns and Christmas and prizes. Nothing makes sense. I finally fall sleep, but not until after Allie Formosa comes down the chimney with no eyes, no teeth, using a big red tarp for a sack.

Twenty-Three

The Honeypot is a half block away from this bench on the boardwalk where I'm sitting. It looks like a shitbox in this blinding sunlight. There are other words that fit. Old. Ramshackle. Neglected. Abandoned. Lonely. The rooftop is uneven, the gray paint on the sides peels away in patches, and the third-floor windows are dull and dirty in the sun's hard light. A couple droops in their chipped frames. It's no place to live, that much is for sure.

Summer's heat has disappeared suddenly before a big cold front that blows down from the north, fall putting out a trailer of coming attractions. The wind whips off the ocean, and white caps froth on a rolling sea and then quickly melt away. The seagulls surf strong gusts that scatter trash, skittering it wildly along the concrete streets. Stop signs creak in the wind. Birds cluster for their meager warmth on the telephone lines. The few people walking by pull coats and hoods tight as they squeeze in some exercise before the weather changes.

The killing of the girls is on everyone's lips. All over the news. Everywhere. And even now, in death, they're perfect. They're just so pretty and perfect. Aren't they.

Eventually they'll all die. That's the real story. But it's taking so long.

It has been hard work over these past years. It's hard, and so sometimes you have to stop and rest, collect yourself and your thoughts. Dig yourself a hole and hide.

And every once in a while things go dark, the overhead switch flicked off. You forget why they must go, why they all have to die, and you have to gather your thoughts again. You do nothing until the passion relights. Then and only then, click, the urge comes back. Because suddenly you remember why.

You start up again. You go on. One by one by one.

You have to finish up your own work. Cross off your own list. When they're all gone, it will be better. There will be relief. Peace.

Sandy seems like ages ago.

The rest are within reach.

Except for Jenifuh.

Grace Giuliani was a lot like Jennifer Botta, so the mistake was natural. Both sheer perfection. Both musical masters. Both the same age. They were friends even.

But Jenifuh, it turned out, was now at Oxford University in England, teaching music and oboe, and when she performed anymore it was in a little academic chamber group. It took time to track her down, but it was all there, her whole story, on the department's web page. Even her office location and hours. And her office and cell phones.

But going there would be tricky. Expensive too. And it would require a passport.

Two seagulls fall suddenly and heavily to the boardwalk in front of the bench, fighting viciously over a large opened clamshell from the ocean, its moist meat gleaming in the sun. The bigger gray one drops its hold on the clamshell and slashes with its thick, sharp beak at the smaller one's eyes, cawing obscenities. The smaller one cowers and then flees on its quick little legs, flying off at last, fast and low over the sand. The victor cries out in triumph. She flies up high into the blue sky with her wet prize, leaving behind the shattered, empty shell on the boardwalk.

Jenifuh will have to come back home. To the shore. Here. It's the only way.

She has a mother down the shore. In Seaside Heights. Jenifuh's mother could get her precious daughter to come back. Something would happen to her, and her precious daughter would have no choice but to return home.

It was easy to do a reverse white page search online and get the mother's phone number. It was easy to find out where she lives. Easy to come up with her photo, lots actually, ones they'd post after their monthly bridge club luncheons. Her bio was there on her church website, when they celebrated her 25th anniversary as secretary for the priests.

Poor thing. She lives alone now, the bio said. Her husband's no longer with us, God rest his soul. But she still goes to the same daily morning mass. Her daughter's in England. She's so lonely. Poor, poor momma.

That familiar thing bubbles up. An ache inside, like after you eat bad food that has to be passed. A burning hurt of an ache, these cramps that bend you over with shooting pain and sudden, heavy sweats. And along with the cramps and the sweat, hate spasms up from your bowels. Over the abandonment. The rejection. The dismissal. The void.

Hate can warm you. It can fill the void. It can make you feel alive. It feels a lot like love.

A tall woman and a little girl suddenly stop on the sidewalk in front of the Honeypot. They came from the other direction. From town. It's Louisa and her daughter. Mother and child. Holding hands. They walk together, and then they laugh as they head upstairs.

They're perfect too in their own way. Aren't they.

They go inside without knocking.

The ache and the pain and the cramping rise again. The desire is back. It's time.

Twenty-Four

"What's up, Ruane?" She's in early this morning despite her late-night shift. Fatigue hangs off her. They sit on either side of his cluttered desk, his office door open.

"I've been working some late nights. Researching online. I found something that doesn't fit with the *Beach Star* stories."

"The *Beach Star* stories? I said you could look into Maureen Logan's disappearance 10 years ago."

"Well, I expanded a little bit."

He's frowning. "This better be good."

"I was trying to come up with a list of unsolved murders or crimes of violence against Jersey Shore women over the last 10 years or so."

He says nothing, waiting her out.

"*The Beach Star* is totally focused on the beach angle. The victims all came from beach towns, so there must be some connection there. That's their thinking."

"So if you find similar cases over the past decade involving women not from the shore …"

"We go down a different path."

"And?"

"And I found a case in Newark. Involving a Grace Giuliani. She was beaten to death with a pipe according to the detective reports. There were microscopic metal flecks in her wounds. Looked like the pipe was swung or plunged into her head and face with significant power and force. It was a vicious, maniacal assault like all the rest documented in *The Beach Star*. And she was a young woman with a bright future, like the rest. She was early 30s, same age range as the rest."

"Unsolved I take it."

"Yep." She looks at her notes. "Sunday, July 6, 2008."

"Where was she from?"

"Born and raised in New Orleans. Lived in Newark for the past few years in an apartment she rented. She lived there the entire time she was in New Jersey. She was an outstanding oboist with the Newark Symphony. No known connections at all to the Jersey Shore from what I can see so far."

"Huh."

"And another thing, captain. She was raped after the assault."

"Totally unlike the Jersey Shore cases." He smelled a break. "Do we have DNA?"

"Yes. But I think there's been a real shitty job of DNA matching here. I mean, they didn't do matches in all the available databases, only a sampling. Pretty shoddy work if you ask me."

"Give me the case number and the investigating officer, and I'll make some phone calls. We'll push for complete DNA matching. But it'll take some time. Maybe weeks."

"I'll email you the info on the Giuliani woman."

"If this leads to a perpetrator we can identify and apprehend, this may shed entirely new light on the Jersey Shore murders. Put out a call to the other departments and have them ready to produce any DNA on the *Beach Star* girls when we need it. Any others like this Giuliani girl?"

She flips loose strands of her hair behind an ear, suddenly stops self-consciously, and then sits straight. "There's one other. But she's from Belmar, and it happened in Belmar."

She tells him about Sandy O'Connor's assault in the Belmar beach condo parking lot in 1999. About the successful prosecution of her boyfriend Timothy Darnall. How it was a closed case but one that now has to be reconsidered in light of the pattern of murders at the Jersey Shore that *The Beach Star* was uncovering.

She watches him stroke the V. "I remember that case," he says. "I didn't believe it was Darnall then, but the evidence disagreed with me. I'll see if we can pull some DNA there too."

"Darby, you keep calling it the *Beach Star's* story, when it's Bernie Ruane who's got the pen there. Your uncle."

Her face reddens. She was hoping to avoid this line of interrogation.

"If you're right about Giuliani, you'll cut Bernie's nuts off. Have you told him what you found?"

"No sir, he knows nothing about the Giuliani case."

"That bother you? That you're holding out on him?"

"I'm not holding out on him. This is police work. I'm not Lois Lane to his Jimmy Olsen."

"Maureen Logan?"

"What?"

"What's any of this got what to do with Maureen Logan? The reason I let you do all this after-hours work, remember? Bernie's old girl friend?"

"She's not a Jersey Shore girl. She's Edison. She doesn't fit the *Beach Star* pattern."

"Except that she disappeared here and was last seen with your uncle, who's from here. She could be like Giuliani. She might point us to someone from the Jersey Shore that a Jersey Shore preoccupation won't."

"She's on my to do list."

"Your to do list."

"Working it!" Darby smiles, stands, and leaves, closing the door behind her.

Rizzo sits quietly, staring at the closed door. She's working it, all right, double time. She's gonna beat her uncle at his own game, no matter what. She's gonna win, no matter what.

He wonders about Darby, how rough she gets. He's starting to see that there's the good, the bad, and then there's the Darby.

Twenty-Five

Sergeant Matt Logan watched the TV reporter go giddy about Ruane's five cold cases. "The fuck," he said to the gloomy black man slumped behind a desk.

The wall behind the black man was a testament to the commander of Edison's Criminal Investigations Bureau. Dozens of photos showed Edison's first and now highest-ranking black officer shaking what looked like every white hand in town, in the state for that matter. The handshaking and grin-fucking were the hard part, he would tell his folks at church, twice as painful as the bullet and knife wounds he got from two gang roundups that put him all over page one of the Jersey papers and resulted in multiple medals of valor.

Commander Mitchell Crombie eyed Matt Logan. He didn't like his creepy ass. Logan was poured into an ill-fitting police uniform littered with rows of bullshit ribbons that had nothing to do with valor. He was wearing the medals on the wrong uniform – the violation was clear. This kind of cheap show was typical of cops known for cracking skulls, for detentions costing thousands in court costs and damage awards, and for building loads of community ill will. So, of course, some dumb shit up top puts Logan in charge of community f'ing relations. That would change one day if Crombie had anything to do with it.

Crombie turned down the TV's volume and swiveled around to thumb through the files in front of him one more time. He looked up.

Sergeant Logan's there to talk about a matter that involved him personally – his missing sister. He brought with him the goon sitting next to him, his bureau's commander. Palma was his name. This guy was just another fat fuck renting space in a uniform.

Crombie got up from his chair, his back to the unsightly duo. "Sergeant Logan, you're asking me to launch an investigation into the disappearance of your sister, who cut out from these parts some 10 years ago. A woman who wasn't legally a resident in Edison."

Logan sat as straight as he could. "Yes, sir. And into the Francine Waterman case as well, sir. I believe they're related, sir."

"You come here on matters entirely outside your areas of responsibility. With no evidence of any foul play related to your sister's disappearance. No proof of this so-called connection?"

"No, sir, but ..."

Crombie returned to his desk. He opened a thin file. "If anything, the file says she was prone to disappearing, had a shit relationship with you and your family, had no real ties to Edison, or maybe to anything on God's green earth. Maybe she just took the fuck off. She was an adult in her late twenties when she left. That's what adults do sometimes."

"Sir ..."

"I'm not done." He opened another, thicker file. "As for Waterman ... Waterman was a hit-and-run, a nasty one, and we haven't been able to prove anything else for over seven years."

"Yessir, I mean, no sir, but ..."

"Stop." Crombie waited until he was sure Logan had shut the fuck up.

"Now," Crombie continued, nodding at *The Beach Star* on his desk, "Waterman is, or was, younger than your sister. By seven, eight years, right? And your sister Maureen isn't from the Jersey Shore like each and every one of the women in the Ruane article."

"But, Mitch ...," Palma interjected.

"I got this, commander, unless this falls into internal affairs or involves Edison's sizable but aging vehicle fleet ..."

Palma shook his head no.

" ... then you're out of it. It's not in the administrative bureau. It's mine now."

He waited for a return volley and then went on.

"To continue. Sergeant Logan, your sister's situation and the Waterman case seem entirely unrelated to me. And I see no pattern in your sister's so-called disappearance that looks or smells anything like the five cases that *The Star* is reporting. Five open cases involving pretty rough, seemingly highly personal assaults against five good women from neighboring towns down the shore, two of whom, Waterman and that other hit-and-run, actually knew each other."

Crombie paced behind his massive desk, his hands clasped behind his back. He stopped next to them. "I'd say Ruane has a real story here, wouldn't you gentlemen? One that been sitting under our noses?"

"And, while I'm on it, guys, frankly, the way this fucking Waterman case has been handled? It just pisses me off. A complete fuck-up. Her hit-and-run investigation is prob'ly the worst botch job I've seen in my 25 years of criminal investigations into vehicular murders. And we found jack-shit? And after finding jack-shit, we put it on ice not even nine fucking months after the incident? What the fuck?"

Crombie looked at the two blank faces staring at him. "Commander Palma, you handled my criminal bureau back then. In fact, you signed off on the final disposition of the Waterman case." Crombie threw the file on the desk. It landed with a loud smack. "You iced it, am I right?"

"I did."

"Well, I'm reopening it. I'm going to make sure everyone knows how badly this case was handled, and I'm going to apologize publicly on behalf of the department to Francine Waterman's family and to the local community about the less-than-exemplary handling of the case."

Palma pushed himself up and out of this seat. "I'm done here. You're way out of your league here, Mitch."

"What league's that, commander? Your bocce ball league?"

"Fuck you." He stumped out of the office, leaving Logan behind. Logan watched him leave with a panicked look and then faced a somber Crombie, alone.

"I'm reopening Waterman, Logan, and you can draft my apology for a press release. After I okay it, make sure it goes to all the right community groups, especially the women's groups and the union shops at the phone company."

"Yes, sir."

"As for your sister, I see nothing."

Logan cleared his throat and swallowed. "But sir, excuse me. This Bernie Ruane, this reporter." Logan stuck his chin in the direction of *The Star*. "He comes from a mental family. His brother is in Rahway for killing his own wife with his bare hands, for Christ's sake. His father was always getting into bar fights. Tried to run down his kids ..."

"Logan! "Crombie shouted, slapping the desk with an open hand. The sound echoed harshly. "Maybe you didn't hear me. I said ..."

"Two seconds, sir. Ruane, this whack job, he was living with my sister Maureen when she disappeared. He's the last known person to see her alive. And he up and left town, left the state, after she disappeared. He's been gone 10 years. Then he suddenly returns. And within days this Formosa chick is killed."

Crombie paused. "How long was he with your sister?"

"More than a year maybe, back in'98, '99. Maureen disappears in mid-2000. Soon after which he takes off. Then he comes back, and one more woman is dead over in that yacht club parking lot. And then he somehow, miraculously, uncovers all these unsolved, forgotten cases that happened during the time he's been supposedly gone, cases involving dead women from towns all within a 10-minute drive from where he was when my sister disappeared and from where he is now. No one's seen the pattern all these years until he shows up and points it out. He puts it all together in a matter of, what, a month?"

Crombie opened Maureen Logan's file again and made some notes on a sheet clipped to the inside front of the folder. "There's been no record of her since 2000? No bank records? No phone records? No welfare checks? No hospital visits?"

"Well, a case was never opened. But that's what Ruane claims. And nothing's ever come to the house in Edison."

"What else you got?"

"Sir, you said my sister didn't come from the Jersey Shore like the other women. That's not entirely true. See, our mother grew up in Sea Girt, a couple towns south of Belmar on the ocean. My mother's family worshipped the nuns there. My mom always helped out with all their nun programs for young kids especially. When we were young, I mean up until high school, my sister and I would help set up and take down chairs and shit like that at the local events the nuns had. There were too many problems and too few nuns, so they went up and down the shore."

"So you're sayin what? Did your sister hang out with any of these dead women?"

"I don't know. Like you said, she's older." He nodded at *The Beach Star* again.

"Your mom alive?"

"No. She died a month or so before Maureen disappeared."

"She dies, and Maureen disappears forever less than two months later."

"Yes."

"Any connection in your mind? My experience tells me that incidents like your mother dying may send you off into strange territory."

Logan grew quiet and looked at his hands. "No. They weren't close."

Crombie studied him. "But you never know. It could have triggered a reaction in your sister. Made her want to get some distance. From here. From whatever. Permanently."

Logan shrugged. "She didn't walk off. Ruane did something to her. I can smell it on him."

"Uh huh. What's that smell like? I could use that superpower in my job."

Logan felt relief and let out a smile.

"I'm not getting an answer. Your sister acted normal after your mother died? Before she split?"

Logan held up replying for a few moments, thinking, looking again at his clasped hands in his lap. Then looked up at Crombie. "Normal for her I guess. But she was with Ruane. I didn't see her. I wouldn't know. She didn't even come to the funeral."

"Your father around?"

"Nope, he died a while back, a few years before my mom."

"Other brothers or sisters?"

"Nope. My mother had a brother. Haven't heard from him in years."

"And you haven't checked?"

"No. I, uh, I don't know even how to reach him."

Crombie grew silent, kicking it around in his head. Nothing really came together, but to ignore Ruane's possible involvement wouldn't be prudent, not with the shit storm of publicity about the Jersey Shore murders and possible police complacency as it was unfolding. It was an angle that, left untended, could bite him in the ass.

Logan sat straight, like a new medal was coming.

"Shit," Crombie said. "I mean, starting a criminal investigation on a reporter who's writing stories about young women whose suspicious deaths the cops have apparently ignored. Fuck. Doesn't look good. To anyone."

Crombie shook his head. "Listen, we got a call later today with the county and the other towns where these girls came from and where they got killed. I'll bring all this up."

Logan wiped sweat from his cheeks. His hair was damp. "Thank you, sir."

Crombie looked at Logan. "I'll take if from here." He sat heavily in his desk chair and picked up the newspaper for what had to be the tenth time that morning.

Logan got up to leave. "And commander?"

"Fuckin what, Logan?"

"You're smart to reopen Waterman. There's something wrong there. And I bet we'll find it. Something that's spelled B-e-r-n-i-e." At that, Logan left in a hurry.

Crombie reached under his desk and turned off the digital recording device he used for meetings like these, ones that could come back to haunt him. You got to protect your ass if you're a black man rising in this department. And that he was. Rising up.

Twenty-Six

Last night I stayed with Isa, and this morning we woke in each other's arms and made quick, hard, wordless love. We fell back onto the sheets. I started to say something, but she shook her head. She got up. "I need a bloody," she said.

After hurried showers, we hit the Belmar Fishing Club for Sunday brunch. Through the windows that filled the end of the room we looked at a fishing pier that reached out to the Atlantic Ocean's thin horizon. The pier was 20 yards wide and extended over 100 yards from the beach toward a small bait house that sat at the end. We were some 20 feet above the waves, and you could feel them underneath us as they pounded the pilings.

Margarita and her uncle Nick were at the pier's railing. He was showing her how to fish. The sky behind them was deep blue with white puffs of cloud scampering from right to left ahead of a breeze from the south that was beginning to whip up white caps below. You could almost reach those clouds. The sky rats dived, cawing for fare. Cool came the breeze, stirring our buzz from several spicy bloodies.

The long, narrow clubhouse had one dark-brown paneled room that was as wide as the pier and extended down it a ways. Inside the room at the near end was a long bar with comfortable couches and chairs near a huge fireplace. At the far end was a cluster of a dozen small, round tables sporting red-and-white checked tablecloths. We took a table near the windows overlooking the pier and the ocean.

It was over a week since my story hit about the Jersey Shore's five cold cases, and the resulting hoopla had died down. As it does. Rizzo cancelled on Bosco and me, telling us there'd be no interviews. The *Today Show*, as Bosco predicted, stiffed me and ran with a former federal prosecutor who had barely read my story. Governor "Piñata" Christie had outpunched the press, formally launching a task force of county and municipal investigators to oversee the investigation, with Belmar and Rizzo coordinating the local towns on the task force. The New Jersey State police were chipping in too after Christie publicly kicked them in the ass. And for good measure, the FBI had sent a small team up to Freehold to offer assistance to the Monmouth County Major Crimes Bureau that was taking the lead on the investigations.

We were waiting for the next shoe. The cops hunkered down. The press milked the sordid storylines for all they could. There was an endless loop of photos of pretty, young, dead women, and videos and life histories, and even NBC's Brian Williams got in on the action, blaming any missteps over the years on budget cutbacks for cops. There were plenty of platitudes from elected officials like the former prosecutor, and local cops pledged to close every last case. The press vacated the Honeypot mid-week, as up north in a single day there were two ugly murder-suicides in Jersey City and a tenement fire in Hoboken that fried 10 sorry souls.

Everyone along the shore was on edge. Even a sweet Indian summer weekend like we were having this late September day failed to woo the usual crowds to the beach for one last summer fling. People stayed home. People stayed in. Christie got mad about that too and told people to hit the beach before it was too late.

Margarita runs up to me through the open door. Her little hand reaches up, and her lips pull back from her perfect white teeth in her version of utter horror. Then she bravely shows me the small black eel they're using for bait to catch the striped bass that came up close to the pier, her face as far away as it could get from her presentation.

"Kiss it, Bernie. Kiss it for luck. Uncle Nick says you like to."

"He did, huh?" I lean in to comply, my lips puckering, and Margarita squeals in delight and disgust and runs off to her uncle who grins back at me. I flash him the bird without Margarita seeing. He smiles and nods.

I turn to Isa. She still hasn't found her smile today. She wears a black T-shirt and tight skirt and black flip-flops. The only color is the blood-red belt at her thin waste that matches the streak in her hair that's pulled tight as shit into a braided ponytail that shoots down the middle of her back and hangs like a blade waiting for my back to turn.

The Belmar Fishing Club has a saying, so I try it.

"'Blessed are they with cheery smile, who stop to chat for a little while. Blessed are they who never say: 'You've told me that story twice today.'"

She narrows her droopy blue eyes. "Uh huh. Nice try."

We get our share of attention from the waiters. It's not just her good looks and growing income. Her granddaddy was the only Italian in the group of local guys who founded the membership-only club more than 100 years ago. Over the years its functional pier in productive ocean waters put food on the table for the locals when it was hard to find work. For folks along the shore lucky enough to know a member, it serves as a primo venue for the great "sport" of fishing. These days, it's mostly used for entertainment, showing off and providing a lark for kids and grandkids. The club is starting to show its age, and the economy's collapse isn't helping with the upkeep.

Being the descendent of a founder means you're royalty among the old-timers. Everyone wants to kiss the papal ring, or in this case the ring of princess Louisa Bongiovanni.

I position my face in front of hers, but not too close. "What's up?"

She looks at me. "Your interview with WRAT last night sucked."

I reach for my glass. Which was of course empty. Hers, of course, was full. Fucking waiters. I wave for a refill.

"You wait until now to say it?"

"Jesus, sometimes it takes a while to process your act. I mean, you minimized the horror of these murders, Bernie. You fucking cracked a joke about the hit-and-runs."

I wonder what she's talking about. Then I remember. "That wasn't a joke."

"You actually said that two of the five murders weren't by, and I quote, 'bat or brick.' They were by, and I quote again, 'bump?' What the fuck? I mean, even brainless Joanie stopped dead in her tracks. She actually went, 'bump, what do you mean by bump?'"

"It just came to me. I was going for alliteration. Then I realized it didn't fit the horror show I was trying to describe."

Isa's eyes grow wide. Like she's suddenly witnessing some mutant life force at her table slurping red spicy liquid from a tall glass. Every once in a while I think it dawns on her that I'm not the perfect catch.

A smile contorts its way onto her lips under thick, dark eyebrows still arched at me. It isn't her nice smile, the one that captivates the beholder. It's more a spastic parting of the lips before razor-sharp teeth sink deep into your neck kind of smile. With the pallor of her skin, and with all the black and red garb and the lipstick and the long nails she's got going on, it's a bit unnerving. Like she's trying out for *The Walking Dead*.

I crick my neck. In anticipation. Like wrestlers do before the bell.

"Oh my God, Bernie. You were going for alliteration. Of course you were." She gazes down the pier, past Nick and Margarita, to the sky and the escaping clouds. She snorts and sips her fresh bloody.

Darby was right. I need Isa to protect me from me. Because last night, on top of my awry alliteration, I had also laid out how Sandy O'Connor's murder was connected. That now we had six, oh yes, count em, six unsolved cases on the Jersey Shore.

Bosco had called me seconds after I got off the airwaves and had a shit fit. A, he began, we had no evidence to support my conclusion that she was part of the pattern. In fact, there had been a convicted perpetrator. B, he continued, I had blown our chance for a *Beach Star* exclusive should Darnall be found not guilty somehow in the coming days. And, 3, I sounded like a lightweight trying to impress a cute anchor.

He loved unloading his As and Bs on me, always followed with a 3, which he knew bugged the shit out of me. Lucky for him, he didn't need to fire me, as I had never gotten around to signing the *Beach Star* hiring paperwork. That's what I told him over the phone. Which of course didn't help the conversation much. But Bosco didn't fire me. He hung up.

The O'Connor mention also got me a phone call this morning from Rizzo, who had rescheduled our cancelled meeting. Now he wanted to "catch up." After business hours on Tuesday evening. Conference Room A on the first floor. No Bosco. I jokingly asked should I bring a lawyer or a bodyguard. "Neither," he had said in a monotone, "at this time."

Isa grabs my hands in hers and looks at me. "Something else you said on air last night," she says. "'Real monsters hide in the light. Not in the dark.' You were talking about whoever was killing these girls. What did you mean?"

I remember that line too. I look out into the bright, hard sunshine beyond the glass at Margarita, at the generations of old and young lining the railings, at the choppy waves beyond, pulsing down below. I turn back to her.

"Whoever's killin all these women. That guy we saw in the Ronnie Landry video coming out of the shadows. That guy not hiding in the dark anymore. He's out here, Isa, with Allie Formosa's murder. He's among us. Sitting somewhere in the bright sunshine. Hunting down his next target, going one by one. Until we stop him. I know this as much as I know anything. I feel him out here."

A troubled look falls over Isa as she searches for Margarita again.

Twenty-Seven

It's still light out when I arrive at the Rizzo's Belmar Police Department on Tuesday evening. The PD is a bunch of offices shared with other municipal departments, like public works, marina operations, and beach passes. They all crowd into a two-story, concrete-and-brick low-rise that could pass for a passport office in East Berlin before the wall fell. It has three holding tanks for the drunks, but Belmar usually has to look to nearby towns for holding cells during the summer bacchanalia when hope springs eternal among beach-bound youth.

Rizzo and Eddy are already at the opposite end of the long table in conference room A when I enter and grab a folding chair. Eddy's the father of Julie the Porch bartender's thick-necked boyfriend. The cop who likes to bring his stick to St. Rose picnics and play with it. He has one with him now, hanging from his right hip. He puts it on the table for all to behold.

Conference room A – there's no B or C – is a windowless office with the largest rectangular table you can find in the department and the most chairs that match. Two of its colorless walls double as storage areas, lined with stuffed file boxes, reams of copy paper, office supplies, cases of Shop Rite bottled water, and boxes of coffee bags.

It's almost six o'clock, so people are clearing out. I hear hurried clip-clops on the cold linoleum floors outside our closed door and the muffled echoes of "night" down the hallway.

I'm all by my lonesome at my end of the table. I put my Hemingway in front of me with my pen alongside it, trying to look journalistic. I have my questions written down, but it doesn't feel like this is my makeup interview. I should have a lawyer with me. Or Isa, who's just as good.

Bosco's right. The cops consider my reporting, certainly my last article on the five shore murders, as an indictment of their dumb asses for missing a serial killer in their midst. At least that's what Rizzo says right off the bat in that cramped room.

It's a story about five, now six missing women, I say, including O'Connor. Cold cases.

It's a story about you saying the police fucked up, Rizzo says. You saying we're incompetent, clueless. Stupid.

We go at it for 20 minutes. Eddy seems to enjoy the verbal fisticuffs, a smile on his face. Rizzo stops berating me long enough to open a folder in front of him.

"Ruane, I'm the Monmouth County lead for all the towns involved in these cases."

"So I heard. Congratulations."

I feel an urge to smoke then and there. It feels like a good time to light up, shoot a plume to the dirty ceiling tiles, and look nonchalant as the yellow smoke in the poor light gives silent stage to the dust motes for their last pirouette. Cool guy, not a care in the world, watching the settling dust, watching life deal from its stacked deck, ready to flip his trump card. Except I don't smile. Instead, I spin my pen on the table perhaps a little too maniacally. It keeps skittering away from me, and I have to bend over in my chair to reach for it and get it back. I pretend to look cool again.

"At the request of Edison, our task force has started a file on you."

"Mind if I ask why?"

"Commander Crombie, head of the Criminal Investigations Bureau in Edison, has opened an inquiry into the disappearance of Maureen Logan. The Monmouth County prosecutor agreed our task force was the best place to coordinate a multi-town inquiry."

Fuckin Logan. "Multi-town inquiry? Is this a criminal investigation?"

"Not yet," says Rizzo. "Just an initial review to see whether there's anything there."

Eddy snickers.

I wonder how quickly I can use that baton upside his face before they tase the shit out of me.

"You told me not to bring a lawyer, Rizzo. I want one now."

"That's it for tonight. No need for a lawyer right this minute. Jes wanted ya ta know."

"Maureen Logan's disappearance has nothing to do with the Jersey Shore murders. It has everything to do with her brother, Matt Logan. A cop who works for Crombie. The cop who, I'm sure as shit, got 'Edison' to come after me."

"If we're gonna discuss it, Ruane, you really will need your lawyer."

My mouth is dry. I make motions like I'm leaving.

"Hold on just a minute, will ya?" Rizzo goes all peace negotiator on me. "I promised you an update. So you just got one. Also, I wanted ya ta know what else we got. Any problem with that? You want a lawyer for that?"

I grab a water bottle through the ripped plastic wrap of one of the boxes lining the wall. I twist it open and take a slug. "What you got," I say.

"Maureen Logan's credit cards and cell phone service were cancelled by the companies in late 2000 because she hadn't been payin. She didn't cancel them, Ruane. Her last call on her cell was to you the day before you say she disappeared. It was a long call."

"She was upset as I recall. Hated the world and everyone in it." I look at their expectant faces. "Except me."

I remember the call all right. She was driving around that day, doing errands she said. She had pulled over and was calling me from the side of the road. We spoke for something like two hours. She couldn't stop sobbing and, in between, she'd say in a low voice, almost inaudible, that we had to leave New Jersey and never come back. Just us. Now, she kept saying. I managed to talk her through it and get her to come to Belmar. She arrived by train that evening, on her own unannounced schedule, and walked the mile to our yellow house at the beach, something she liked doing. We barbecued, drank some beers, and enjoyed each other. That last night turned out as sweet and good as it ever had been. Funny how those nights come and go.

I remember that our last month hadn't been as good as that last night. Her mother had died in mid-April, and a week after that Mo took a deep nosedive. She never explained it, and we never got into it. Maybe it was about her mother – sadness, grief, guilt, whatever. She stayed in bed all day every day. It was springtime at the beach, but it was dark inside. While she rested up, I left her water, soup, and grilled cheese sandwiches, sitting by her side and using a washcloth on her face and neck, her arms and legs. Then one Saturday morning, fresh and showered, it was over. She was better. She came downstairs and into the kitchen with her big smile. Her face had that look she got when she slept too long, crinkly and pink. A few weeks later she made that long cell phone call to me, another nosedive. The day after that call she took a walk with the dog and didn't come back.

I'm about to tell them all this, right then and there, but I look again at the two of them and decide I should zip it.

"Ruane?"

"Yeah, I'm here."

"Like I was saying, in this update I'm giving you, her cell account got closed down. The debt collectors went after her but came up empty. Couldn't find her. No evidence she used any of her credit or ATM cards after she disappeared. Nothing. Poof. Her bank put her checking account into escrow six years ago. It had all of $67 in it, although something like three grand had been taken out during the two weeks before she called you and then disappeared."

I think about the money. I never knew she had any. Rizzo, having heard my request for a lawyer, didn't ask me if I knew about the money. He wasn't asking anything. He was talking.

"Her car was found in the parking lot at the Belmar train station. Let me put it more correctly, Bernie. It was found in the Belmar Mall parking lot that runs into the train station parking lot."

"She told me she took the train to Belmar and walked from there. Like usual. She didn't park it at the Belmar train station. She would've parked it at whatever station she got on board the train, not off it. Rizzo, something's wrong there."

"I'm not asking questions, but, shit, man, you didn't look for her car when she disappeared?"

"No. I knew it was not in Belmar."

"Her car sat there for a few weeks after she disappeared. The police were called to impound it eventually. It was sold at auction after lotsa tries to reach her at her registered address."

"The cops who impounded it. They didn't know I had filed a missing persons right in Belmar? They didn't connect the car to my report?"

"Guess not. It was a private contractor that impounded it for the Belmar P.D. They're not in business anymore."

"You lookin for the car now?"

"Yeah."

"You have a record of my missing person report on her, right?"

"We do."

Eddy drains his Styrofoam cup and wipes his lips with a sleeve. Rizzo looks in the folder in front of him. "The car was in her mother's name, Bernie. The mail went to her. Matt Logan says he knew nothing about it. But someone filled out a card they sent the mother. Filled it out in her name. Lettin them sell it at auction. It's on file."

"Anything on any video cam showing her parking it in Belmar?"

"We're looking. The mall's system is pretty shitty. They probably don't have records going back that far anyway, presuming they even had a video system back then."

"Any indication she actually took the train? Either the night before when she came to town or the day she disappeared?"

"If she bought a ticket it was with cash. No credit card record exists. And it's too long ago to see if anyone has a recollection."

"She just disappeared, Ruane," adds Eddy. "Poof. Gone. Yer the last to see her I guess."

I eyeball Eddy. White hairs grasp at the edges of his gaping nostrils, trying to pull themselves out and take the final plunge. He's busting out of his well-worn uniform. And he's digging this shit. I know he wants to grab his stick and thwack it.

Rizzo scrutinizes my face. He leans over to make a note in the folder. His sharp features point at the scent he's sniffing, and that's straight at me. "Ruane, we're going to want to know where you were, and with whom, for all these dates and towns."

He pulls a large index card from the folder and flips it across the tabletop to me. I look at the typewriting. I know the dates by heart.

August 13, 1999. Belmar. ... Sandy O'Connor.
July 11, 2002. Avon. ... Rosemary Prelia.
August 29, 2003. Edison. ... Francine Waterman.
August 20, 2004. Bradley Beach. ... Mary Angliotti.
August 21, 2009. Philly. ... Veronica Landry, in the parking lot.
August 7, 2010. Shark River. ... Allie Formosa, with her pink shirt.

"August 13, 1999," I begin.

"That's Sandy O'Connor," replies Rizzo. "You know, we heard you on the radio with Joanie. Brick, bat and bump? Wow, Bernie, you have a way with words. You must be a reporter. A fuckin writer even."

I wave him off. "Isa found Sandy's obit. I put it together and called it out as a Jersey Shore murder. But why's it on your list? You got a convicted perp."

Rizzo closed the folder. "You said this Sandy's part of this. So let's proceed on that assumption. And I want to know where you were the night she was killed."

I was still in Belmar in 1999 when Sandy O'Connor was killed. I was in Philly when Prelia, Waterman, and Angliotti were killed. An hour away. I was in LA by the time Landry was clubbed to death in Philly. And then back here at the Jersey Shore live when Allie Formosa got crushed with cinderblock.

I put the index card in my notebook.

"You have a car back then, Ruane? When Maureen disappeared?"

"I did. I sold it before I left."

"You remember who you sold it to?"

"Bosco's brother."

"He still got it?"

"It hasn't come up."

"We'll find out." Rizzo starts packing up.

"That it?"

"Don't leave town, okay?"

"Where am I gonna go?"

Rizzo gives me a one-shoulder shrug. "Don't ask me. I stay put. This is my home. Not you. You move around. You run." He points a thin finger in the air. "One more thing, Bernie."

"What?"

"We found another one."

He tells me about Grace Giuliani. On July 6, 2008. I retrieve my Hemingway and take lots of notes as he's talking, which Rizzo regards with interest. When the quiet in the room tells me he's finished, I close up my notebook. "So? Why are you telling me this?"

"You didn't know about her?"

"No."

Rizzo sits back. He's studying me, checking if I'm telling the truth. "Giuliani's murder," he says at last, "smells a lot like what we see in your cold cases."

"And?"

"And, you may be dead wrong about someone going after Jersey Shore girls. Your whole storyline may be for shit."

I wonder what he isn't saying to me right now.

"Rizzo," I say, "read more closely. I'm not sayin there's a serial killer going after Jersey Shore girls."

"But that's where you're goin with all this. Come on. We all know it."

"So let's say that's the theory. I'm not saying it right out loud in my stories. I'm completely silent on that. But, what's wrong with that theory? I mean in light of this other case."

"Grace Giuliani's from New Orleans. She lived in Newark. Rented an apartment there. Never got close to the Jersey Shore from what we can see. Hated the beach. Hated water. She lived through Katrina and got her ass up north as quick as she could."

I open my Hemingway again and write it all down.

"And one more thing."

I look up.

"She was raped, Ruane." He pauses as if expecting me to say something. "We're investigating DNA matches now. We may have it all nailed down very soon. We may have our Jersey Shore murderer. Who might have nothing to do with the Jersey Shore at all." Rizzo smiles then, a flash of white teeth from the dark end of the table.

"This Giuliani information is embargoed, by the way, 'til I say otherwise," continues Rizzo. "You write nuthin 'til I say so."

"Looks a lot different than the story yer pitchin, Ruane," says Eddy.

"Thanks, Eddy. That's some good insight." I turn to Rizzo. "Let me know what you learn, chief."

"Add July 6, 2008 to your list of dates where I want alibis, wouldja?"

I close my notebook and get out of the building as quickly as I can. Fall's coming fast, and it's near dark already. I walk to the Honeypot. Along the way, I call Bosco on my cell, telling him what happened, including the news about Grace Giuliani.

"Fuck," says Bosco. I know he's smelling his Pulitzer going up in smoke along with my carcass. And then, "you got alibis, Bernie?"

"Hell if I know, asshole. But thanks for the confidence. And if I did, my alibis would be drunkards, cheap tricks, petty criminals, or reporters."

Bosco goes silent.

"I'm fucked, Bosco."

"Ain't we all."

"I might not beat this rap."

149

"Find out who's doin it. Find out about that Giuliani DNA. Use that damn niece of yours. That's your out, solving this shit before they pin it on you. It'll help my paper out too."

"Yeah, right. Just solve it. Easy as shit."

I ask him if his brother still has my car. He thinks it's up on cinderblocks in their mother's backyard over in Wall, inland and south from us. And he thinks she's pretty pissed about it.

We hang up.

I keep walking, my hands in my pockets. I pull my sweatshirt hood over my head. I pass a few bars on the way. I have to. I might not come out.

A couple times I stop and turn around. I feel Rizzo following me or maybe some steroid-laced knucklehead from the force. But I see nothing back there in the darkness. Belmar's streetlights are for shit, and back the way I came it's more shadow and night than pools of dim light. I keep walking.

When I get back, I sit on the Honeypot porch for a while, ping-ponging conversation with some of the guests. We pass around a bottle of cheap tequila that burns its way down and slug back iced beers to soothe the aftermath. We talk about the murders. Not a few of the lowlifes claim they have some inside word on who might be 'offin' the chicks." I listen to their investigative insights. I'll take all I can get.

The guys finish up and move on to scrape up dinner, and I sit there alone. An early half moon shoots up from the ocean at the end of 12th Avenue. It lays down a golden path that stretches from the shoreline to the horizon. I think about Maureen. I squint to find her on that golden path and see through it instead to thick, black, silent water surging and quickly falling. I think about Sandy O'Connor, who died in a dark parking lot only a block south of here. I pull out my notebook and my pen hovers over the page. And then I close it up.

I got nothing to say.

Twenty-Eight

Matt Logan guided his Edison police cruiser into an empty spot in the Belmar police lot. He grunted his way out of the front seat and got his paperwork out the back. He wiped at his upper lip. It was getting darker earlier now, and he liked it. At least tonight.

He introduced himself at the front window and found himself waiting 15 minutes for Rizzo to get free. Rizzo himself retrieved Logan from the lobby, and they went to the breakroom. Rizzo poured what was left in the coffee pot for him and Logan. They sat at the table.

"What's Commander Crombie got for me, sergeant? I'm trying to wrap up a shit day here."

"We did a run on my sister's car like you asked. We tracked it down to the current owner in Jersey City."

"And?" Rizzo stirred in his seat. He could've learned this via a secure email. A sit-down like this was a waste.

"We took the car apart. We found this under the seat. The original's with forensics, but I thought you'd want to see what we got."

Logan pulled out of a plastic, see-through folder a copy of an article torn from an old edition of the *Newark Star-Ledger*.

Rizzo squinted at the faded text. "Says Maureen Logan came in second at some Catholic girls track meet held in Newark. In '86. How old was she then?"

"Sixteen. She was still in high school."

"And you found the original article in her car that she left in the train station, what, in 2000? Fourteen years later? When she was 30?"

"That's when she disappeared."

"Were you involved in taking the car apart by chance?"

"I took a look at what they produced after the fact. I wasn't involved in the search."

Rizzo picked up the second copy in its own plastic folder. He squinted. "And this? The *Star-Ledger* again. Front sports page. July of 1989."

"Just after she got out of high school."

Rizzo kept reading. "Your sister went to Bishop George Ahr High School in Edison. And got named to some 1989 top ten list for women's track and field."

"For all the northern New Jersey Catholic schools."

Rizzo put the copy of the article down. "And this means what?"

Logan presented another plastic folder with three documents. Rizzo pulled them out and thumbed through them. "Certified copies of death certificates for three women."

"Three of the women on that top ten track and field list are now dead. One died about one month before Maureen disappeared."

"I'm not getting this. The first one died of natural causes, or so says the certificate. Fell while rock climbing in New Hampshire. And the second one …"

"Black chick from Elizabeth. Tiffany Jones. She was suffocated in her bed one morning when she didn't show up for work. On January 30, 1999."

Rizzo stroked the V. as he held the Jones death certificate in his other hand. She died about eight months before Sandy O'Connor died in that parking lot behind her parents. The Jones case was still open but not listed as a homicide. The family had been pressing all these years for a determination one way or the other, to no avail. Rizzo shook his head.

"And the third one, chief, Alisha Sanchez," said Logan. "From Bayonne. She was beaten to death in Asbury Park in April of 2000. On the 27th. And penetrated repeatedly with a blunt instrument. A vicious attack like the rest. You can see the coroner's report there. No one's been questioned, much less arrested."

"This third victim. She was the one that beat your sister in '86. As in came ahead of her, I mean."

"Yup. I think we need to check into these other two. They might tell us what happened to Maureen."

"I guess we should investigate," Rizzo said. "And I guess we should get alibis from Ruane on these new dates." He paused and then looked at Logan. "Jones and Sanchez don't seem to have any connection to the Jersey Shore at all. Your sister, maybe, but not Ruane's storyline."

"No. Nothing obvious at least."

Rizzo frowned. "All the others on this top ten list, they're alive?"

"Confirmed," Logan said with a nod.

"Send me the department confirmation by secure e-mail. I want it to be independent. You know, by the rules."

"Sure."

Rizzo squinted at Logan. "Your sister's car. Was there any blood, any evidence of a crime there?"

"No trace yet."

Logan waited a couple of heartbeats for more questions, and then swept his hand over the tabletop. "You can have all these. They're your copies. I'm gonna head back north."

Rizzo reread what Logan had dropped off, sipping his crap coffee. He'd have to accelerate the task force's investigation into Ruane. All the heat coming down forced his hand.

He opened a file on his desk. He found Ruane's cell number and punched in the numbers, checking his watch.

Twenty-Nine

I end the call. It was Rizzo asking if I have a lawyer yet and giving me two more dates to add to my alibi list when I say no. I open my laptop and my Jersey Shore murder chart, adding Rizzo's dates to round out the timeline. I'm keeping this chart, adding to it here and there, putting the Jersey Shore murders, Maureen's disappearance and Rizzo's track & field names in the same timeline. I look at it.

Event	Hometown	Where Killed	When	How	Occupation
Formosa story in print/Darby's back			8.26.10		
Allie Formosa dead	Neptune	Shark River Hills	8.07.10	Cinderblock, parking lot	Librarian, reading activist
I'm back			8.05.10		
Veronica Landry dead	Philly/Belmar	Philly	8.21.09	Bat/pipe, parking lot, voicemail	Local TV anchor
Grace Giuliani dead	New Orleans	Newark	7.06.08	Metal pipe, parking lot, raped	Principal oboist – Newark Symphony
Mary Angliotti dead (knew Waterman)	Bradley Beach	Bradley Beach	8.20.04	Hit-and-run, fake phone call/setup	SVP – real estate, Town Council
Francine Waterman dead (knew Angliotti)	Neptune	Edison	8.29.03	Hit-and-run, dragged to street, repeat hits	Strategy planning, phone company
Rosemary Prelia dead	Avon-by-the-Sea	Avon-by-the-Sea	7.11.02	Blunt/bat, back porch	Local actor, singer
Danny convicted			8.29.00		
Darby gone			7.04.00		
Flamingo dead			6.30.00		
I'm gone			6.22.00		
Mo walks out			5.27.00		
Rizzo addition #1	?	Asbury Park	4.27.00	?	?
Sandy O'Connor dead	Belmar/Princeton	Belmar	8.13.99	Head crushed, parking lot	Intern at *Trenton Times*
Rizzo addition #2	?	Hoboken	1.30.99	?	?

The April 27 date in 2000 is interesting because it falls between the time Mo's mother died and Mo's meltdown, a time when Mo started to unravel. I go online and see that a woman named Alicia Sanchez from Bayonne got murdered in Asbury Park the night of April 27.

I sit back and think. Alicia Sanchez. I've heard that name before, somewhere, long ago. Before Mo left, before I left.

I close my laptop and leave a voice message for Isa asking if she knows this name or anything about the Sanchez case, which is a cold one according to a follow-up story published a few years ago. Alicia Sanchez, another young woman, this time around Mo's age, bludgeoned about the face and head, then penetrated vaginally with the same weapon most likely. And her name rings a bell.

On the table next to my laptop are print-outs of credit card and phone records going back over 10 years. Earlier Isa and I had plowed through these reminders and indictments from darker days, drinking nights and fuzzy recollections, trying to find alibis for Rizzo's dates. But I didn't leave a lot of tracks, and so far we were coming up with nothing. The night Sandy O'Connor died, we had me buying Mexican takeout for two in Belmar, for Mo and me, and we ate it at my second-story apartment across from Jack's near the train station. But that didn't cover the times the coroner figured Sandy was murdered that night.

I find my buddies lined up on the shelves under the window. Outside, fall is knocking, and night's been around a while. I grab the remnants of a Macallan 18 and pour some over a glass half full of ice.

Tomorrow morning I might not remember today.

Thirty

Anne Botta heard a noise. It was after 10 p.m. She had just pulled her garbage cans down to the street for tomorrow's pickup and was walking back up the driveway, enjoying the hint of October in the air. The noise came from near the detached garage behind the house.

She heard it again. She approached slowly, looking into the shadows on either side of the garage. The garage door was down, so no animal could have gotten inside. But was someone there? Leaning against the wall? She squinted and scanned the area.

A new noise stopped her in her tracks. Dry leaves crunching. She moved closer to the garage, peering into the blackness. She regretted letting the spotlight over the backyard burn out. Her husband, rest his soul, would have taken care of that in a jiffy. And then she would have gone back into the house and just flipped it on. It was probably a dog or a raccoon back there. It would have skedaddled with that spotlight coming on.

A sudden movement caught her eye. From the garage a shape taller than she rushed out at her and then stopped inches away. Wide open eyes stared out at her from a dark ski mask. Then something else moved, swiftly. She heard and then felt a horrible crack on her forehead, and then she was down on the ground on her knees. Oh … Oh … mygraciousgodthepain, ohmydearlord, the pain. Something dark and sticky burned down her face, but she couldn't move her hands to wipe it away. It dripped off her there was so much.

The shape stood over her. Anne Botta tilted her head to look up and then tipped over onto her side and then her back, facing upward. The shape eyes were looking down at her. She couldn't wipe the wetness now pooling in her eyes. There was so much. The shape crouched next to her now, again watching, just before Anne Botta stopped seeing everything. Just before it all went black.

Thirty-One

Darby turned into the Belmar police parking lot about five a.m. It had been a long night. She put her hand to the back of her neck and worked on the kinks, rotating her head sideways. She let out a deep sigh and swung out of the car.

She spied an official cop vehicle. Edison Police Community Relations. It had been there but empty, like it was now, when she started her night shift. When she radioed back to the station about it, she had learned Logan was meeting with Rizzo.

She wondered where he was now. She found her answer in the hallway outside the female officer locker room, waiting for her. He looked up from the metal bench where he was sitting and smiled at her. His eyes were glassy. His uniform was rumpled. Had he been waiting all night? This was fucked.

She stopped. "What do you want?"

"Good morning, Patrol Officer Ruane. I was waiting for you. I missed you last night."

"You waited here all night?"

"I slept some in the car."

This time of day the place was empty, folks either changing into their gear to go out or changing out to go home and sleep. She forced her way around him into the break room.

"I'll join you."

She filled her travel mug with fresh-brewed coffee some angel had made. The place was empty.

Logan slithered up behind her. She spun around. "Back off."

He kept this glassy smile on his face. "I'm working a case you're involved with."

"Community Relations from Edison? I don't think so."

He moved closer. "Listen, Darby" he managed. "We got off on the wrong foot. You're not your uncle or your father. I know that. Let's you and me be friends. We're cops."

She looked at him, disbelief on her face. "It's Patrol Officer Ruane. You had it right the first time."

He put his left hand against the cabinet she had her back to. She didn't move. She lowered her hands to her side, flexing her fists while he concentrated on her face and breasts.

"You jes like Flamingo, Darby, you jes like her, " he half- whispered. "Come on you know it." He leaned in. He touched her arm and kept it there, pulling her to him slightly.

She kneed him swift and hard in his balls while raising a fist with middle knuckle extended into the fleshy part of his chin. The jaw clicked like it had snapped. As he went down, she directed his head with two hands so she caught his nose with her rising left kneecap. The nose broke, she was sure. It had that mushy feeling when she landed it. And there was a satisfying, sharp crack followed by equally sharp groans.

He fell flat onto his back on the linoleum floor, his face pointed at the camera. She squatted down and spat softly at him. "See that camera on the wall behind me right now?"

Logan spotted the camera over her shoulder in the corner and groaned again.

"You're fucked Matty. And if you think at all you're gonna mess with Bernie, let me remind you of what I told you back in your office. All your macho boot boys will be digging on the YouTube version of me beating the shit out of your sorry, fat ass in the break room. I'll be sure they get the link. And I guarantee it will go viral all over Jersey. Then I'll file sexual harassment and assault charges with the Edison Police Board and a civil case against you. You'll lose your manhood, your job, your pension, and a bunch of coin. You'll land in jail for a coupla nights with some of the guys you put away. Sexual assault is a serious matter, especially when a cop's the perp."

He was trying to breathe through the pulp that had become his nose. He emitted a liquid wheezing noise. Blood spurted in thick gobs onto the floor.

He grunted something. She grabbed his chin and pulled his face up, blood flowing onto her wrist and hand. She arched her eyebrows, and her bright green eyes glowed hot with menace. "Got it, asshole?" She was about an inch from the hole emanating his shit breath.

He slowly turned his glassy eyes on her. She saw his hate gathering. As if he could do something with it. She smiled at the poor shit and thrust a thumb hard and deep into his right eye socket. He let out a defeated, muffled cry. She dropped his head to the floor with a wet thud. The camera behind her wouldn't have been able to catch that given the angle. It would look like all this time she was huddled over him, making sure he was okay. Still all cop, ever the protector and servant.

"Are we in agreement? You leave Bernie, and me, alone from now on? I need affirmation of our contract. Now."

He sobbed something that sounded enough like yes. She shot her right knee sharply into the side of his face again as she stood up. He blubbered.

"And that?" she said down at him. "That's for Flamingo. Don't you ever say her name in my presence again. You're not worthy."

She called Bernie later that day.

"Uncle B, I cut off Matt Logan's balls! Tell me what you want me to do with them."

She told Bernie everything in an excited torrent of curses. After she hung up, she considered calling back to make sure Bernie knew Logan was actually alive and breathing, balls intact. Nah, she thought. Let him wonder.

Thirty-Two

October brought with it wind gusts off a surly gray ocean and solid sheets of rain. The Honeypot's windows rattle in their frames, and the swirling mist outside obscures the boardwalk lights below.

I finally have the two of them, Darby and Isa, in the same room. They're sitting at my table, on opposite sides. In the middle I've put a coffee carafe, some cups and a bottle of Henry's Jameson's from downstairs. Just in case anyone needed it. Anyone besides me, that is.

I hadn't planned on this meeting. I invited Darby to tell her something she needed to hear from me face-to-face. No quick text or email. Darby agreed, and arrived through the hotel's back alley. She didn't want to be seen with me right now given Rizzo's sudden interest in my alibis.

Isa had sprung a surprise visit. She had just returned from Rahway, where she had interviewed inmates who had known Darnall, Sandy O'Connor's purported killer. She had some news she wanted to share with me.

They sat and sized each other up. I sat. Behind me News 12 New Jersey is on the TV.

A news alert comes on. We listen and I realize I should've started this little meeting a wee bit earlier. The anchor starts quoting an unnamed source involved with the Monmouth County task force investigating the so-called Jersey Shore Murders. The source says the task force is expanding a previously undisclosed investigation into the background of the *Beach Star* reporter who broke the story – Bernard Ruane of Belmar. That's it. Flash to the next story.

We all look at each other. The reality of it hangs over us in the cramped room.

I pour Jameson's into my coffee. "This is what I wanted to tell you, Darby. Part, at least."

"This is Crombie?" asks Darby.

"Yup."

"That fuck."

We share our visit with Matt Logan with Isa.

"The day you borrowed my car."

"Right."

"Would've been nice to share this was coming, Bernie," says Isa. "Why is this Crombie going after you, Bernie?"

"Logan convinced him I'm nuts maybe. Cause of Danny. And my father. Now he's trying to stick me with whatever happened to Maureen."

"But you reported her missing," says Isa. "You, we, we banged on the cops, everybody, back then trying to find her."

Darby pours some Jameson's into her coffee. "Well, what other good news did you have for us, Bernie?"

They're both looking at me, knowing it isn't good what I'm about to say.

"I was in Edison the night Francine Waterman got run down."

"What?" They say it as one. "You're certain?" adds Isa.

"I found the credit card receipts online a little while ago, and I remember. I rented a car and drove from Philly to Edison the day Francine was run down. I looked for Maureen, and then I drank a ton in some bar. I was sleeping it off in my car just about the time Francine was run down. I drove back to Philly the next morning. Stupid night in a long line of stupid nights. But there you have it. I let Rizzo know earlier today."

"This was, what, when?"

"2003 is when Francine Waterman got hit-and-run. August 29."

"You were looking for Maureen in Edison?" It was Isa, her face clouding up. Darby watched the change, saying nothing.

"I got wind that Mo was working at a trucking company. When I got there, they told me I was wrong."

I tell them what I remember. I had found a Maureen Logan tagged in a photo on the web site of a trucking company in Edison. It came up in a global search. On one of those late nights that started too early in a bottle. It was a photo of a company event, including one woman who looked to be in her thirties. The photo was blurry, but it could have been her. It was so close. She was thinner than she should have been, but she was smiling her smile. I called Matt Logan to see if he knew anything about the company or Maureen working there, and he had strange answers. A strange tone. He said he had no idea what I was talking about. So I drove there to check it out.

"Holy God, Bernie." Darby was shaking her head. "So Matt Logan knows too. And that's what he was going on about in his office."

"He had no clue I came to Edison after I called him."

"I think he had a clue, Bernie."

Isa's quiet, her eyes find the window behind me. I know what she's thinking. Fucking Maureen is still fucking present. She's still fucking up her life. Her eyes go wet for an instant, and then she blinks it all away. She comes back dry-eyed and blank. It's not a good look.

"Did you find anything for any other of the dates Rizzo gave you?" Darby's voice has gone quiet, almost respectful, like at a funeral.

"I have nothing – one way or the other – on any other night. Where I was, who I was with. Except for that night Sandy O'Connor died."

"Also with Maureen," says Isa.

"It gets worse," I say.

Isa blinks. Darby's almost self-satisfied, like she's happy I'm proving Isa wrong and foolish with her heart. Something Darby knows to avoid, exposing your heart like Isa.

"The Edison PD tracked my old car down, the one I had sold to Bosco's brother when I split town, and seized it. It was sold at auction and resold, but they got it."

"And?"

"There's blood in my old car. In the backseat. It wasn't there when I sold Bosco's brother the car, or he would have howled and dinged me down another five hundred or a thousand. But it's there now and I'm betting Bosco's brother will say it's from me, my time. Rizzo has impounded the car and is doing forensics on it."

"Wonderful," says Isa at last, rousing herself.

I'm feeling like space grows between me and the tabletop, with Isa over there on the other side. I'm feeling anxious like she'll walk out, like Mo. I'm waiting for Darby to say something nice. Why I don't know. She pours a straight Jameson's shot instead and comes back wiping her mouth with the back of a hand.

I blurt it out about my visit with Rizzo and Eddie the baton thwacker. About Grace Giuliani being bludgeoned and raped up in Newark. I tell them that Rizzo thinks the Giuliani case may show that there's no Jersey Shore murders going on, that I'm speculating all that. There may be a serial killer, maybe, someone who comes and goes, like me maybe, but someone who isn't limiting himself to Jersey Shore victims.

I look back and forth at them. "Rizzo's thinking this Grace Giuliani case blows up my storyline in my face."

"Giuliani's my goddamned investigation," Darby says. "Rizzo told you?"

Isa points a long finger at Darby. "Wait a minute! You knew about this Grace Giuliani murder? And you didn't tell Bernie?"

"I'm a cop first, Isa. I'm not here to bail his ass out. That's your job."

They eyeball each other across the table. Isa's now pissed and shedding her stunned reaction to me looking for Maureen in Edison the night Francine Waterman is killed.

"So Bernie goes with a story about his five Jersey Shore girls last week," Isa says. "and you know he's going to go with a full Sandy O'Connor story this week, and you say nothing about the Giuliani case? Nice, real nice, Darby."

"He's a big boy, and I'm not his copy girl," Darby snorts.

Isa shakes her head and cranks a thumb in Darby's direction. "Un. Fucking. Believable," she adds.

Me? I'm used to Darby. This is who she is. Who she has had to be in a family that included Danny and Flamingo. And me. Tough. Self-reliant. Self-protective. Crazy. As shit.

"Have you gotten anywhere with the Giuliani DNA? Rizzo told me," I prod. "At least tell me that?"

"Fuckin Rizzo," snarls Darby.

"You owe him an answer, Darby. Some morsel."

"Fuck you, Isa. I owe him shit. He left me high and dry. 10 long years ago."

"Oh my God, Darby," Isa snaps. "Stop crying over Bernie leaving a decade ago. He didn't kill your mother. Your fucking father did. Bernie's back, like you, to make some sense of what happened back then, to both of you. To all of us. Stop punishing him for doing exactly what you did, run, run away, run far, far away."

Isa's crying a little but she swallows the bitter tears. She freshens her coffee and pours a quick hit into it. "I shouldn't but I can't … You two..." She drinks. "Fucking Ruanes."

We're each sitting ramrod straight now, breathing some, Darby and me choking the shit out of our coffee cups. We know she's right. Fucking Ruanes.

"Darby," I continue, "if I'm going out with stories suggesting one sort of perpetrator, but there's another sort they should really know about, I need to know. People could get hurt."

Isa reaches over and grabs my hand. "I have something to add here."

I put both my hands around hers. She's still reaching for me, I think, just as she pulls her hand back. "Sandy O'Connor. Timothy Darnall up in Rahway. I talked to inmates who knew him."

"Do they think Darnall killed Sandy?" I ask.

"Nobody. Said Darnall insisted he saw someone in the parking lot that night. Someone in dark clothes. Someone who killed the woman he loved."

"Sandy's one of the Jersey Shore victims," I answer. "I can smell it."

Darby purses her lips a minute and then starts talking, choppy at first, the words painfully tip-toeing into the light. And then they run over each other. "So, with Giuliani, I think we have a DNA match on some gangbanger who's serving time in Trenton. We're awaiting verification, but I think he's the one who raped her."

Isa's watching Darby's face. "Anyone talk to him yet?"

"He claims Grace was dead when he found her in the parking lot. Says he was just walkin by on his way to a shelter. Says she was just there waiting for him, dress up and all. Dead as shit but still warm. Says he left her where he finished her."

"Any priors?" Isa asks.

"Rapes, yes," answers Darby. "But no prior murders, assaults, whatever. Giuliani's murder would be his first violent offense that wasn't a rape." She pauses. "Nothing in his past suggests he killed her. Everything in his past suggests he's repulsive enough to rape her. There's the very real possibility there were two perpetrators that night. As sick as that is."

"Or this was his first rodeo," says Isa. "And he killed her first."

"Darby, can I quote you as 'an unnamed source?'"

She flips me the finger and drinks her spiked coffee. "Of course not." Her eyebrows arch in abject incredulity I would consider such a thing.

"Fuck, Darby. Come on ..."

"No. As in fuck no"

"Well, then. What do you got on Grace? Anything in her New Orleans past that's come north to Newark to hurt her?"

"Nothing yet."

"She lived in Newark or just worked there?" Isa was checking her notebook as she asked.

"Lived."

"She rent or own?"

"Rent," said Darby.

"Rent or sublet from a primary renter?"

"Sublet actually. Some new yuppie/buppie building."

"Who'd she sublet from?"

"No idea. Haven't gotten there yet."

Isa sits back. "OK, since she's back on the table again, Darby, what about Maureen. What have you learned that's relevant?"

Darby watches Isa pull my hand to her and, for once, doesn't let a sneer or a mumble escape. "I knew they found her car, Bernie. Rizzo knows, so I know."

I look at her. "So what?"

"They found something."

I wait. She's got something to say.

"The Edison forensic team came across two newspaper articles tucked in the cushions of the car." Darby summarizes the articles, about Maureen coming in second in a track meet, about her being on a top ten New Jersey athletics list of one sort or another. She tells us the buzz is that at least two on that top ten list are now dead, victims of violent crimes yet unsolved.

"Three, if you count the fact that Maureen's unaccounted for," I say. "If Darby's right, the dates of the articles are way before I knew her."

"But they were in her car the day she disappeared?" Isa's face shows puzzlement.

"She never mentioned the articles or her track career to me. I knew she was a hot shit runner in high school. College, I don't know. She quit after her freshman year. That's all I knew. I didn't even know she had her car in Belmar the weekend she disappeared on me."

Isa looks from me to Darby. "How well did you know Maureen Logan?"

"Why?"

"You're the only other crazy Ruane here who knew her."

Darby allows a smile to hit her lips at that one. She watches my face as she answers. "I met her a few times. I thought she was very fragile and when she got cornered or in a jam she got very, very nasty. Especially to Bernie."

"How nasty?"

"Get-the-club-and-taser nasty."

"Darby and Mo met maybe four or five times," I add, "and got into a 'fuck you' shouting match at least half of those times."

"You'd never confront her with how she was her own worst enemy. She crippled herself with pain and blame and you never challenged her on it. You let her go on and on."

"I saw her maybe once or twice with Bernie, but I didn't know her," Isa says. "One day she was there and Bernie was with her and I didn't see him much again."

"Till she left and then he asked for your help."

"No, Darby. He was hurting and I wanted to help him. Period." There's no emotion on Isa's face as she says this. She's serious as stone, as if she's wanted to lay her case out with Darby for way too long.

"Such a saintly woman," says Darby.

"Do you Ruanes get along much with anyone on this planet? Ever?"

"We try," Darby and I respond in unison, smiling small, genetically similar smiles.

Isa sits there, pale, black, and crimson in my darkening room, one knee pulled to her chest, her arms encircling her bony knee. I turn on a floor lamp. I put a few more inches of Jameson's into my cup and then warm it with coffee from stove.

"Darby," says Isa in a low voice, "you were first in your class at St. Rose's High School. You were among the top ten scorers in the state for high school women's soccer in 1999, your senior year, and all the years prior at St. Rose's. You were first in your class at John Jay. As a rookie, you took a bullet in Freehold when you responded to a domestic disturbance. It entered your upper shoulder but ended up mere inches from your heart. Despite that, you still seized the gun that shot you and soothed, subdued, and cuffed the shooter. Pretty impressive."

"Wanna tell me why you know this?"

Isa's blood-red lips form a slit as she lets it out. "Like I said. You're the only other crazy Ruane around, and, apparently, I have a thing for Ruanes." She keeps going. "The Freehold paper said you were the toughest cop in the field. Year in, year out. That was your reputation."

"I just asked why you're fucking investigating me." This time louder, more aggressive.

"Look, Darby, you pop back in town after 10 years, just like Bernie. The day Bernie breaks the Formosa murder in the paper, here you are. Almost exactly 10 years after your father was convicted of murdering your mother. I'm just curious about you, Darby." She pauses.

Darby is eyeing Isa from across the table.

"You never got any college offers? Scholarships? Nothing? That strikes me as odd."

"Listen, Lou-*eeez*-a. My 'personality' issues sorta got in the way. My advisors and coaches found it hard to recommend me, as I'm not a team player, you know? They'd say I was rough and tough in Freehold, but they never said I'd make a good partner. You notice that? I'm not too much of a foxhole buddy if you get my drift."

"Listen, I get that, Darby. You're tough. You take no prisoners. You go it alone. You'll get all the awards for bringing in the true Jersey Shore murderer, fuck Bernie."

"Fuck you, Isa."

My eyes find Isa's. "Why are you investigating Darby?"

"Because I don't trust her, Bernie. I worry she may hurt you. I don't know where she's been or what she's up to."

"Listen," Darby snaps. "You're the one who got dumped by Bernie because he couldn't get enough of Maureen. It's your sad ass that followed him around like a lost puppy while he looked high and low for her. And it's your sad ass following him around now while he continues his hopeless mission to find and bed her."

"Darby ..." I give her a what the fuck look.

"Shut up, Bernie. And Isa, guess what, bitch? I got no respect for your sorry, sad, Bernie-chasing self because I can't. And I can't trust who I don't respect."

Their backs arch, their stomachs press against the tabletop, and their hands go flat on the table. Their eyes are aflame.

Darby gets up to leave, saying good-bye to no one. She's out the back door to circle back to her cottage. She calls me when she gets there.

"Bernie? I've been thinking. Isa's all right."

I look at my cell. "What?"

"Fuck you. Tell Isa I'm glad she's helping you, okay? You know that day you liked how I fought for us in that shitbag Logan's office? I saw that fight tonight in her. She's fighting for you. For the two of you. I like that. Don't hurt her, Bernie, or I'll hurt you."

"I'll tell her. You two remind me of each other sometimes."

"Whoa, wait. Don't compare her scrawny scarecrow ass to me."

I laugh and hit end.

Isa hears it all because I take the call in bed, and she's stretched out next to me. She flashes the bird at my cell and makes a face as I set it on the side table next to us.

To Isa I whisper, "You know what? I think she's starting to like you."

Isa snorts and thumps my chest with her fist. But looking into her eyes right then? I see a million new reasons she's running through, right that moment, to steer clear from the Ruane freak show. From me. I reach for her fist on my chest. I open it and flatten it to my heart and hold it with my two hands. We lie quietly like that for a while, her eyes closed.

I don't deserve her. She's known that for a long time.

A while later Isa calls her brother and asks him to stay overnight to watch Margarita. She's going to stay with me, and I thank the deity out there in his blackness for small favors. She falls asleep in a second, her head on my shoulder and her hand on my heart. I feel hers beat strongly, and I smell her fine hair.

I conjure up the pantheon of my Irish aunts and uncles long dead and gone. Rose, Father Joe, Monica, Jimmy, May Belle, and the Bernie I'm named after. I always convene them in an Irish bar with low lights, all of them lined up on their stools with dark green cushions and me on the working side of a shiny brown mahogany bar. I beg them now like I do when it's bad for me and getting worse. I have no pride with them.

"Listen guys." I half whisper into the room. "I'm in trouble again, and I need your help. I'm about to blow things up again. Is there anything you can do? Make a few things break my way? I mean you gotta have some pull up there by now."

Isa stirs, and I pull her closer and turn out the light. I let the rest of them up there carry on and carouse around me. I fall asleep without an answer.

Thirty-Three

The next morning I wake to the sound of distant voices in my head. And an idea.

"Let's see that nun who talked to you about Sandy," I say to Isa.

"Why?" Isa had slipped on a skirt after her shower and had gone back into my excuse of a bathroom to comb out her hair. She curses the foggy mirror and wipes it with a squeaking towel. I listen to the soft flap of her long wet hair against her naked back.

"She said Sandy had won some sort of prize or award."

"Right. Year-end 1998 or early 1999, the year she died."

"There's something about prizes and awards, about competition, going on here." I remind her about the articles found in Mo's car. "We need to figure out the connections."

Isa comes out of the bathroom with her brush in her hand. "You may be right. There's something about prizes and winners and losers here."

She writes down the nun's number for me and kisses me. I call the nun. Sister Seton Margaret answers and says she can see us anytime. I tell her we'll be there in a couple hours. She says no worries, she's busy praying. I ask her to put in a good word for me. She laughs and says she will but promises no miracles. I say I need some. She says don't we all.

Then it's my turn to take a shower and curse the mirror.

Isa and I head out from the Honeypot. Henry's on the porch and pulls me over by my arm before I head to the curbside where Isa has parked.

"Ain't no way she'll be turning into a Kitty in her old age, my friend," he says. "Keep that in mind. Ain't many like her. She's a keeper."

I thank Henry for his psychic predictions, and we leave.

Bosco calls me as we hit the Garden State Parkway and says I'm sinking his Pulitzer chances with the task force now looking at me. On top of maybe, with the Giuliani murder it'll be shown there's no Jersey Shore murders going on here, just regular, random murders. I remind him that the Pulitzer committee loves stories about the persecution of truth-seeking journalists and that I was probably increasing his odds. Bosco lets that one bounce around.

"Just get me an update for this Thursday's edition," he says. "Something that'll make me smile for once, okay?" I punch off.

Isa pops in a Bluetooth earphone. She speaks a phone number into her cell. "I'm going to find out who leased the apartment to Giuliani," she says to me as she waits to be connected. "I've got an intuition."

She gets to a fellow bail bondsman in Newark who has a huge business. He has a brother who works in the New Jersey Department of Housing Inspection in Trenton. He hears her out and then makes a call. In 10 minutes Isa is talking to the guy who handles safety and health inspection for the building where Giuliani had lived. He promises he'll be back in touch by the end of the day. "That building has lotsa issues," he says to Isa. "The landlord will move mountains to get me the name."

She ends the call. "Now, one more thing. What's the name of that place in Edison where you said Maureen might have been working?"

"Why?"

"If she worked there and was off the books, maybe nothing. If she was an employee, I got a guy in the New Jersey Department of Taxation who can check socials ..."

I wave my hands in the air. "I don't want to know. I don't want to know. I just got a job on the paper and this kind of reporting is not acceptable ..."

She pivots and looks impatiently at me, shutting me up. "Name?" she asks.

"It's Cusack Moving and Storage," I finally say.

Fifteen minutes later, we park on the shady street where St. Benedictine Academy sits in Elizabeth. The spot is far from the trashed, darkened streets of downtown. Out here, the trees are already pimped out in early fall red, orange, and yellow leaves. We walk across the cut grass to the low-rise building that fronts the campus and check in at the admin office. We find the nun's office down the hall.

Instead of a habit, she's wearing an above-the-knee tweed skirt and a form-fitting, business-like matching jacket and white blouse with a big gold cross hanging like Jesus's own hand-me-down bling around her neck. Her blond hair is short and spiky. She says call her Seton. I say maybe, but I always had trouble calling priests and nuns by their first names. She gives me a weary eye. There's nothing I'm gonna tell her that she hasn't heard before.

She brings us coffee and tells Isa how much she loves her heels and black dress. "Very dramatic," she offers. She looks past my rumpled brown corduroy sports jacket, my wrinkled white shirt, and my washed-out jeans with fraying cuffs.

I tell her where we are in the case. I tell her how all the victims are young, promising women of the same age from towns along the Jersey Shore. Or at least most of them.

"I've watched the news," she says. "I follow your stories."

I tell her about Maureen and the articles found in her car. She nods now and then.

We move on to Sandy O'Connor. You can tell the nun is going back in her head, thinking about Sandy. At a pause in my monologue, she starts up with her stories of Sandy, just like she did when she spoke with Isa. All Sandy did for others. All she meant to everyone. All that terrible, meaningless, God-forsaken tragedy and loss. We listen and take notes.

"Tell us about the award Sandy got," Isa prods. "The one you told me about."

"Okay, I've dug around and I know more now. This award she got was part of a whole program called the 'Ladder.'" She put her finger quotes around "Ladder." "It was a big deal for a time. Such special girls got involved in that program. I spoke with some of the other sisters here since you called me, Louisa, to fill in my memory gaps. Throughout 1999 the Ladder sponsored a series of awards for young women, and Sandy won one."

"What for?"

"I'm not sure. We weren't ones to keep records back then. The Ladder had all kinds of activities going on. Awards. Dinners. Citations. It's hard to piece it all together so many years later. But we will. We'll find something that gives us the answer. God will guide us. He will answer our prayers."

We sit there in silence, frustration rising instead of prayers.

"What was the Ladder all about?" I finally ask.

"There was this Sister Helen Molson who lived in our convent for maybe four decades. I knew her well in her later years. She was a social activist. A real radical in the day. Hung with the Berrigans, you know the anti-Vietnam priests in the '60s and '70s, and all that. Drove the priestly hierarchy, especially the local archbishop, absolutely nuts. I loved her. We all did. She's dead now, God bless her. It grew like crazy at the beginning and had affiliates or chapters all over New Jersey at its peak. The goal was to help vulnerable adolescent girls, teens between 13 and 19. Sister wanted to provide them role models and programs so they could rise above the poverty, the abuse, and the hopelessness of their sad lives. She would go from parish to parish, town to town, and city to city in New Jersey and reach out to young ones who weren't living up to their potential. When she found girls with nothing to reach for, Sister Helen gave them their "Ladder."

"But these girls who were killed, including Sandy, weren't the kinds of girls that Sister Helen was trying to help. These were accomplished young women. They were achievers."

"Well, hold on. Sister Helen ran programs for young girls who joined the Ladder. Sure enough. And these programs were all about enrichment. Empowerment. Can-do-itiveness." Finger air quotes again.

"Sister Helen was firmly of the view that the only real things these kids were missing were basic coping mechanisms and an awareness that other girls and women from their own hometowns had succeeded, risen up, and climbed life's ladder. And that's …"

"That's where girls like Sandy came in."

Seton smiles and nods. "As a role model for the young Ladder girls."

As I listened to her, I was actually feeling a warm spot of inspiration inside me, the glimmer of hope that hope could soar. As if she was leading me to the Promised Land. In silence, I firmly instructed my Irish consigliores to cool it and stick to pulling my ass, not my soul, out of a sling. I could hear them clucking and chuckling on their barstools.

"So to close the loop, Sandy was to receive a sort of mentor award at the Christmas dinner in recognition of all her work and sacrifice. And not just Sandy. There were other New Jersey girls who were to receive awards that year."

"Other girls? Like mentors?" I ask. Isa is looking at Seton.

"Yes. Other mentors. Girls from down the shore."

Thirty-Four

I take the wheel this time, and we fly back down the highway to Belmar. Isa's slouched down with her knees on the dashboard, and she's going on and on about what we just heard, her hands flailing. Her heels lie discarded on the floor in front of her. A spot of crimson is blossoming in her ivory cheeks as she carries on.

Seton told us there was a series of awards in 1999 in different regions of New Jersey that recognized the achievements of young women from those regions. One set of awards for Newark, one for Trenton, one for Camden, one for Cape May way down south at Jersey's tip. And one for the Jersey Shore. There was to be a dinner in each of the five regions at the end of 1999 where the recipients would get their awards. The kids Sister Helen was targeting for help would come with their parents, siblings, and entire extended families. Or they'd come by themselves, as happened too often. And the stories and the tears would flow. Phone numbers and emails and mailing addresses would be exchanged, and lifelong bonds would form. And with all that, hopefully, the climb up the Ladder begins.

The program came to a screeching halt with Sandy's brutal murder in late summer of 1999. Sister Helen and all the other sisters were traumatized by the event. From then on, Sister Helen cancelled the end-of-year award dinners and instead asked each award recipient, her angels, to reach out to an assigned handful of kids needing a hand and a vision.

Seton couldn't find a single list naming who else won awards that year either at the Jersey Shore or elsewhere. Not even a list of girls who had joined the Ladder. Not even a list of who would have been invited to the 1999 awards dinners.

"One of those kids could be Sandy's killer," I say out loud.

Isa thumbs through a small pile of Ladder papers and brochures from Sister Seton. She looks over at me. "You serious?"

"Sure. Jealousy. Rage. Just pissed off that a girl named Sandy from down the shore was getting the award and all the attention and the good times, leaving them behind in their dirty, shitty cities and dead-end small towns. Same old."

"I guess it fits the idea of vengeance," Isa offers.

"And it fits with the voicemails that Veronica Landry got in Philly. The ones saying, 'I found you.' It was someone from Ronnie's past. Someone who knew her."

"I guess. Bernie, if Sandy became a target because she was on that list, how many others are still alive and are targets too?"

We hear in answer only the sound of air rushing by us on the parkway.

"Jesus," I say. I hit the accelerator and do 85.

"Who was on the Ladder board?" I ask.

Isa scans one of the papers in the pile. "Big Catholic muckety-mucks full of guilt," she says. "Suits. Bishops. Women with nothing to do but spend their husbands' money."

"You sound like Darby."

Isa shrugs. "Sometimes that bitch is right. Like about me." She smiles and then fishes her phone out of her bag, smacking my arm to shut me up.

I squeeze in what I'm thinking before she starts dialing. "I'm going to rewrite my story on Sandy. 'Sandy's Story.' I'll talk about the award from the Ladder. That she has to be the sixth victim, as I said on the radio. And that there could be more out there waiting to get killed by this monster, maybe even more Ladder women. It might get the attention of people who know something. Remember something. You know, spook them enough to speak up."

I call Bosco, and he buys the idea. It will fill Thursday's paper, making up for the Sandy O'Connor scoop I lost with my radio interview. He asks if I've been indicted yet.

"Not since this morning, asshole." I end the call.

Isa grabs my hand. "I like 'Sandy's Story.'" She breathes in audibly and shakes her head. "It's so sad these young women were just … extinguished like this. Who would kill them? One of the young girls they were trying to help? I just don't buy it."

In little over an hour I drop Isa off at her office. I park her car on the side street without meters, only a few steps from her back door, which opens onto the sidewalk. She has some business dinner she has to go to later on and needs the car for then. It's why she has on her good-looking gits. I walk back to the Honeypot, thinking about a lot of things.

Thirty-Five

Isa sits at her desk and flips off her shoes. She slips on her sandals and inspects a chipped, crimson-colored toenail. The business dinner at Matisse's on Ocean Avenue starts in an hour. It's a five-minute drive. She's got time to check in.

She begins with her snail mail and then fires up her email. Next, her voice mail, deleting most after hearing the caller's name. Two call-backs were mandatory before she left.

The first is to her contact at the department of taxation. There was no one named Maureen Logan at Cusack's for the month in question, he tells her. If he had her social he could be sure, but without it they'd have to rely on names. She thanks him and goes into her paid Hoover's database. She pulls up Cusack's and reads the company profile.

She finds the CFO's name and direct dials him using her office's phone system, which blocks her Caller ID. She looks through her front windows to Main Street as she waits for someone to pick up and notices the neon lights lit up in the bar's windows across the street. She curses herself for forgetting to bring a light jacket.

The CFO answers. She isn't surprised. In her experience, small company CFOs are always working into the evenings and at such times answer their own phones because a spouse or a boss, someone, was always hounding them.

She tells him she works for the Benedictine Academy's alumni department and is trying to find a Maureen Logan. Isa tells him that Ms. Logan's last reported workplace is Cusack's. Would he possibly have her home phone or address? Her reunion is coming up, and the nuns would love to see her there.

The CFO notes it's an odd time to call, and Isa explains that the evenings are the only time they can work the academy's phone banks. Her voice conveys some attitude.

He asks when "this woman" worked there, and Isa gives him a range in 2003 that includes August when Bernie went to Edison and Francine was run down. He replies quickly, too quickly, that, nope, no Maureen Logan worked there at that time. Or at any time for that matter, near as he could tell. He must have realized he was working it too fast as he says hold on, let me confirm, puts the handset down on the desktop. A minute of drawer opening and closing and paper shuffling later, and, lo and behold, he comes back on and confirms he was right.

She asks if it's possible Maureen Logan worked off the books and there might be some other way to find her information. He sniffs. No, of course not. No one's off the books at Cusack's. That would pose legal issues.

Right. A moving company. In northern New Jersey. With no one's off the books. Really.

The CFO hesitates and then asks Isa her name again. She hangs up and calls her new contact at housing inspection.

"Jennifer Botta," says a man's voice thick with an Eastern European accent. "B-O-T-T-A. She sublet the joint to a Grace Giuliani from November of 0-7 until the end of June of 0-8. Let's see. July's when Giuliani picked up the lease in her own name."

"Any contact data for Botta? Any profile information?" Isa holds her breath.

"Nothing. They say they destroy tenant data one year after you move out. Who knows. But they give me nothing on that."

"Shit. … Do you trust them?"

"They wouldn't lie to me. They would regret it. Believe me."

Oh, she believed him, all right. He wasn't one to mess with. "So the mailbox, the front desk, the parking space, the telephone directory for the building, everything would have been in Botta's name right up until the end of June 0-8, right?"

"I asked them. And they said yes, at least. When was Giuliani killed?"

"Six days after she took over the lease." She looks at her notes. "July 6. 0-8."

"Mistaken ID? Is that what you're thinking?"

"Could be. Happens a lot. Thank you. You've been very helpful."

"No problem, chickadee. You going to help my nephews with their visas, right? Get their papers straight? Snap snap?"

"I promise. You know how to reach me."

She checks the time and hurries to the bathroom. A little blush, a little brush, and she's ready. She needs some corporate clients bad, some regular income, and this gig tonight had better produce something. Time to pull out the charm.

She pauses and looks at herself in the mirror. She smiles and notices that, except for Margarita, that simple act had so eluded her when Bernie was gone. But he's back now. And so is the smile he brings. She wonders how long he'll stay. She inhales and then blows out her expired breath through puffed cheeks. Why can't it be a little easy now and then? Just a little? Huh?

She looks for her shoes under the desk, finds them, checks the front door, and turns off the lights. She puts on the alarm, locks the side door after exiting, and clacks briskly to her car, checking her phone. In the driver's seat, she looks out her rearview, and after blinking a couple times confirms what she's seeing. In the darkened portico entrance of an empty storefront, she sees someone's watching her. The figure turns suddenly and spins into an alley directly behind her building. The alley extends to the next block. There's riff-raff from time to time in Belmar, particularly on this side street, but this felt different. Real different. Suddenly she thought of Margarita's bogeyman outside her window.

She turns the ignition and spins into a quick U-turn. She drives down the block and turns right into the alley. She slows then and begins to inch her way in deeper. Whoever was watching her has to be right here. She stops and then squints into the darkness gathering against a tall brick wall that stretches down the alley on her right. On her left are trash bins against a rusting chain link fence with barbed wire curled atop and beyond that the beat-up back stairs and platforms of more forlorn low-rent shops and offices.

She flips on her high beams. Someone in a hood stands with legs apart and facing her at the far end of the alley, almost on the next street, hands in the front pouch of a sweatshirt, head lowered to avoid the beams, but looking at her from under the hood. Defiant, it seems. daring her to come closer. Waiting for her to come closer.

She feels the urge to gun it and run the shit down. She curses and flips the high beams a few times. A fuck you to the guy. She backs out, watching him stand there, and hits a trashcan and curses again. It falls over onto the asphalt behind her, its aluminum top separating from the can. She pulls forward and from her side mirror sees the can lying on the ground.

"Damn it," she breathes. No way she's getting out of this car. She backs up quickly, knocking the can out of her way. It clangs loudly to the chain-link fence. She spins back into the side street and stops to look back down the alleyway one last time. Shadows rule. The fucker is gone.

She pulls out, running the light at the corner of Main. She calls the babysitter. Lock the doors she says in a strained voice that is not hers, and set the home alarm. And pull the shades. Call the cops and tell them a prowler's outside if you hear any kind of noise or spot anyone strange. "Fuck my meeting," she finishes. "I'm coming home now."

She dials another call, and leaves a message. "Bernie, it's me. Somebody was outside my shop near my car. Wore a dark hoodie like the guy in the Landry video. He was watching me, Bernie. I gave chase, but he beat it. Call me quick. I mean it."

Fifteen minutes later she pulls into her driveway and gets out of her car. She remembers her hasty exit from the alley and goes around back to see if the trashcan she rammed left any dings. She didn't need the expense of dings. She stops short.

Deep craters pockmark the trunk of her car, as if it had been slammed with a crowbar. Repeatedly, by someone in a goddamned crazed frenzy. There are maybe a dozen deep crevices that weren't there before.

She folds her arms across her chest. She's worried. And pissed.

She looks around. It's her neighborhood but it doesn't feel like that tonight.

Thirty-Six

Matt Logan looks in the mirror and winces when he touches his nose. Hot pain explodes in his sinuses and up his forehead.

He stares at the mess she has made. Fucking bitch, he thinks. And then she calls Cusack's, and she gets his uncle. The CFO. The bitch was looking for Maureen. Someone from her high school. Right. Sure. She's been off that call list a long time now.

It had to be Darby Ruane who made that call. Without a doubt.

He studies his reflection. Disgusted at himself, he closes his eyes.

Women like Darby take what they want, wreck and empty you in the process, and won't back down ever. And then they leave. They just fuckin flip the bird at everyone in their rearview mirror without looking back, their victims, like him, dragged under their wheels. They leave the rest behind to cope with the nothingness, the nowhere to go.

It's all too much. Sometimes you got to fight back. That's the way it is.

Maureen's mother, his mother, she was the same. Always pushy. Never accepting. Never congratulating. Never so much as a look in those blank eyes that made you feel noticed or special. No, her own children just weren't ever deserving enough.

She walked over his father. No wonder he punched back. Logan tensed, as usual, at the memories. His father never meant to hit her. Surely he never meant to. Didn't plan to. She, she just pushed too hard and he snapped. His father had to fight back. Didn't he? To remain a man? You punch, right? You fight back? Hard like, and final.

Well, that's what his father did. He punched back when it got bad with her. He would hit them all, but mostly he hit his mother and Maureen. Punched them like a boxer, body blows sometimes, thick fists striking fleshy bodies. He still could hear, when it would get bad, the heavy thuds of landing fists, from behind closed doors. He still could hear the muffled blows in the dark. He could still hear the low moans floating down the hall to his room at night. But it helped bring calm. Put things back into place. Back in their boxes, right? It was to protect them from their own selves and what was out there. Isn't that so? Is that so bad?

He swallows two more Percocets, trudges down the stairs and out the front door. He locks it and looks up to be sure all the lights inside are out. The house is black. No need to attract anybody in this neighborhood. It's no longer a good neighborhood. If they thought you lived alone and you had a light on, they knew you were there or you were gone and pretending you were there. Either way, they'd think about breaking in. They'd come one day. To his home. That day was coming soon.

His head throbs, and his lungs hurt. He can barely swallow the pills, there's so much swelling. But they'll stop the pain. He starts up the car. This drive will make him feel better. Getting away in the safety of his locked car. A secure little world, alone, the air shushing by outside. It was good to drive. It would be quiet, peaceful in here.

Things will be right soon. It couldn't last much longer, could it?

His thoughts turn to Darby Ruane as the streetlights watch him pass. The bitch.

Thirty-Seven

Darby Ruane looks out the front window of her Belmar bungalow. Julie's late.

They both took tonight off. Tonight, the first Saturday in October, is Give Back Night at D'Jais. Free admission and $10 covers all you can drink for anyone showing a Belmar ID, electronic dance music and booze pumping all night long. It was D'Jais's way of saying thank you to the community that weathered the summer months of rowdy drunks and associated bacchanalia, a Rio Carnival, Jersey style.

She dressed the part of hot D'Jais chick. Micro skirt that barely stretches over an ass tight from gym duty. Tube top that swells her breasts. Stilettos. Watch out.

She spins in the window and sizes up her reflection. It had been 10 years since her last Give Back Night. But with her new, shorter hair-do, she sorta looks like she did back then. Just stronger and more confident. And since she wasn't drinking much with the job and all, she'd lost weight.

It's gonna be a good night.

She thinks about the Matt Logan video. She claimed it easy enough. Then she downloaded it onto a flash now hidden under a floorboard in the attic crawl space over her head. There's another flash with a copy taped to the bottom of her headboard.

She thinks about Bernie, about how he's still looking for fucking Maureen. It's hard to believe she's as alive and real to him as she was back then. Ten years after.

Back then, Maureen had trouble relating to pretty much everyone but Bernie. She would just stare at you with those big empty eyes, dark patches hanging underneath. She could fly into spitting fits of untamed anger in a hot minute. Darby knew this because she'd seen it. Poor

Bernie, she'd remember thinking, how did he put up with her? Where was she taking him that it was worth the trip?

It wasn't destination love. Fucking love doesn't exist, not really. Or if it does she sure hasn't found it. And when you get close to something halfway good, it always goes bad. For her. For Bernie. For her mother. Love doesn't keep you going. It lifts you up to drop you. It breaks you. It steals your breath away. It stops you dead.

Bernie had pissed away so many years, chasing Maureen, chasing his idea and ideal of her. Maybe it was guilt with Bernie. Guilt he hadn't save Maureen from whatever fate had reached out and taken her away. Guilt can move mountains. Darby knew that. Or maybe it was anger. Maybe Bernie's consumed by his anger at what Maureen Logan did to him, leaving him cold and forever. Maybe he's back to make sure she's really dead and gone. Or to end it once and for all. Anger, that's even more powerful than guilt, and more deadly. It lasts forever.

She looks down the street. No Julie.

She checked up on Bernie in those late hours Rizzo had given her. Checked his past 10 years using Belmar's computer system. Got his license records. Checked PACER for court cases. Searched arrest records and misdemeanor and felony convictions in Philly, St. Louis, LA, New Jersey. Nothing implicated him or put him anywhere close to any of the crimes he was now writing about. In fact, there was nothing that tied him to any unsolved young female homicides. It was possible he had gotten his offending records and crimes expunged, but even that leaves a trace in the system, and she couldn't find one.

Rizzo told her he was coming up dry too. His special assignment from the task force was to look into Maureen's disappearance and Bernie's role, if any, in it. He had nothing so far. They still couldn't locate her, and they couldn't point to anything Bernie did to make her disappear. He was coming up dry and if no leads popped he'd shut this tangent down and move on.

She checked Danny Ruane, too, while she was at it. Except for a handful of medical visits overseen by attending state troopers, he hadn't been out of prison since he was arrested in the kitchen of their home in the first hours of Saturday morning, July 1, 2000.

But, to be honest, finding nothing on Bernie or Danny didn't surprise her.

Blinking lights come down the road. It's Julie. She turns on a light for later and heads out.

Thirty-Eight

"Sandy's Story" came out early in the Thursday, October 7, morning print edition of *The Beach Star*. All day it was crazy. This was big news.

The article got rapid pickup by the AP and UPI and News 12 New Jersey. It hit all the nightly news reports coming from New York and Philly and all the cable news outlets. I got calls from journalists and bloggers all over the country who'd read or heard about it. Sandy's Ladder award got good play, and the reports uniformly mentioned *The Beach Star* was seeking tips on the award and the names of the awardees. Once again, the cops, the task force, the county, and the governor were taken by surprise by the breaking news and had to dole out a slew of "no comments." Bosco warned me again about keeping my nose clean and keeping any and all hooch out of my glove compartment.

That night I'm sitting in my room at the Honeypot, a new, celebratory Suntory Yamazaki 18-year single malt on my shelf and in my glass, one ice cube floating. A red bulb on the wall over my desk goes off. It means someone's dinging the bell at registration. I take a long sip, swirl it, smack my lips, reluctantly put the glass down, and head downstairs.

Rizzo's sitting in the lounge, today's *The Beach Star* on the coffee table in front of him. His cap rests upside down next to it. "Good article today," he says to me. "You're gonna hit the big time."

"It's almost eleven. A little late for you, no? What happened, the wife throw you out?"

Rizzo smiles despite being clearly dog tired. The dark beard says he hasn't shaved in a couple days, and his puffy eyes hint he hasn't slept for even longer.

"The award thing," he begins.

"The Ladder?"

"Yeah." He looks intently at me. "Maureen Logan won some awards too."

I sit across the table from him, waiting for him to go on.

He flips two clear plastic folders onto the surface between us. I read two articles from the *Newark Star-Ledger*. He hands me another folder that contains copies of two death certificates.

"These two deaths, I guess, explain the extra dates you wanted alibis on, right?"

"Yup. You know either of them? Tiffany Jones or Alisha Sanchez?"

"Don't think so."

"Alisha's the one who got beat to death in Asbury Park and penetrated by the same blunt instrument that killed her. We've learned that Maureen knew her. See that first article? Where Maureen came in second? Alisha came in first. You knew Alisha too."

I look at her death certificate and then at him again. I knew I knew Alisha, at some point in time, but I still hadn't figured it out. "How's that?" I say.

He flips another clear plastic folder onto the table. It's a 5 by 7 color photo. Me, Maureen, Matt Logan, their mother, and a black couple, all of us looking miserable. We're in the Logan living room in front of a fake white Christmas tree with red lights aglow. There's a slight blur where Matt had just squeezed back into the photo after setting the camera's shot timer. The date on the back says December 17, 1999.

I remember Alisha Sanchez now. I look back at Rizzo.

"That look on your face. It's all coming back to you?"

"In a flood. She was a friend of Mo's. We shared the same birth date."

"So Alisha's killed on her birthday? We hadn't quite gotten there yet."

"Yeah, that's right."

"So we got this gathering around Christmas." Rizzo gestures to the photo. "Then, four months later sometime, like mid-April, Maureen Logan's mother dies what looks to be a natural death. We're checking now, but it looks legit. A coupla weeks after that, Alisha gets herself clubbed to death. A month after Alisha dies more or less? Maureen Logan disappears."

"May 27, 2000."

"The day Maureen leaves town never to return."

"Yes."

"And then your ass vanishes a month after that."

"Yes."

"The week after you pick up and leave, your brother beats his wife to death. A few days after that Darby goes AWOL. Like you, she's not to be seen for the next 10 years." He pauses, lets me take it all in. "Do I have this all right?"

I breathe in some stale air. Suddenly this place stinks. I nod.

"From December of '99 through the summer of 2000, one hell of a few months in the Ruane clan. No?"

"Point of clarification. I went to work in Philadelphia. Darby ended up at John Jay. We both left. We both had our reasons. But we didn't vanish. We didn't sneak off and hide."

"Uh huh, sure. You and Maureen ever hook up after you two left Belmar?"

I shake my head. "Never. I looked, but I never saw her, spoke to her, nothing."

Rizzo shakes his head. "So many fuckin possibilities in this case, Ruane." He studies me.

"The Sanchez case is unsolved," I say.

"Yes."

"All those alibis you're looking for from me. You think I would have killed her? Alisha Sanchez?"

"Stranger things have happened."

"Why would I? Because she beat out Maureen over a decade earlier in some bullshit track event?"

Rizzo shrugs. "Who knows, Bernie? Anything can happen in this world, that I've learned. Just about any fuckin thing. It could have been love gone mad. Some sick pact between you and Maureen. Fuck, I dunno. But I feel something's going on here, Bernie. Connections are forming. Alisha happened to get herself killed in the same way all those other Jersey Shore girls did."

"More or less."

"Mostly more."

"And, earlier, in August '99, I'm killing Sandy O'Connor? Why? What's the connection there? And what would that have to do with Maureen?"

"If there's a link, Bernie, we'll find it."

I hear movement on the porch and turn back to see over my shoulder a Belmar cop looking back at me through the glass.

Rizzo's rubbing his eyes. "Why were you in Edison August 29, 2003, the night Francine Waterman was run down?"

"I already told you. I was looking for Maureen."

"Tell me again."

I explain how I had found a Maureen Logan tagged in a photo on a trucking company web site in Edison. I tell him that when I called Matt Logan to see if he knew anything about the company or Maureen working there, he was strange about it. Not evasive, but speechless. Not hell no, not get fucking lost. I explain how her brother Matt made me suspicious, so I checked out the company myself. How I went there and they blew me off. How I started some heavy drinking because I was wondering where'd I go if she didn't take me. How I slept in my car.

Rizzo shakes his head. "See?"

"See what."

"You remembered something new this time."

I look at him. "That I called Sergeant Logan about this back in 2003."

"Good one, Columbo. You sure about this call?"

"Yes. And I'm sure there are phone records. But why not just ask Logan?"

"I intend to do just that. Cause he never mentioned it before either. Amazing."

"Where'd you get the Christmas photo?" I ask. "From him?"

"Yup. Couple days ago."

"My, my."

Rizzo pulls on an earlobe. "You got a drink?"

I look at him to see if he's serious, see he is dead serious and then go upstairs for that sweet-ass Yamazaki scotch. Back downstairs, I put a cube from the mini-fridge into each of two short glasses and pour them half full.

"To my Irish aunts and uncles," I toast.

Rizzo takes a long, slow drink. "Nice. Real nice. Smooth." He lets out a big breath. "All right, listen. The blood in your old car is inconclusive. It's human, but right now we can't say whose it is." He takes another pull.

"With Bosco's brother, it could be anything. Including from one of his buddies throwing up his guts in the backseat. That's happened. Believe me. I've been there."

Rizzo smiles at that. It flashes across his face like a crack of lightning and then it's gone. "Logan wants to pin all this on you."

"He can't stand me. Never could. But I can't tell you why he's so sure I did this."

"I've asked Edison Police to pull Logan from your inquiry. And the entire Jersey Shore investigation for that matter."

Rizzo's cell goes off. He listens. He closes his eyes. "Shit on me. Time of death?" He looks at his watch. "I'll be right there." He returns the phone to his pocket, letting out a sigh.

"I was going to arrest you tonight, Bernie," he says.

I look at the Belmar cop still peering inside and then back at Rizzo. "And now?"

"I've had a couple men following you today because we wanted to know where you were when we made our move. They've been watching the Honeypot entrances. You've been here since five p.m."

"Right, but ..."

"I thought about what Louisa Bongiovanni called in last night. About someone watching her. Someone who beat the shit outta her car."

Fuck, I think. I've been so wrapped up in Sandy's Story that I didn't call her back about being followed. I shake my head at how much I can fuck things up with her.

"I didn't think it was you watching her or beating up her car."

"Her car?"

"You didn't know?"

"No. She left a message but she didn't say anything about her car. What happened?"

Rizzo explained.

"I was here. I was making changes on this story that came out." I nod at *The Beach Star* on the coffee table between us.

"Louisa couldn't raise you on your cell."

"I shut if off sometimes when Bosco's driving me nuts. Like he was last night. All night."

He considers my answer in his head but gives no hint if he believes me. "So while my guys are watching this place tonight, I get a phone call myself. Logan's fingerprints were on the originals of these articles back in Edison." He waved his hand over the paperwork scattered on the tabletop. "They lifted one full and two partials. But they're his for sure. The oils from the prints were pretty fresh too. Like recent. Certainly not over 10 years old."

"So?"

"Sergeant Logan says they were discovered in Maureen's car by Edison forensics. That he never got close to the evidence. I heard him say as much to his Edison commander on a recording that was made."

"So Logan either lied and planted the articles or ..." I begin.

"There ain't no 'or.' So arresting you tonight wouldn't have made much sense. You weren't goin anywhere anyways. And then I got to thinking about why he shoved this photo of you and Alisha Sanchez in front of my face. And I didn't like what I was conjuring up."

I take a drink. "What was that?" I point my chin at his cell phone.

He drains his glass. He pulls Scope from a pocket and sprays it into his mouth. "That? That was about Bernadette Twill."

"Was?"

"She's been beaten to death with a blunt instrument. In what used to be her parents' home on 3rd Avenue in our fair town of Belmar, near River Road. About nine blocks from where we sit right now, Bernie. Less than an hour ago is the early guess."

He sets the lonely, empty glass down like he's sad to let go. "She was 30 years old, Ruane. She was a rising star. She was another Jersey Shore girl, now beaten dead like the rest." He assembles the folders on the table and tucks them under his arm.

He puts on his cap. "Looks like you finally got yourself an alibi, Ruane. But if you print an-nee-fuckin-thing about an-nee-fuckin-thing, including how I was here? With some officers outside? When Twill got killed? With me with a cup of hooch in my hand? I will not be happy. Nor will you, my friend."

The first thing that crosses my mind as he shuts the door behind him is that whoever is killing these girls has just made a sudden, desperation move. Like they're looking to finish things up. Someone's feeling squeezed by all the attention. I know that feeling and how you act when you get that feeling.

I remember to call Isa. She tells me about the hooded figure in the alley and the deep dents in her call. She doesn't bother to ask where I was or why I didn't call her back. I try to tell her. She cuts me off.

"Bernie, just stop, please."

I tell her about Bernadette Twill.

She tells me about Jennifer Botta, Grace Giuliani's friend and landlord.

"Whoever's killing these girls made a mistake."

"Yes. And was probably in my alley denting my car."

"I'm sorry I didn't call ...."

"Bernie, hold up. I got used to you not being around. You haven't been around a lot, you know. I can manage. I have to manage."

"I won't shut the phone off anymore. Not for you."

"Let's just get this fucker, Bernie." She hangs up.

I go to the door and look out the glass at top into the night. The cops are gone. The streets are empty. I walk to the back door and step out onto a small porch, looking up and down the Honeypot's alley. It's empty except for a dark cat that's suddenly on it haunches staring with glowing eyes at me. Like I'm the jinx.

Thirty-Nine

I half run the nine blocks to the Twills. By the time I get there, the place is an explosion of cop cars, ambulances, and emergency lights. I call Bosco on the way to tell him what's up.

I next call the woman who works in Belmar's Deed and Title department and doubles as the secretary for the town council meetings. I get her at home. She complains about the hour, but she owes me one. She agrees to check out the Twill property from her home computer.

Turns out it was once Bernadette's parents' place, the family home where she and her older sister grew up. According to April, the parents died, and the home was probated to the Twill girls, who now share it. It overlooks the Shark River Inlet that runs from the Atlantic Ocean into the Shark River basin. Across the water to the northwest is the Shark River Beach & Yacht Club where Allie Formosa was killed. On the north side of the river from the Twill home lies Avon-on-the-Sea, where Rosemary Prelia was beaten to death one warm summer night on a back porch of an empty rental. For a fleeting moment I wonder again what kind of sick place I've come back to. I promise April a couple beers at Jack's in gratitude and end the call.

I learn Rizzo is inside the Twill house from one of the cops setting up a perimeter. They won't let me onto the lawn, so I stick to the street. I scan the house. It was built in the roaring 20s, I learn, around the time the Honeypot was built, when money flew into town for a time. An open porch crosses the front of the house while a gazebo sprouts on the left front lawn. I bet the Twills sat in that gazebo and watched nice sunsets over the river. Once upon a time. On the right, the house shoots up almost in the shape of a barn. The bedrooms are up on the second floor of the barn. One glows with brilliant forensic light.

I wave over a young cop who doesn't know he should be avoiding me like the plague because I'm the newspaper hack writing about all the dead women his peers and superiors missed.

"You see the body?"

"They don't let us juniors onto the front lines. I'm here to make sure folks like you keep a distance."

"Any word on the crime scene?"

"Blood everywhere. She was fucked up pretty bad." He looks around and catches a couple of cops looking at him. "That's all I can say."

The canine unit pulls into the driveway. The dogs tumble out of the back of the van, catch a fresh scent, and then with a chorus of barks strain against thick leashes, leading their handlers into the backyard. Cops are up and down the street, flashing wide torch beams into the bushes and down darkened driveways, their free hands on the guns at their belts. Several have crossed the street and a wide expanse of grass down to the Shark River Inlet, where they're walking the shoreline. A helicopter thunders overhead and shines blinding shafts of light down into the woods behind the houses. It looks like a war zone.

Allie Formosa's pulp of a face pops into my head again. Fresh and moist. I exhale hard, hoping to expel her for good.

I wait, scanning the blank faces of the cops coming and going, looking for someone who will talk to me. Around me, lights blaze behind thin shades in a few of the surrounding houses. A few neighbors gather in the street, their arms uniformly folded around their chests, holding in their fear.

Forty

We went live online with the Twill story around three a.m. The news was nationwide about an hour after that, and bright-eyed reporters were already on the scene in Belmar in time for their Friday morning news reports. *The Today Show* even sent Savannah Guthrie 90 minutes south to Belmar for a live shot in front of the Twill house, the sun rising over the tranquil Atlantic.

It was a beautiful, early fall day, Guthrie intones at the top of the show, but not for Bernadette Twill's sister. I turn off the TV right then. Pretty shitty day for Bernadette Twill too.

My cell goes off. It's an international call. Country code 44.

"Mr. Ruane?"

"Yes?"

"This is Jennifer Botta." A crack in her voice. "I know all these women who have been killed."

I'm thinking who the fuck is Jennifer Botta calling me from some other country. I remember Isa's discovery. "Grace Giuliani's friend."

Jennifer sucks in her breathe. "Oh, God. Listen, I'm from Seaside Heights, Mr. Ruane. But I've been living in Oxford, England for the past few years. I've just heard about what's been happening. I just read about Bernadette Twill." Her voice breaks. I hear her spill a soft cry.

I grab a pen and a yellow pad and sit at my desk. "Go on. How do you know these women?"

She swallows a deep breath. "I mean," she continues, "I never met all of them. But the Ladder award … I know about it." She stops. "I got one too."

"Like Sandy O'Connor."

"That's right. The Ladder named us 'Young Women of Power and Promise' for the Jersey Shore. There were others like us, you know in other parts of the state, from north to south. Like you wrote."

"When?"

"When what?"

"When did Ladder announce the award?"

"God … It had to be about the middle of January. In the last year before the millennium, I remember."

"1999."

"I..., most of us, we were sophomores in college then. Maybe one or two of us were juniors. We were all involved in volunteer work, and all of us won something or other. Most of us were Catholic, but not all."

"How many of you were there?"

"Ten from the Jersey Shore. It was the same for the other regions, I think. That's the thing. I went back today after reading about Bernadette. She was one of our group of 10 from the Jersey Shore. I remember her, Mr. Ruane. So sweet. We all got close back then. Sandy, Rosemary, Francine … all of them."

"Mary Angliotti? Veronica Landry? Allie Formosa?"

"Yes. All of them."

"What about Grace Giuliani?"

For a moment I thought I lost her. She came back flat. "She … was …"

I waited, remembering to breathe. "Take your time," I say.

"The year … the year I left for London, I sublet to her. She was a friend. We met somewhere along the way as we each chased the music. She was from New Orleans. She was murdered in Newark while she lived in my apartment. Clubbed one night after a symphony. She was lead oboe in the Newark Symphony."

"Someone killed her …"

"… thinking it was me. Had to be. She was killed right after July 4th. I remember. Back in 2008. I thought it was just a horrible thing. Such a vicious attack. I never thought it was me he was after. I just didn't know about the other girls. But now with all this … Oh my God!"

She takes her turn to breathe now. "And she was raped after he beat her to death."

"It may have been someone different than the attacker. " I explain my theory.

"A year before Grace was killed, I saw Whitney Dickerson," she continues, with new wind, coming to full tilt. "Whitney was on the Ladder list too. She's a lawyer. She had a roommate who wasn't on the lease and was crashing with her. A woman she had gone to law school with. She was beat up in Brooklyn in the summer of 2007 and left to die in some alley."

"Whitney?"

"No, no, her roommate." She stops again and I hear the space between us hiss.

"I … I just never thought what happened to Whitney's roommate might be related to what happened to Grace. I never put two and two together. I didn't know."

"You couldn't have known," I say. I stop because I don't know what else to say.

"Whitney told me her roommate actually survived her attack. I forget the girl's name, where she was from. But she wasn't from the Jersey Shore. It was the Midwest somewhere."

"Where was Whitney from?

"Sea Girt." A couple of towns from me going south on Ocean Avenue.

Someone was visiting vengeance upon the top ten Young Women of Power and Promise on the Jersey Shore from 1999. One by one. After tonight, maybe three were still alive or at best unaccounted for. Jennifer Botta, Whitney Dickerson maybe. And the last one they hadn't talked about. The murderer. I was suddenly convinced of that.

"Who was the tenth Woman of Power and Promise, Jennifer?"

"The last one was Dabny something. Or Daffney. I can't remember."

"Was she white or black?"

"Dabny, or Daffney, was white. Whitney was the only African-American woman."

"Were any of the girls in the Ladder – the ones you were supposed to help – the type who might do this? Anyone who stands out as especially odd, angry, unbalanced?"

The phone line's hiss takes over as she thinks. "Well, not really," she says finally. "I mean many were sullen, unhappy, bottled up. Defensive. At least at first. But they warmed up usually. It was just such a wonderful experience with these kids. I mean across the board. Their hearts were so big and yet they got so little."

I wanted to tell her that a big heart can be as twisted and ugly as a shriveled one, that a big heart can pump blood to a sick mind and a murderer's hand just as easily as it pumps life to a healthy mind and a helping hand. But I didn't press it. She didn't need my insights on life just now.

"Who knew about the Ladder award, Jennifer? How big a deal was it? How much publicity? No one seems to remember anything, not even the nuns who gave it away."

"It wasn't a big thing. It was the first year they gave out the awards, and things were pretty disorganized. The Ladder wasn't really capable of publicizing it much beyond their own community and those they served. Not yet, anyway. There was a newsletter with our names and all that. The Ladder was doing it, you know, to pump us up as role models for the kids. The award dinners never happened, you know. Because of what happened to Sandy."

Role models. Rising stars. And now most of them are dead. Extinguished, as Isa put it.

I ask her about Oxford. About security over there. She's on someone's kill list, I needlessly remind her. She has to talk to campus security. I make a mental note to talk to Rizzo about it.

"But I won't be here long." She chokes back another surging cry. "Someone attacked my mom the other day. And I'm coming back."

"Your mom? Where?"

"Seaside Heights. She's in the hospital. Someone clubbed her over the head with a pipe from our garage. When she was taking out the trashcans for the next morning's pickup. That's what the police tell me. She's touch and go right now, but they think she's going to be okay."

I go cold right then. Attacking her mother was a surefire way to get Jennifer Botta back to the Jersey Shore, where she in turn would surely be stalked and killed, like all the rest. I ask her where her mother is. Jennifer tells me Jersey Shore Medical over in Neptune.

What Botta says next doesn't surprise me.

"I'm on the first flight out from Heathrow today. I'll be there by the evening."

She gives me the flight details. I tell her I'll be sure there's someone to meet her at the airport to escort her to a secure place to stay. "It'll probably be cops," I finish.

"I don't mind that. But, Mr. Ruane? My mom still has the newsletter from the Ladder. The one announcing our awards. I'm sure of it. It'll be in her house. It'll still be in the big bookcase on the back wall of my old room in a notebook of clippings and stuff."

"We'll find it."

We say goodbyes, and I think about calling Darby. Then I stop, thinking about this Dabny or Daffney or whoever. I suddenly have doubts about what to do next. If Darby is Dabny, then she's the tenth person on that list. She could be the next victim. But there's also the possibility she could also be something or someone else I didn't want to think about.

Isa's questions about Darby bounce around in my head. Darby's volatility hits me too. Did I know what finding her crushed mother on the kitchen floor back then did to her? Did I know why she came back to Belmar? Did I know Darby after all? Was she possibly a Ladder girl? Could I have missed that too among all the other things I apparently missed back then?

I don't call Darby. I need to find that newsletter. I call Rizzo for help and then Bosco.

Forty-One

Bosco agreed to a special Sunday morning edition of *The Beach Star*, its first ever. In real print. On real paper. Two pages of news and commentary about the shore's Women of Power and Promise and some sober and appropriate ads hurriedly solicited. It would be delivered to stores and *The Star's* vending machines along the shore at roughly three a.m. Sunday morning. About three hours from now. Pulling this off was no small task, but we did it. Bosco and me.

We meet at the Porch with his copies hot off the presses. We grab a table looking out at Ocean Avenue, our backs to the bar.

It's mid-October, and the nights come chilled now. The Porch has lowered its see-through tarps, and the flames of the heating lanterns keep us toasty. Patrons in the dulled photos on the walls watch us, craning in and listening solemnly, not liking what they're hearing, drinks in hand. Heavy waves we can't see pound it out in the dark.

Julie not only kept the bar open for us, but she also sets us up with some steak frites and our own bottle of Macallan 12. Her eyes are red and gleamed vicious wet. Sunday's story hit her hard.

Isa joins Bosco and me and dips into the scotch. "Just one," she says as she picks up the early print of *The Star* open on the table.

"I'm glad you came," I say.

"I literally forced you to shout out to me when the paper was ready."

"But I'm ..."

"Quiet, I'm reading." Her big blue eyes go small and black as she scans the front page. I watch her, thinking about all the young women of promise and their mothers, and all that those mothers had done and were doing for their little girls.

When I got Rizzo earlier, I briefed him on my call with Jennifer Botta. Rizzo said he would have Newark airport police pick Jennifer up this evening and escort her to the hospital where her mother was recovering. He also arranged for Seaside cops to go into her mother's house first thing Saturday morning, over 18 hours ago. Rizzo had a copy of the Ladder's newsletter hand-delivered to us by yesterday evening.

Soon *The Beach Star* would be telling the story to Belmar and Neptune and Avon and Seaside Heights, and everyone would come to know why their young women went missing.

Besides Whitney Dickerson and of course Jennifer Botta, the last missing Young Woman of Power and Promise was a Dabny all right, just like Jennifer Botta almost remembered. Dabny Famula. I had let out a long sigh when I saw that name in print in the Ladder's newsletter. I didn't tell anyone what I had feared. Not Isa. For sure not Darby. I might not have survived the telling.

Besides the Ladder newsletter announcing the Jersey Shore awards, the Seaside cops found a hold-the-date card sent to the Bottas by the Ladder. It was dated early in August, 1999, the month Sandy O'Connor was killed. The card said the big Ladder dinner would be December 17, 1999, at the Breakers on the ocean in Spring Lake just down the boardwalk from Belmar. Not far from where we sat now.

According to the newsletter, there was a Dinner Committee organizing the Ladder awards that year. And Charlotte Logan, Lottie as she was called, was one of the stalwart matrons on the Committee and chaired the Jersey Shore dinner.

Anne Botta's hold-the-date card had a familiar return address in Edison, New Jersey. Charlotte Logan's. Rizzo told him about what they had heard from Matt Logan about his mother's work with the nuns. And here she was, a big shot in the whole Ladders program.

Mo might have seen the Ladder newsletter. But if she did, she never mentioned it to me. I couldn't remember when she ever talked about her mother for that matter. It was her father she hated. And it was her brother that she constantly tried to avoid.

The newsletter went on to feature short, inspirational, heart-tugging stories about each of the award winners. Sandy O'Connor remembered sitting on the Jersey Shore watching the stars overhead with her father, the waves shaking the sand beneath them. She remembered he would point out Venus and tell her that not even the sky was her limit, nor was Venus beyond her reach. Jennifer Botta loved her music, and the best part was seeing how her oboe lifted others up, how both she and her audience could rise above the hard times that troubled them. Whitney said her mama taught her that worry and tears got you nowhere. When her father left her, Whitney was young. No one cares if you have a sad story, her mother told her back then. Every girl has her sad story. Everyone has a world of reason to shoot up, get high, get lost, disappear. But only a very few have a story of resilience and triumph. A story about rising above all that drags you down. A story about trying your hardest and making a difference in your own life and the lives of others.

Their stories bring Isa to silent tears. She wipes them away with a long pale finger as she sits at an ungodly hour at the table with Bosco and me. She slaps some more from the bottle into her glass. I know she's thinking about her own promising girl.

The last person on the Jersey Shore list, the one Botta couldn't remember, is Dabny Famula, a woman whose last known job was as a sultry-voiced disc jockey at an indie rock music radio station out of New York City. Dabny was from Neptune, like Allie and Francine, and had her poetry and short stories published in literary journals at a young age. A quick call to Francine's mother made clear that Francine "didn't know no Dabny" despite their being of the same age in the same town. Francine's mother was slurring her words early these days, probably more since Edison announced they'd reopened the case of Francine's hit-and-run.

With Isa's help we had managed to track down and contact Whitney Dickerson yesterday afternoon. She was still practicing law out of New York City. She told us she was too busy to keep up with "your" Jersey Shore murders because she's been in litigation in Buffalo for the past year. Whitney hadn't returned to Sea Girt in years. She sounded like she was never coming back to Jersey, much less the shore. She had moved on. Stepped up one more rung of that ladder.

Whitney told us about Sara French, a woman she had met at Howard Law School in DC. Sara looked a lot like Whitney, same coloration, same height, similar body, same long, dark, straightened hair. Sara had been attacked and left for dead in an alley in Brooklyn after she left too late from a litigation clinic that served the locals there. It never occurred to Whitney that perhaps she herself had been the target. Rizzo confirmed to us that no one has yet been arrested in the Sara French case. Nor could French remember anything about the incident.

Whitney and Jennifer were once young women of promise from the Jersey Shore, and over the years they had lived to deliver on it. Others had paid price for their recognition. Death. Dabny, however, was off the grid as far as we could tell after a long Saturday evening of Isa pounding the internet pavement looking for information.

Isa puts down *The Beach Star*. "Rizzo needs to haul in Dickerson and Famula and question their asses. Like he did it to you, Bernie. Where were you, give me alibis, prove 'em, you know - the whole nine yards. Now."

"He's going to question Whitney as soon as she gets her ass down to Belmar."

"Good," Isa nods.

"Whitney insisted that Rizzo get on a call with her to the law firm security office. And you know what? She didn't express a word of concern, shock, or outrage about the carnage. Not a word about the women dead and gone. She just made sure her ass was covered."

"Lawyers have no blood," Bosco offers up. "Cuz they have no heart."

"And I just don't believe this is the first she's heard about these murders," I say. "There's no escaping this story."

"Seems like a cold bitch to me," Isa replies. She takes a last sip and gathers up her things. "You coming home with me, Bernie?"

I beg off. I owe Henry the rest of the night and tomorrow. And tomorrow will come early with phone calls. Isa nods.

"What about Lottie Logan?" Isa tucks a copy of *The Star* into her shoulder bag. "She knew all the Ladder girls. She's the mother of an Edison cop, where one of the Ladder girls got killed. And the mother of another woman missing from Belmar, Maureen Ruane."

"It's an angle," Bosco says. "We're gonna pursue it. But what do we say now?"

"You got Lottie's son, the Edison cop, trying to stick this to Bernie. You don't think that's odd?"

"Isa, we'll work it."

She kisses the top of my head. "That's where I'd look, Johnny Bosco. Matt Logan. He's the monster hiding in the sunlight. Just like Bernie said." She heads out the door.

Julie watches the door close behind the departing Isa, then yells at me from behind the bar. "Romeo? What's with you? You're not escorting the woman who loves you out of this fuckin bar, asshole? Especially with everything goin on?"

I jump up and run outside to open the car door for Isa. She thanks me with surprise on her face, and we hold each other, kissing long, deep, and hard. I pull her silent warmth closer, and then I let go.

"Call me when you get home," I say as I close her car door.

"Pick up this time," she says. She pulls the door shut.

I go back inside to finish up with Bosco.

He looks at me. "I can't hold off on Lottie Logan, Bernie. We have to get to that part of the story."

"I know. Let me work it."

"You are working it, right?"

"Good night, Johnny. Talk to you tomorrow."

Forty-Two

The Beach Star from Thursday and Sunday sit open next to the laptop. Their headlines shout out loud. They scream.

Time is running out.

Sara French in Brooklyn was a mistake. Just like Grace Giuliani in Newark. Sara sure looked like Whitney Dickerson. Sure dressed like her. Sure walked like her.

But she cried a lot in that alley in Brooklyn. Maybe that should have been a clue. Because Whitney never cried. That's what she bragged about, right? "No Tears" Whitney was another perfect one. She was strong. Whitney's mother raised her to be the proud woman she became, told her time and again that no one could ever hear her cry, no one could ever see her tears, and no one would ever care even if they did. Whitney had to be strong. And Whitney was.

But Sara wasn't. She cried. She begged. She wet herself right there in that alley in Brooklyn.

Whitney Dickerson. She's with a law firm in New York. The laptop screen glows with her phone number. And her photo. Wow, she hasn't changed much. Of course not. Does perfection decay? Does it grow old? No, it doesn't. But it can cease. It can die.

A few more clicks, and the story in the *Ocean County Gazette* pops up about Anne Botta's attack. Even has what hospital she's at. Jennifer will be home soon. She might be at the hospital right now.

Need to move quickly now.

Forty-Three

Crombie pointed Logan into the empty chair in front of his desk. It was Monday morning. He was going to waste no time. His concerns had been borne out. Rizzo was right.

Crombie liked Rizzo. He spoke plainly, drawing sound conclusions based on fact and cautious inference. And he didn't back down. They both agreed on Logan.

"At minimum," he began, "you broke the chain of control on the evidence found in your sister's car. We probably can't use any of that shit now even if we felt we could convince a jury how those two articles got there."

Logan's face glistened red where it wasn't already black and blue.

"How'd the articles get there, sergeant? Did you put them there? Did you plant them as part of your vendetta against Bernie Ruane?"

Logan's eyes widened. "No way. I, uh, uh …."

"You fuckin uh uh what?"

He couldn't stop wringing his hands in his lap. "I wanted to see if they might help find my sister."

"You didn't care about her when she first went missing years ago. You did nothing all these years she's been gone. You showed zero emotion when before, in my office, we spoke about it. But now you care?"

"If Ruane did it, I care. He's made me, all of us, look bad on the Waterman case. If he did Mo too? And is blaming us? Damn straight I care."

Crombie's mouth worked like he had just tasted something foul. "If he 'did' your sister? Curious f'ing answer, Logan."

"Listen, asshole, I would turn this whole pile of shit over to internal affairs, but it's in the same damn bureau as your unit. And I don't trust you shits. So I'm asking the county to take this up. You're stinkin like shit in all this. That's why I've asked Lieutenant Sanders to be here."

Logan eyed the woman next to him. He looked back at Crombie. "Am I suspended, sir?"

"Yes. For now. Your admin officer will handle the paperwork later when I get you the fuck outta my sight."

"With pay? Better be with pay, or I go to the union."

"I don't think we have a choice. The lieutenant here is going to want to know why you didn't tell us Ruane called you the night Waterman was run down. That would have been pertinent in the inquiry you asked me to initiate against him. Very pertinent. That you excluded it is suspicious. Very suspicious. The lieutenant is also going to want to know the particulars of the complaint that a Patrol Officer Darby Ruane has filed against you. Sexual assault and harassment."

Logan froze. She broke her promise. She's gone public. "She, she attacked me," he manages.

"Rizzo tells me she's thinking hard about filing a criminal complaint against you too. Says there's a video of the attack. Says he's seen it and you're cooked."

Logan shrunk into his chair, looking like he was trying to disappear.

Sanders smiled. "It appears that she wiped the floor with you, sergeant. That itty bitty thing do all this to big ol' you?" She pointed a finger at him and did a couple of figure eights over his body, her eyebrows arched in mock surprise. She shot a glance at Crombie, who's shaking his head, a slight smile on his lips wanting to bust out.

"Sergeant Logan, some other things Rizzo mentioned."

"Yes sir?"

"Your mother was organizing the dinner for the Shore girls who won the Ladder award."

Logan said that sounded like her. And he remembered the Ladder bullshit and all the fuss she made over the star girls who had won. He remembered all the time she spent working with the nuns on those fuckin dinners.

"Logan, is there something you wanna tell us about the dinners. About those girls?"

He looks at the two of them. "What I got?"

"Who's killing them, Sergeant? Where were you when Twill was killed on Thursday?"

"Dunno. Gotta check."

"Why did Alisha Sanchez and Tiffany Jones have to die? They weren't Ladder girls."

"No …" he begins and then stops.

"The union will get you a lawyer for the internal affairs inquiry. I guess you might want a lawyer for when Darby comes after you too. You might be needing a whole mess of lawyers."

Crombie dismissed him with a disgusted wave. Logan took the cue and slipped quickly out the door and down the hallway.

#

Logan packed up his locker and drove home. He'd call his admin officer tomorrow. Same for the union legal call line.

It was dusk, and the street was empty. He pulled himself up the front stoop and headed into the house and upstairs. He paused at Maureen's old room. The room that still has her bookshelves with some of her stuff from long ago. A couple of hangers of her clothes still occupy her closet, the door half open. A pair of slippers hides under her bed. Alongside balls of dust.

He moved on to his bedroom. He stopped and listened to the house creaking, clunking and clanging. He knew its constant noises and sighs. It was empty now.

He packed his own bag. Belmar was his destination tonight. He'd get there a little after 10.

But first he'd eat. Down a few brews. Pop some Percocet.

She would not get away with this. She fucked him. Bad.

Next time wouldn't be him on the ground, looking up at her. No sir. Next time he'd take care of her for good. Real good.

Forty-Four

Matt Logan hid in the shadows a block from Darby Ruane's darkened cottage. He was wearing a dark turtleneck and jeans. His issued Glock was in its holster at his belt, and his baton hung from the other side.

He got her address from a contact on the Belmar force. She was getting off at midnight, the contact volunteered. At the station, everyone knew her comings and goings. She was like the weather. On everybody's minds and lips.

He jogged over to the house and slipped into the shadows along the side. The cottages on either side of hers were dead, For Rent signs out front. He got up close to a grimy window and peered in.

In the dim light from the moon he can make out a living room with two hulking couches where the summer people probably crashed, a couple of big, stuffed armchairs, and a table. The one room with the shade drawn, probably her bedroom, he couldn't see into.

He put his face to the window in the back door and spotted a basic table and two chairs in a crappy kitchen. He tried the door. It was locked, but maybe with a heavy shoulder he could crash through.

He decided to wait out front until she returned. He'd go right up to her and then hit her before she could say shit. Hard. Quick. She wouldn't have time to react, to lure him and cut him down like last time. He wouldn't wait for her blubbering, for her answer. He'd hit her with his baton with his full weight behind it, and she'd go down. And then he'd hit her again. He'd hurt her bad. No one would gaze upon that angel face of hers the same way again. Not anytime soon.

He remembered passing Bar Anticipation up the road on his way here. It would be a good place to refresh his buzz and work out his moves step by step. He had a couple hours until she would return anyway.

Logan left his police gear on the front passenger seat after parking at Bar A. He grabbed a booth in the back, next to idle pool tables and dartboard alleys, and sat facing the square bar in front and the entrance.

His pitcher came, and the waitress, a young thing in white short shorts crawling up the crack of her ass, courtesy poured his first mug. "Anything else for ya?"

"Not right now sweetheart. Maybe later." He winked big at her.

Her lips slipped into a rigid grimace of death as she turned away.

He downed the first beer in three gulps. Real cold. He filled his second and thought about something to eat. He checked his watch. Still an hour before Darby's shift ended. He started thinking step-by-step.

Emergency lights exploded in the Bar A parking lot. Then a second and a third wave of lights mashed up outside. Intense orange beams swept across the windows, playing off the ceiling and walls inside the bar, accentuating his buzz. He peered out a window to see what was goin down.

The front door to the bar crashed open. In stepped Darby Ruane and two other officers. Thick guys with muscles bulging under light blue Belmar PD shirts over sparkling white Ts. Rizzo came in behind them.

They scanned the room, Darby flashing some paper at the manager who had come out from the back. They swiveled their heads across the dozen patrons and then spotted him in a back booth. They fanned out. Rizzo beelined toward him.

"Hey, Logan. Whatcha doin here?" Rizzo squeezed into the booth across the table from Logan. He took off his cap and laid it upside down on the table, running a hand through his hair.

"Havin a beer. Problem?"

"I mean here in Belmar."

Darby moved into the back area where they sat, her thumbs latched behind her utility belt at her hips. The other two cops stuck near the front entrance. Logan figured there'd be another couple outside at the back exit and near his car. He knew the drill.

Rizzo gestured to Darby to move back up front, away from them. She knew Rizzo was right but she sneered at him and Logan anyway, out of spite if nothing else, before she left.

"How'd you know I was here, Rizzo?"

"Commander Crombie told me he'd taken you off the Jersey Shore murders. Put you on leave. Said to keep an eye out for you what with the Darby Ruane incident and all. We got a call from one of our finest driving by that he saw somebody reconnoitering Darby's house. I mean, Jesus, man, you've lost the feel for the street in your comfy office. The guy who spotted you followed you here. He's up front. Bad form, baby. Bad form. Also not good form to leave your gun and gear visible on your front seat. Violation of procedures."

Logan took a long drink.

"Tell me Logan, what you got against Bernie Ruane?"

"He's a piece of shit."

"That it? Just bad vibes?" Rizzo slid a photo across the table, the one he had shown Ruane. The Christmas photo with Alisha Sanchez, Bernie, Maureen, Matt and their mother in it.

Logan eyeballed the image.

"Why'd you send me that?" Rizzo asked.

"Showed Bernie Ruane knew the Sanchez girl."

"Shows you knew her too."

Logan finishes his beer and sets his mug on the table with a thud. His eyes fall again on the photo between them.

"Those Ladder girls," said Rizzo. "You never saw that list?"

"Nope."

"You knew about the Ladder though."

"I guess. There was lots of inspirational shit like that goin on with my mother. Lots my mother got involved with. Pilgrimages. Retreats. Holy Roller sing-alongs. Shit like that galore."

"You never knew about the dinner and the awards and all that?"

"I musta. But who knows?"

"Is that a no?"

Logan shrugged. "Why's it matter?"

"You said your mother was knee deep with these nuns down here. But she never talked about the Ladder awards and her big, upcoming dinner?"

"She talked about the nuns a lot. Yeah, Ladder was big with her. Took up a lot of her time. She liked the idea of helping other kids escape their hellholes. The fuck with us. So, what about the Ladder awards?"

"She had a big heart, your mother?"

"Big enough for some."

"What happened to your mother, Sergeant Logan? Did you do something to her? To any of those Ladder girls?"

"She fuckin died. Her heart or somethin."

"What happened to your sister?"

Logan put his forehead down onto his crossed arms on the table. His shoulders started heaving slowly and silently as he cried into his sleeve. When he looked up he was wet. He blinked at Rizzo.

Rizzo signaled to his cops up front. When they got close, he pointed to Logan. "He's done for now. Take him. And Darby? You touch nothing. Do nothing. Al, you do the cuffing and the handling at the station. Leave Darby out of this."

" Matthew Logan, you're under arrest," said Al moving along the table. Darby crossed her arms and watched the show. She noticed then that Logan's eyes were black spots in tiny red seas in a room gone orange from the swirling police lights outside.

"You shoulda read me my rights earlier, Rizzo," snapped Logan, a little smile playing on his wet lips. "Everything I just said can't be used against me, you know."

"Well shucks, Logan, I ain't arresting you for all of that. I'm arresting you for sexual assault and battery. Remember? It's caught on film, and our Miss Darby's going to press charges. We'll hold you in Belmar until we transfer you up to the Monmouth prosecutor."

Logan spat on the floor. A different man in the blink of an eye. "Fuck you. Fuck all of you."

Darby followed the parade that led Logan out to the scattered applause from the room. Outside she waited for Rizzo to turn and head off to his car and then she quickly grabbed a sweaty handful of Logan's thick neck and shoved his head into the roof of the flashing squad car they eventually put him into.

"Oops," she said.

"Fuck you, bitch," he snarled back as he looked up at her from the back seat.

She spat in his face. "You wish, limp dick. Ain't never gonna happen."

Forty-Five

Darby sat back at her Belmar PD desk and smiled. That punkass Logan sobbing like a baby at Bar A was priceless. What a pussy.

Darby sat straight and suddenly clicked into her computer. She remembered that Rizzo was talking to Jennifer Botta and Whitney Dickerson in the next day, maybe two. Only Dabny Famula was unaccounted for among the Jersey Shore award winners. Dabny Famula.

She headed first to the Belmar police resources page to grab the low-hanging fruit. County marriage records in New Jersey would show if Famula had hooked up or changed her name. Then, if Dabny had a driver's license, the DMV would steer her to a wealth of information.

Darby struck out with the marriage records. Nothing. But it was bingo at the DMV. Dabny's last issued New Jersey driver's license was in the system, but had expired almost two years ago. No renewals.

Darby peered at the photo image on the license. It was in color but Dabny's face looked pale white under some nasty black patch of punk hair. Her face was caved in like it was getting sucked down a sinkhole, and her neck bulged veins and ridges.

The old license had a familiar street name, Spray Avenue in Ocean Grove. Ocean Grove was one town up from Bradley Beach and one town over from Neptune where Dabny Famula was born. Close.

She kept clicking through various links and scrolling down opening pages quickly. The state courthouse records in Trenton gave up zero cases from 2000 onward involving anyone named Dabny Famula. Westlaw showed no liens or estate filings in her name. National Student Clearinghouse had Dabny graduating from CCNY in New York City in 2002, right on time with the other Women of Poise or Primp, or whatever they were. And, lo and behold, Dabny was in default on her student loans to the tune of over a hundred grand. That was a ton of money to get out from under.

Darby stretched in her chair. What else, she thought.

She searched Monmouth Country records for convictions and came up empty, then checked adjacent counties. Nothing. She needed higher access clearance to be entirely sure the County records held expungement orders and New York City arrest records. She wrote a Post-It note reminding her to do that tomorrow.

What else.

She pulled up Ocean Grove's current phone directory. No Famulas. She searched for all landline and mobile numbers allocated by the phone company to residents at 10 Spray Avenue. A Dabny Lane had a mobile number billed to Apartment 11 a while back. Another Dabny, no way. How many deranged mothers could have named their sweet peas Dabny?

She Googled the address. The apartment sat at the corner of Ocean Avenue and Spray, overlooking the beach and the ocean. To the right, when you looked at the apartment from Ocean Avenue, a large, empty, weed-and-kudzu-choked lot stretched north to the beginnings of the Asbury Park waterfront area. There on the horizon was Asbury Park's circular old casino and pony carousel house that Bernie loved so much, a hundred yards beyond a now-abandoned power plant, with its looming tower. Bernie once told her that the power plant had generated steam and electricity just for the Asbury Park boardwalk where Bruce Springsteen hung out along with his Madam Marie and those corner boys. Greetings from Asbury Park and all that shit.

She smiled at the sudden memory of Uncle Bernie belting out *It's Hard to Be a Saint in the City* at some family backyard barbecue. He knew the song, every nuance, cherishing each and every angst-filled word. It's so hard to be a saint when you're just a boy out on the street.

She studied the Google photo of the apartment. There was space for parking alongside a side road that had a direct line of sight to Dabny Lane's apartment building. Darby figured she could get there in 15 minutes.

She logged off and grabbed her bag, her officer's belt, and her hooded sweatshirt from her John Jay days.

Forty-Six

It's close to two a.m. I can't sleep. A lot has happened since last Thursday night when Bernadette Twill was murdered in her bed.

Then came Rizzo's call a little while ago. He's arrested Matt Logan who's sitting in the Belmar jail.

Rizzo tried to convince me it had nothing to do with Maureen Logan, nothing to do with the dead Ladder women. It was simple criminal sexual assault and battery against Darby. But I know he's bullshitting me.

So I ask him. "Why are you telling me this?"

"I need you to think real hard about that night with Alisha Sanchez, Maureen Logan and her mother. What happened that night? What does it tell us about Logan? Anything at all that took place that might shed light on who killed Sanchez, and why his sister left town. Anything that might tell us why his mother's Ladder girls have been getting themselves killed."

I start asking why he thinks that night might hold hidden clues to all that, but Rizzo cuts me off. "Start thinking. Stop talking." He hangs up.

I'm with Isa at her place. Henry's sleeping over at the Honeypot to help manage the residents and all the fucking reporters banging on my door since the Sandy O'Connor and Ladder stories.

I look at the ceiling and think about that night back in December of 1999. It was forever ago. I need my memory shook. I need to go to Edison.

I turn over and hold Isa. She gives me a low moan. "Not now. In the morning."

"I need to take the car. I got something Rizzo wants me to do."

She rolls onto her back. She's as white as the sheets in the moonlight, her dark hair framing her smooth face. "Rizzo's asking you for help? That's fucked."

Her eyes squeeze shut, and she kisses her pale bony fingertips and plants them in the air somewhere near my cheek. "Kiss. Kiss." She turns over. "Hurry back. And don't make me late in the morning."

I smile and smooth her hair back from her face, watching her breathe softly for a minute.

I dress quietly in the bathroom after rubbing my face in stone cold water. I peek in at Margarita, who's sound asleep, translucent and skinny like her mother.

An hour later up the highway, I park in front of Logan's three-story walk-up in Edison. I park so the driver side is against the curb. The street is safe enough, but the brothers on a stoop a few doors down keep an eye on me. I'm pretty sure they generally steer clear of Logan who reeks of Edison cop creaming in his starched pants to crack skulls. I'm pretty sure they apply that technique of diplomatic avoidance to any of the creep's visitors. Like me.

I roll my window halfway down, letting in the cool October night air. I look up at the house atop a slight hill with a set of concrete stairs that take you to the front stoop. Thinking about Maureen. About her brother. Trying to picture their mother and father and what had happened here. I never knew what really went on in that house. Maureen never said much.

I think about the Christmas before Mo disappeared. Christmas 1999. The one in the photo Rizzo hit me with. It was a strange night. Strange gathering.

That Christmas, Mo wanted Alisha and her fiancée, that was it, her new fiancée, to come to a holiday dinner at the house in Edison. Alisha and Mo had run across each other somewhere or other, maybe the mall, I can't remember, and the two of them kicked around old times.

Some things didn't fit. Like that Mo was celebrating old times or glory days. She hated old times. Hated glory days worse. That she was celebrating an old friendship. I was her only friend. That she wanted to host a dinner party with her family in Edison. Perhaps the strangest thing of all.

Her mother, Lottie, was totally out of it by then, gone deep into the endless caverns of her foggy mind. Matt Logan did the cooking for reasons that still elude me. He served up a dried ham and freezer-burned vegetables, along with a salad of sliced cucumber and vinegar. That salad selection mystified me. Almost epicurean.

Mo pranced about in a red sweater and red tights. She was hyper with happiness, almost cute. She played some Christmas tunes from a lousy cassette player and butchered "The Little Drummer Boy" with her singing and two wooden spatulas. She talked about the old days. Alisha and her fiancée sat there, desperately drinking as much of the cheap beer being served as they could, thinking, I'm sure, what the fuck.

I remember something snapping Lottie out of her coma. It was something to do with church or going to church or Jesus or something.

It came to me.

Alisha had brought something up, something about how young folks like herself were moving back into Asbury Park to give it new life. How her local church was chipping in to help.

I check out my rearview and that stoop with the local crime watch. Across the street a sign stuck in the lawn reads "For Sale. Buy Out of Foreclosure. Act NOW! Brought to You by the Edison Housing Development Agency."

Something clicks in my head, a door unlocking, as I study that sign. Alisha and her local church. She had talked about working back then with her local church group, which was connected to an affordable housing program in Asbury Park. Alisha was a do-gooder sort. And Lottie came alive, thrilled by it all. She tried to enlist Alisha in something some nuns were doing in Asbury Park. Or somewhere. Helping other girls who were lost.

That was when Logan and Mo snapped in syncopated time. They got angry and loud. They yelled at Lottie and then at Alisha. Not tonight, they shouted, not tonight. Not now, not now. Stop, stop. Back and forth like that they went.

Alisha was smooth, quick on her feet. She laughed it off, or tried to, whatever it was that was happening in this crazy house, saying she was Baptist anyway and that she didn't work with nuns. I remember now how I laughed way too hard at that. Everyone else simmered down and sipped their lukewarm beer. Lottie went silent. The tension began to thaw.

Alisha and her beau left real soon after the commotion died down. I trailed them out as soon as politely possible. Mo insisted on staying. She made me go back to Belmar alone. I remember being confused about that.

That was one of the last nights she stayed over in Edison before she moved in with me and then left for good later that summer of 2000. The mania she showed that night in December of 1999 was all gone when I saw her next, two or three days later. She was quiet, emptied out.

I tap the steering wheel as I picture a timetable in my head. Early in 1999, the Ladder puts out their Young Women of Power and Promise program for the Jersey Shore and four other areas in the state. The whole Ladder thing catches on, with girls reaching out for hope and mentors looking to lend a hand. In August, Lottie's mailing out hold-the-date cards for a big year-end awards dinner to occur mid-December. That would have put the Ladder's special dinner right about the time we were in this house I'm looking at, that night with poor Alisha Sanchez and beau.

But that awards dinner didn't happen. It got cancelled. Because in August of 1999, right after the hold-the-date cards went out, Ladder poster girl Sandy O'Connor got herself murdered.

Maybe that explains Lottie's depressed state of mind that Christmas and her rapid deterioration over the prior months. Her heart was plain broken. But it doesn't explain the outburst from Matt and Maureen when Lottie invited Alisha to work with her nuns. Or maybe, somehow, it does. Maybe something happened to Alisha because of that night. Because of Lottie Logan's pure joy at Alisha's charitable works. Something that didn't end with Alisha's brutal death. Something that continued to wipe out the Jersey Shore Ladder girls.

A guy on the sidewalk passes by my car window. He rocks side to side as he walks. He's got a golf club with him, and he's using it like a cane, the club in his palm and the handle hitting the ground. He passes me, muttering something about something that didn't work out in his life. I know from that. Lord, I been there. I'm there still.

I gaze at the house again. One day I'll go back to our old summer house where Maureen left me, and I'll look up at our bedroom window where I loved her and down the street where I lost her. And I'll say goodbye there too.

I remember a night long ago. I kissed Maureen good night as we sat in a car almost in the same spot I'm sitting in now. It was early on in our relationship, and I had to drop her back home because she had no place else to stay. It felt like a high school date. I remember the kiss, and I remember her saying she wanted us to stay forever young, frozen in time like we were right then. Time, she said, isn't forgiving. She burst into Dylan's song about it and then kissed me for what felt like forever. Like she badly needed what I had inside. She got out of the car and climbed the concrete stairs to her front stoop. She smiled at me before she disappeared into the dark inside.

As I peer up from the car, a third-floor light turns on. I blink up at it. The light in all that black above stings my eyes. I shake my head to be sure I'm seeing right. I watch and wait. A thousand heartbeats later the light goes off. Then nothing more except the fading bright flash at the back of my eyes.

What the fuck was that? No one's supposed to be here.

A minute later a dark shape slips out of an alley two houses down and zips down the street toward me. The figure stops abruptly at a car and gets in. The car light doesn't come on.

The car comes to life and hurls in my direction. I'm down face first in the front seat when it passes. I hear it slow down when it goes by.

I pop up. The third floor is still dark. I make a decision. Five blocks behind me, right off this street, is the entrance to the turnpike. I start the car when the other is two blocks down and pull a U-turn. I follow it, keeping two blocks behind, my lights off. Just another beat-to-shit vehicle driving Edison's streets in the bleakness of its long night. The brothers say their goodbyes, grabbing their crotches at me.

The car takes the ramp to the turnpike south. I switch on my lights as I get to the ramp. I accelerate, and the car ahead goes the speed limit in the right lane. I do the same a couple cars behind.

Another light goes on. Inside the deep recesses of my brain this time.

That December night with Alisha, Lottie kept asking about Alisha's work in Asbury Park. Alisha told her about the affordable housing project. And she added that she worked with poor kids on the weekends or something like that.

Lottie lit up like the Christmas tree. She wanted Alisha to meet her nuns.

Lottie was trying to enlist Alisha in something. She was trying to get her to be a Ladder mentor. Lottie was not giving up on the Ladder even though it had seemingly died with Sandy's last breathe on the pavement of that parking lot. That's what got Matt and Mo so agitated. That's what brought the night to a screaming crescendo. The Ladder.

The Ladder was alive and well.

Forty-Seven

"Is that fuckin Logan making all that racket?" Rizzo looked up at the night sergeant who's just dropped the Logan file on his desk.

"Yup. It's a harvest moon tonight, and Logan's starting to howl. But check the file, chief. He's got a union lawyer springing him as soon as he gets here."

"Guaranteed that gives us a few hours by the time he gets here."

"No, contact's been made. Dude's on his way."

"Fuck." Rizzo got up from his office chair and turned into a hallway. He signaled the guard to open the door and headed down to the cells. Only one was busy tonight. Matt Logan's.

Logan looked through the bars. His hair was wet with sweat, and his face was freshly puffy and red. Like he'd been banging his head on the bars before Rizzo walked in.

"Logan, what the fuck is wrong with you?"

"I can't be in here tonight."

"Where do you need to be?"

"Home. In Edison."

"It's getting near dawn. What you need to do is shut the fuck up and let me get a little work done so I can get home to my wife, who's plenty pissed off at the hours I'm keeping."

"I can't be blamed for what will happen tonight."

"How'd you get a lawyer so fast?"

"I can't be blamed."

"Meaning what?"

"You'll see. You'll see. Just don't blame me. I've been trying to keep a lid on it. I've been trying. But it's out now. It's out." He sat on the cot at the back of the cell and then slumped over on his side, pulling up his feet. "It's done."

Rizzo watched him. The guy was seriously troubled. Textbook troubled. Rizzo needed to call Crombie. Time to make sure this guy doesn't ever see his name on a duty list again, and time to make sure he permanently loses his department firearm.

Rizzo scanned the wreckage Darby had done to Logan's face. Guy never had a freakin chance. Rizzo smiled. Couldn't happen to a better guy.

He headed back to his office and opened Logan's folder. He saw that Darby had given a careful statement documenting her non- involvement in the Logan arrest tonight, omitting the shots Rizzo knew she gave at the police car. She had signed and timed it. He squinted at his watch. Twenty minutes ago.

He punched into his computer and opened the JSM file. Jersey Shore Murders. He saw that Oxford University and Dickerson's law firm had already filed their daily reports on suspicious activity, arrests, and other noteworthy items that have occurred in or around Botta's and Dickerson's work and living spaces. Nothing today. Good. He clicked out.

He called security at the hospital where the Bottas were holed up. All was quiet.

He checked the daily log. He spotted a report from Darby Ruane. He looked closer. She filed an update in JSM. What the fuck' she doin in JSM?

He scanned her notes. He caught the Dabny Lane entry and the Ocean Grove address. He clicked through a few more pages and saw that minutes ago Dabny Famula's Social Security Number has been updated in the database after Darby's entry triggered an automated SSN search. He hit a link and saw a dozen other databases he could now search using Dabny's newly entered SSN. He picked the Ocean Grove police database and selects a search range that extends back 12 months. He scanned the results and then called the Ocean Grove night officer.

"This is Captain Rizzo from Belmar. My code is skydoor00."

"Confirmed, Chief. You up late or starting early?"

"Both."

"What can I do for you?"

"I'm doing a records search. You can check my credentials if you pull the scan data up."

"Yes, sir, I see you."

"Your records say you arrested a Dabny Lane last month. I want to walk through what you got and confirm what I see. Same for a Dabny Famula. Use this social to limit the records you pull." He read off the numbers.

"Call you back in five."

It was ten.

"Your Dabny Lane. She got herself arrested on possession charges on the boardwalk in Ocean Grove. Preliminary motions in a couple of weeks."

"That it?"

"Not really. She's got a pretty big file, captain. She's been Dabny Lane for a year or two. She was Dabny Daily for a year. She was Dabny Coleman for a few. I mean, funny girl, right?"

There's a pause, then Rizzo heard some keystrokes and the beeps of programs opening up and data being entered.

"She did time in New York City for meth possession. Three years. Got arrested for possession several other times. Got off. Several assault arrests. One conviction for a nasty assault. I mean, damn, this girl's rough."

"She's one Woman of Promise who's lost her way."

"'Scuse me, sir?"

"Nothin. Just thinking out loud. … She lives on Spray?"

"Far as we know."

"I want you to arrest her."

"Pleasure. What's the charge?" Rizzo hears typing and clicking in the background.

"Murder One. I think she may be our Jersey Shore murderer."

"Fuck a damn duck."

"Yeah. Now move it."

Next he called Darby. She picked up immediately. "You in Ocean Grove?" he asked

Darby pulled the cell from her ear and stared wide-eyed at it. Fuck me, she mouthed. And then she put it back to her ear. "Yes sir," she said in a flat voice.

"Surveilling Dabny Lane?"

"More like Dabny Famula."

"That's her, Ruane, number 10 on the list. Keep an eye out. If you see her leaving, detain her. Ocean Grove officers will be there in a few minutes to arrest her."

"On what grounds?"

"She's a hard addict and has a violent criminal record. She may be our murderer."

"Or our next victim."

"Maybe. But either way? Don't leave. Don't let her leave. I'm there in a few."

Forty-Eight

Darby tossed the phone into the passenger seat. She sat outside the apartment off Spray. She reached behind her to the backseat for her nightstick, warmed it up with her hands and laid it across her legs. She clicked her pistol's safety off and set it next to the phone.

Her eyes went back to Apartment 11, which was on the ground floor facing the street. A light had come on inside maybe ten minutes ago. She counted maybe a dozen apartment doors on each level of the building. Two more levels rose above Famula's. A couple of interior lights glowed in various apartments behind drawn curtains. Three feeble parking lot spotlights shoot dim shafts from the eaves of the building to the spaces assigned to the apartments.

She was parked across the street in a small, unlit lot across from the apartment. Behind her spread the overgrown lot that reached to the old power plant and carousel of Asbury Park.

The moon, nearly full, lolled overhead and drooled faded yellow light into the streets that intersected at the corner of the apartment building. Ocean Avenue to Darby's left headed south to Belmar. Rizzo and his cavalry would probably come that way.

A rising wind whipped up fine spittle from the ocean a short walking distance away. Her windshield gleamed with tiny droplets that refracted the light. She looked through insect eyes like from one of those old horror movies. She pulled her sweatshirt arm down over her hand and rubbed the inside of the windshield to remove some fog.

She spotted movement behind the drapes covering 11's window. Then the light went out. Suddenly a parked car started up to her right, high beams on, and moved down Spray in her direction. Two pale hands gripped the wheel, a white face hovering eerily above. The car's high beams flashed off and on several times as it rolled slowly.

Darby turned the ignition. Her car roared to life.

The door to number 11 opened. In the doorframe stood Dabny Famula, 1999 New Jersey Shore Woman of Power and Promise. Now an emaciated beach punk. Her arms hung thin like rolling pins. Her neck was too weak to hold up what used to be a strong, proud face and a thick head of hair.

Famula peg-legged into the apartment's dimly lit lot. The oncoming car suddenly roared in a mad burst, steering sharply off the road and straight for Famula. Famula swayed in an unseen wind and shielded her eyes from the oncoming high beams.

Forty-Nine

I follow the car from Edison to a darkened street in Ocean Grove that leads past a tired apartment building at the corner of Ocean Avenue. Ahead, down Spray Street and beyond the sand, the dark and unruly ocean awaits. Off in the distance to my left are the sad, hulking memories of Bruce's Asbury and my wasted dreams.

I slow as the car I've followed pulls over to the left side of the road and dies. I pass it, turning my head away, and continue down Spray, making a quick right onto Ocean like I got someplace to go. I pull over a half block down on the right, out of sight of the parked car.

This feels like where we were going from Edison. To confirm my thinking I wait a few minutes to see if the car I followed makes the turn behind me onto Ocean. Nothing.

I reach for my Ozzie Smith bat in back and open the car door. I sprint from the car to the apartment wall facing the ocean and slide along it until I reach the corner. I take a quick look around the edge of the building. The car I followed is still there down the street. Dark. Brooding. Waiting. A pale, watery shape shifts in the driver seat. Something is about to happen.

I pull my head back and wait. Who's driving that car? I look at my watch. Did they let Logan out already? I peek around the corner again. The pale face stares straight in my direction through a misted car window.

Another car slowly comes down Spray and passes the car I had followed from Edison. The new arrival kills its lights and then backs into an empty spot across the street from the building I'm next to. That's Darby's car. When she stops backing in, when she cuts off, I see her inside, scoping out the building facing her.

I pull back and put my head against the wall. What the fuck is Darby doing here?

The three of us wait like that, the cosmic clock tick, tick, ticking. I listen to every drip down the apartment's rainspout, every gasp of wind off the growling ocean, every desperate wave pounding an empty shore. The heavy ocean in the air thickens in the damp darkness.

A car engine suddenly cranks in the night. I can't tell which car, Darby's or the other. Then a second engine comes to life.

I look around the corner and see Darby's expression locked into a tight grimace. The Edison car is suddenly moving down Spray. Its high beams blind me, flashing once and then again, as it bursts forward squealing over the wet pavement. Darby's muscle car, a 3.5-liter monster engine inside, almost goes airborne at the same instant, screaming out of its spot.

I burst around the corner, then stop when I see for the first time the target of the car hurtling down Spray. She's a gaunt figure swaying in an empty, dark lot, her hunched back to me as she waits in the oncoming lights for the beast bearing down on her.

Darby's car knives hot and fast into the driver's side of the oncoming car with a screeching crash of metal on metal. Airbags punch the two drivers quick and hard in the chest and face, thrusting them backward. I hear a muffled gunshot and then Darby's car suddenly accelerates again as if a foot's been planted onto the gas pedal, pushing the tangled wreckage further toward the apartment. The cars sputter loudly into a heap of thick smoke now rising in the mist.

The scarecrow girl sways in the lot, her hands now scraping at her face, screaming. She gimps away from the steaming hunks of metal and back into apartment 11.

I run to Darby as a siren screeches behind me. Tires cry hard and sharp around the corner on wet pavement. A cascade of emergency lights bounce off the night. Brakes squeal. A car door opens, and a voice comes at me from behind.

"Drop the bat, asshole! Drop it! Stay put, or I shoot!" It's Rizzo.

"Help Darby," I yell as I drop Ozzie. "Make sure she's all right."

I fall to my knees, my hands locked behind my head. I'm assuming the position. I'm not fuckin around.

The driver I had followed emerges from the wreckage in a hooded sweatshirt that obscures any and all signs of hair or face. He suddenly shrieks like a banshee and tears off toward Apartment 11.

"Stop," screams Rizzo. Another cop riding with Rizzo runs in a crouch toward Darby's car.

The hooded driver's at the apartment door now, pulling at the handle, pounding on it with two clenched fists. We watch the frenzied, unproductive display as the crouching cop gets to Darby's door and pulls it open. She leans out sideways, anchored to her seat by her seat belt. She's unconscious.

More cop car lights scream past me going the wrong way on Spray and swing to a skidding halt near the smoldering cars. Rizzo runs past me now to grab the flailing arms of the hooded driver at the apartment door. He twists the figure around and rushes it roughly toward the wrecked cars, ripping off the hood. He slams the squirming attacker face down on the Edison car's hood, his right hand now forcing the guy's neck hard into metal. Ocean Grove cops surround them. They point greased and shiny guns with muscled arms that tremble for release.

Lights are popping on randomly in apartments. Curtains draw back to let occupants watch the show.

From our midst comes a feral sound I will remember to the day I die. It rises up above all the shouting and cries, spewing hoarsely, inhumanly, from the body Rizzo has pinned against the car. It rises up amongst us. As from a cornered animal crazed with bloodlust.

Two Ocean Grove cops move to either side of Rizzo, and together they struggle to hold the creature's flailing arms. They force cuffs on one wrist and then another. Rizzo steps away, hunched over at the waist, breathing in big gulps of air.

There, growling, blood dripping from the head-banging Rizzo gave her, bent at the waist, poised to lunge, there, a gray face turned to me, haunted eyes in deep holes. There, crazed in the night's mist below a near-full harvest moon. There, my Maureen.

Her head tilts upward. Her lips pull back.

She howls long and loud into the night.

Fifty

The Ocean Grove cops put Maureen Logan into the back of a squad car. They put her in ass first, handcuffed wrists behind her, manacles now at her ankles. She sits there, quiet now, breathing deeply, her feet dangling outside the car above the shiny wet pavement. Rizzo and two Ocean Grove cops squat in front of her, stanching the flow of blood at her hairline, giving her her rights, asking what's going on, what's up, trying to get her to talk. Three more cops stand off to the side. I'm watching over the shoulders of one of them, breathing hard.

I looked for her for 10 years, and there she is. Right in front of me. I barely recognize her.

She watches the cops blankly, her dulled face moving from one to the other. When they stop talking, she sees me and squints. Her head tilts to one side.

She grimaces. Maybe it's a smile. Her once wavy-brown hair has gone stringy. It's short and bright yellow now. There are patches where you can see her pale scalp. And there's scalp where you can see bloody, painful welts. Like a cancer is eating away at her from the inside out.

Her hollowed-out cheeks form craters where her smile once poked dimples. Her thin, taut, bloodless lips are smeared across her face. Her eyes, still upon me, are small, glassy orbs bobbing in blood-shot. Only the spotlights from the apartment building and the flashing light bars atop the police cars give her eyes any glow of life.

She'll face even more questions and body probes tomorrow, but tonight she's under arrest for attempted murder. I'm the principal witness.

The EMS guys work on Darby and figure she has suffered a concussion and maybe a fracture in her left cheekbone, given the swelling. In a few minutes they'll take her to Jersey Shore Medical over in Neptune where the Bottas are.

Rizzo tells me he's going to the hospital with Darby. The Ocean Grove cops got this now, he says, but he wants to make real sure she gets treated as a cop injured in the line of duty. That's how he's going to write this up. She's going to get a medal for valor.

I ask him about the gunshot I heard. He tells me the airbags came out with such force they triggered the pistol Darby had on the seat next to her, its safety off. She's lucky the bullet didn't hit her or the gas tank. Or both.

I find Darby awake, her big eyes blinking. She's lying down with her head elevated on a couple of pillows in the back of the EMS van.

"Romeo, Romeo," she says as her eyes fill with tears. "Time to shake that Juliet. Look at her. Look at what she became. You see that, right?"

I grip her hand and kiss her forehead. "Let 'em take care of you, okay? Please?"

Her tears refuse to fall. She's looking into my eyes, gripping my hand. "Let her go."

I brush away some hair that's fallen over her eye. She's still searching my eyes, worried now on top of being concussed.

The EMS guy asks if I'm coming. I say no and jump out the back. I tell Darby I'll check in on her later. She nods and lifts a hand. Another EMS guy shuts the rear doors and they take off. The van's siren and lights shoot down Spray to Ocean.

The remaining Ocean Grove cops work the crime scene. It's going to be a long night. A couple of them are just inside apartment 11, talking to tonight's intended victim. They let me hang in the doorway and listen in.

Best I can figure, Dabny Famula has been saying she's Dabny Lane. She's high as the moon tonight, still swaying in a breeze of her own making.

Turns out Maureen had approached Dabny downtown earlier in the day, and they arranged a buy tonight. Dabny was to be in the parking lot at an agreed-upon time, look for Maureen's car with the flashing headlights, and have her money out to swap for Maureen's promised meth bag.

But that was not to be. Maureen was settling old scores, not settling up on deliveries.

Dabny tells the cops she has no idea about a serial murderer going after the Women of Power and Promise. She laughs at that one and puts her hands out, palms up, inviting the cops to check her out. "I mean," she says, "you see any promise here? Huh? Any power? Yeah? Maybe? Well, then, whachu gonna pay for it, bitches?"

She flashes me a smile with too much black space between too few teeth. She makes me the same offer. "Hey boy, you see anythin promising over here that you wanna pay for? Huh?" I'm thinking no, and I back out of the door.

I call Bosco from Isa's car, and we agree to do an online story about the capture. No speculation, just facts. We'll let it all sit a couple days until the Thursday print edition where we'll add some content on how this might be the end of the line for the Jersey Shore murderer, Maureen Logan. "We gotta make it good, Bernie. Work on it."

The night keeps misting, wanting to rain, as I head back to Isa's car. I sit and watch as the wind off the ocean pushes sheets of suspended droplets inland, past the lamp lights on the boardwalk, over the black street, around the houses heading down Ocean.

I feel empty. As empty as Maureen's eyes, as hollow as her unearthly shriek to gods unseen and unknown. I wonder who those gods might be. I wonder where they went.

I turn the key and drive off. I want to get back to Isa's warm bed. I want to hold her tight. Juliet is dead. By her own poison, not mine.

Fifty-One

I am in bed with Isa when I get a call from Rizzo. She turns away from me and onto her side as I swivel around to sit at the opposite of the bed, my bare feet on the floor.

Turns out Matt Logan's union lawyer didn't quite finish all the paperwork that was needed to spring him, so he's still locked up. Turns out Logan wants to talk. To me. Rizzo can't guess why but tells me to hurry up if I'm going to do it.

A little while ago I had told Isa about finding Maureen after all these years. At least what was left of Maureen. I told her Maureen was the Jersey Shore Murderer. Isa had quietly listened to me, staring blankly at my lips, almost reading them, as I told her how I had followed Maureen back from Edison to Ocean Grove.

"A powerless woman goes after women of power," she said. "Ain't that the way."

I turn on my side after hanging up on Rizzo. I tell Isa's back that Matt Logan now wants to talk to me. Isa says nothing.

I dress and grab the car keys off her bedroom bureau. I say see ya later, hoping for something back. I turn and leave with nothing, hoping there is a later, thinking there may not be.

I get to the station and hear that Logan already knows his sister has been arrested in Ocean Grove. One of the Belmar cops had let it out.

I sit on a bench across from his cell. He says nothing. I remind him I'm not with the cops and that talking to me is harmless. He knows that ain't true, but it breaks the ice.

I tell him I followed Maureen from their house in Edison to Ocean Grove.

He nods, his head heavy with his thoughts. "That's what I wanted to tell you. Then the cop told me she'd been caught. So you know what I was gonna say. You can go now."

"You were going to tell me she was there? That's it?"

"I kept telling them here that I needed to go home. I needed to be there."

"To stop her tonight?"

"To be with her when it was over. When she was done with all of them."

I sit back against the wall. He wanted to, what, celebrate with her? What a pair. I tell him about the light I saw on the third floor of their house.

His eyes are bright wet now. "Yes."

"She's been living there with you all this time." It wasn't really a question.

Matt Logan nods again, drawing closer to the front of the cell. "Not long after she left you down in Belmar, she came back to Edison."

"Why?"

"Who knows. No place to go, man. No money. Who knows."

"She had me."

The Matt Logan I knew would have fired off a salvo of insults. Anything but you, shithead, that sort of thing. But he was done with me. He was all done. "Not anymore."

"What's that mean?"

"Lots of stuff went on, man. Things got fucked up pretty bad that last month."

"After your mother died."

"Yeah."

"What happened that Christmas when Alisha Sanchez and her fiancée came over and you cooked dinner and all?"

He studies his socks.

"Rizzo says your mother didn't help you out of your hell hole. You were her failures, right?"

"We weren't her anything. We were nothing at all."

"When did Maureen start killing?"

His lips tighten. "It wasn't like that." Then he shakes his head.

We wait in silence some more, then I prod. "You took care of her all these years."

Nothing.

"You kept her safe. You covered for her. You dumped her car off in Belmar. Not to go after me. That turned out to be an added benefit years later. You helped make it seem she had disappeared or come to a bad ending.

"She always took the train to Belmar. So if they found her car there, they'd know you were lying. It would look like she disappeared from Belmar. Disappeared when she was last with you."

"You planted the articles when the car was later found and seized?"

He nods. "I got rushed when I was planting the shit. I was piling on. I shouldn't've."

He walks around the cell, and I wait for a few slow turns.

"Matt, why."

He stops. "Huh?"

"Why did she ..."

"Fucking why? Jesus. That fucking Ladder list."

He starts walking in circles again, his pace stepped up. He talks quickly into the middle of the circle. I stand and walk to the cell to hear better.

"You need to know how bad it was," he's saying. He repeats himself.

"When?"

"Back then. All of 1999. It was all about the Ladder and nothing else in our house. About the fucking chicks of fuckin promise. It got up inside Maureen and ate at her. It got worse and worse. Our mother abandoned us for them. For her Ladder girls. Mo took it bad."

"But she was in her late twenties by then. A full-blown adult. Why did she care so much?"

Matt shakes his head furiously as he walks. "It didn't start with the Ladder girls. They were just the latest beautiful and pure thing our mother obsessed over. Just the latest gift from her God to make up for us. Maureen just wouldn't any more. Not after you showed up, Bernie."

I'm hearing the words he's saying and then I hear what he means. "You wanted to talk to me right now so you could blame me for Maureen. That's the real reason. You wanted to say I did it."

"You made her feel special, Bernie. That made her very pissed off at how it had been up until then. She acted out."

"Fuck you." But I thought about it in that dank hallway.

The night before she left me, Mo told me my love made her new. Gave her life. I had finally gotten around to being convinced that that was a good and noble thing despite how we ended up. I was feeling good about that. Feeling good I made a difference in someone's life.

But I realize something now. And it's like a freight train ramming through. I've been searching for Mo not to find her, but to find what proved I made a dent in this world. That I wasn't just passing through.

I made a dent all right. So forceful I punched a hole unleashing Mo's vengeance. Her righteous crusade to expunge all that had pained her in this world. It may have started with Sandy, but I had sent her on that crusade to kill her attackers and unbelievers. My love did that.

"Maureen started hating the Ladder girls after me?

"She hated them since the beginning. The perfect girls, she called them. She started, well, acting out, after you showed. She got really got focused on it about the time she left you.

He stops. And then comes a low voice. I push between the bars to hear.

"She found Sandy first. It just happened that way. Sandy was the first Ladder girl to go. And that ended the Ladder awards that year. No awards, no nothin."

Logan suddenly stumps to the front of the cell. I recoil.

"Sandy's death about killed my mother." He's smiling now. "She died in the spring of 2000 some months later, but she went lights out with Sandy. Maureen killed the Ladder awards and my mother the day she killed Sandy. I actually thought it might end then. That Mo was finished."

"But Alisha Sanchez showed up."

"That night, Bernie. It snapped that night, forever."

I think back to that night with Alisha Sanchez and her finance. "So Alisha pops back into Maureen's world that December around the time the Ladder dinner was supposed to happen," I begin. "Your mother, despite it all, despite her losing Sandy and the Ladder dinner she had worked so hard on, your mother came alive that night with Alisha, right?"

"You saw it. She was all back in business. She started making another Ladder list."

I remember the disgust on Maureen's and Logan's faces that night. That was it. Disgust. Revulsion. Their cries were screams of no more. *No more.* I should have seen it in their eyes.

I step back from his jail cell and lean against the wall behind me. My love made Maureen new, a brand new killer.

Logan grabs the cell's bars in his two beefy hands. "That night Mo realized, we both knew, that the line of perfect girls would never, ever end. They'd keep coming back. Again and again. So, yeah, Alisha was next. She was killed even though she wasn't a Ladder girl."

"So she kills Alisha right before she moved in with me at our beach house."

He nods. "True love."

"Why didn't you stop her from killing Alisha?"

He blinks at me. He's not hiding it. He wanted those perfect girls gone too.

I head back down the hall. I remember one last thing, and I head back.

"Matt." It comes out as a whisper and I realized I'm tired, but it sounds more pathetic than tired. "Was she working at that trucking company in Edison? That night I called you?"

"You never gave up, Ruane. She knew you never gave up on her. They teased her about her ex showing up the next day when she came into work. Her poor, lovesick, scorned boyfriend. She had to quit the job because of you. She wasn't too happy about that. It was a sweet gig, working for our uncle, and he paid her good cash off the books. But she knew you'd never give up trying to find her. She knew she had to move on. But she liked that you chased her. That you still loved her."

I heard his accusation. I heard hers. "I validated her mission to kill."

Logan's smile cut me like he wanted it to. "She was on cloud nine, Bernie boy."

Fifty-Two

After talking to Logan, I briefed Rizzo. He listened quietly. We both knew that no prosecutor would use what I learned. Even a moron defense lawyer could convince a judge and jury that what I did was nothing but a police setup with Logan having no counsel.

"Yeah, there's that," says Rizzo. "But now we know Matt's role. And that she did it alone. I'll rest easier."

"But the only evidence you got against Maureen is in Dabny Famula's attempted murder. You got nothing on any other of these Ladder girls."

"We will. We got that Ronnie Landry tape. We'll find that bat. We'll show it was Maureen who swung it. We got some good clues in that Francine Waterman hit-and-run, including the witness who saw a car lookin awful like the Logan kids'. And, up in Edison, the cops searching the Logan house found Allie Formosa's car keys in Mo's desk."

"That's huge."

"Can't use it yet. But you're right. Step by step, my man. Step by step."

Rizzo tells me that by noon today the cops in Edison would wrap up their search of the Logan place. He tells me he's arranged with Crombie to let me into the Logan house for one last look-see when they finished up.

"We need your eyes," Rizzo says. "I want you to walk every room and think what it says about Maureen. Especially the top floor where she lived all these years."

He tells me that anything I put in a story, including photos, has to be pre-cleared with him and Crombie. I agreed. What choice did I have? I needed to get inside. I needed to prove, to me, that Mo's carnage all these years wasn't me. It wasn't me. I gave her love. She did herself in. I had been Romeo at last.

So I'm back in Edison. Once again, I park in front of her house. Once again, I remember her walking up these stairs to her front door.

Fuck it, I say out loud, and I lock the car behind me and head up the concrete stairs.

The place is a torn-up mess. I head straight to the second floor and stop by her old room. I hadn't noticed the slippers underneath the bed the day after she disappeared. They were there now. I wonder if every so often Mo would come back here, to sleep, to dream her little girl dreams before things got bad.

I head down the hall and reach for the pull-down ladder in the ceiling of the second-floor hallway. It falls down noisily, with it dust that floats in the weak sunshine that even heavy curtains can't block. I climb up and look around like a gopher coming out of its hole. It's roomier than you'd guess from street level. It's a room I hadn't known about.

The ceiling, the exposed wood of the roof above, comes to the shape of an A. A solitary light bulb with a pull string dangles from the pinnacle. A runner covers the wood floor from the ladder to the window overlooking the street below. Otherwise it's exposed wood planks. There's a bed in the far corner, the mattress now lifted on its side. An empty refrigerator squats in the corner. A desk and computer paraphernalia are covered with fingerprint dust. Lots of weights, stretch bands, and running shoes hang out, waiting for action. A punching bag droops from one of the rafters.

Rizzo told me that the Edison cops had seized Maureen's laptop and her drugs. The drugs were potent and plentiful, guaranteed to combat depression and rampant anxiety with delusion or stupefaction. The laptop had been wiped clean. The hard drive was removed and was nowhere to be found. They were going to send the laptop to the FBI to see if anything might be salvaged. They held out little hope.

Her closet is a metal valet rack on wheels. It's empty now but Rizzo told me they held a bunch of jeans, a few short skirts, some Ts and blouses, a winter coat. I look at the list of items I wrote down as he was talking.

They also found a couple of black hooded sweatshirts that sounded an awful lot like the one worn by the assailant in the Philly garage video. I make a mental note to tell Rizzo they also sound an awful lot like the hoodie worn by the person who shadowed Isa that night she discovered the hammering to her car.

A small bureau of drawers held what was left of her sweaters, blouses, and underwear. I lean down and smell the inside drawers, to breathe Maureen in maybe. The odor that assaults me is sour, rancid. I try to bring back how sweet Mo smelled the day she left me for good. The day she told me she had been reborn with my love.

I can't remember. I don't want to.

Maureen was always writing something, so the loss of the hard drive is bad news. The cops found nothing – no journals, books, drives, or flashes in her room or anywhere in the house. That wasn't right.

I scan the top floor for hiding places. I know she kept her story somewhere. If she had destroyed it, it would have been because there was nothing left for her to accomplish in this life, no more story to tell. Which didn't ring true. She'd write her story 'til the bitter end, I'm betting. Even if she had killed Dabny, there were still two more on her list. She wasn't done with the killing spree I had launched her on.

I lower myself into her desk chair and gaze at the study lamp she must have flipped on last night. The surprise, the sudden contrast with the black of night, the fact that I was looking right up here when it came on, all of that made it seem like this little lamp was atop a lighthouse. It was a beacon in the night. Nothing mystical here, right?

I look out the window to the street below. I was parked almost exactly where I had parked two nights ago. Right below Mo's window. That night I would have been in plain view, staring up like a goofball at her house.

Had she seen me?

I eye the lamp again. She had had it on for a good 10, 15 minutes. Had she been writing a goodbye note? A last entry? Sending up a search flare?

I look under the desk and chair. Nothing. I look at the two-by-fours nailed to the ceiling. Nothing loose. I look at the beacon lamp. Inside it's dusty shade there's nothing taped. I turn the lamp over. Nada. I rummage through her desk drawers. Nope. I sit back. And breathe. And let thoughts fly.

I pick up the lamp again. It sounded funny when I just put it down. I knock a knuckle on the base, which is a little larger than a CD. Something clunks inside.

I slam the base of the lamp against the desk a couple of times and then pick at the bottom panel. It snaps off and spins to the floor, along with a single USB flash drive the size of a thumb tip. Velcroed to the top of the panel are seven other drives.

I shit a brick and call Rizzo before touching anything else.

Fifty-Three

A little more than 12 hours after Maureen's arrest in Ocean Grove, *The Beach Star* shouted the news from a banner headline. "JERSEY SHORE MURDERS SOLVED". It went national and international as soon as we put it on the wires. ABC, NBC, CBS, PBS, and CNN each did two-hour-long specials this weekend. MSNBC and CNN's Anderson Cooper did background reports on "what really happened." Every damn nun in New Jersey, all 57 of them, did interviews and for once scored more headlines than the priests.

Sister Seton Margaret called to thank me. The Ladder was receiving hundreds of donations, and she was getting pressure from the archbishop to step into the shoes of Sister Helen Molson and resurrect the group. She was thinking she would do it. I told her that Sister Helen up in heaven above would be damn proud of her protégé. I know that to be true because one night in a dream my Irish relatives told me so, and Sister Helen Molson was right there with them, downing a pint atop my glistening bar. When I told Sister Seton about my dream, she said she had to go and hung up. I don't think her saints in heaven clustered at Irish bars. Pity.

For days you couldn't avoid the media's histrionics about the Jersey Shore Murders. The booze flowed, and the women danced on tables. Fireworks lit up the night skies after days of parades. Ribbons and decorations festooned the streets of small and large towns alike. Medals got pinned. Chests swelled. Children ran through the streets strewing rose petals behind them.

Case closed. Justice done. Life, it goes on.

Bosco spent the next week nominating his paper and me for every single award that moved. And figuring out how to get to Stockholm, Sweden, to accept his Pulitzer. "I got to write my speech, man. It's a once-in-a-lifetime thing, you know."

I broke it to him that the Nobel Prizes were awarded in Stockholm. The Pulitzers came out of Columbia University in good ol' New York City. It actually made his day. Just a train ride north. No hotel charges. No buying rounds for people he didn't know anyway.

I needed a break and got away for a few days.

For the first time since I got back, I went to see my older brother in Rahway. I arrived unannounced, so I waited forever, and then we just sat and looked at each other through the thick plastic partition. After a half hour, I left saying I'd be back. He asked which decade. I said I was stopping by Flamingo's gravesite. I said I missed her. He said nothing to that. He didn't ask about Darby, and I didn't tell him anything either. His loss, not hers.

I went to Flamingo's gravesite and softly sang the lyrics on her tombstone that Darby belted out in my car that day. I told her I would keep an eye on Darby. I promised to return with her.

I went to see Francine Waterman's mother in her four-room, one-story Sears house on 7th. She was day drunk again. I wanted to tell her in person we had her daughter's killer. I wanted her to see some light ahead. She said she'd try. I got up to leave, and she gave me a hug so tight I had to pull her off me to get out the door. I promised to come back. I knew that was a lie, but it got me out of there. And maybe I would.

I visited Anne Botta at the hospital. I got to meet Jennifer Botta. I promised to see her and her mother in Seaside before Jennifer went back to Oxford in time for the spring semester. Another lie, but I'd try.

The flash drives I found in Maureen's room were analyzed. Turns out they contained musings, mutterings, electronic doodles, and artwork, mostly nonsense. Over 1,000 poems, with dozens near the end, the last couple of years when I was around, having one theme – I'm someone loved, I am alive and to be cherished, and no one can deny that, and if you do it's at your peril.

One drive was quite useful, however. I wondered if it was the one that leapt from its Velcro perch when I banged the lamp on the desk, risking everything to be discovered. It contained Maureen's journal entries for the murders she had committed. Each and every one. Her confessions in her own writing saved from her laptop onto the disk.

Confessions for each of the Ladder women she killed plus those she mistook for Ladder women and killed plus one more from an old *Star-Ledger* top ten list, Alisha Sanchez, that she killed. Maureen would write an entry telling dear reader how her next victim would die. And then she'd write an entry telling dear reader how it actually went down. On the same flash drive was a copy of the Ladder newsletter announcing the awards to all the girls and containing their interviews.

There was nothing blaming me. And I felt weird relief about that.

Sandy O'Connor was Maureen's first off the Ladder list. Maureen crushed her face and head some eight months after she was included with nine others on the Ladder's Young Women of Power and Promise list for the Jersey Shore. Maureen's last entry was for Dabny Famula. Dabny was going to meet the same fate as Francine Waterman and Mary Angliotti. Hit-and-run. Maureen confessed she'd be tempted to be done with her list, even if she had to take two substitutes for Botta and Dickerson. Perfect girls were all the same, so substitutes were perfectly acceptable according to Maureen's twisted logic.

Matt Logan talked once the Monmouth County prosecutor put the screws to him by threatening to charge him with the Jersey Shore murders himself. As in life in prison in some dank hole where inmates plan special surprises for cops gone bad. He broke down in a heartbeat and told them what he told me when I saw him in his cell, and more. After a proper reading of his rights. He accepted the lesser charge of accessory to murder. He'd get some time but not as much. He was getting off light, probably, but at least they were putting him away for a while.

Matt talked about the Ladder kills. It started with Sandy and he did nothing then, and nothing after. The night Maureen killed Sandy, she had come home covered in blood, weeping, a demon raging inside her. Their mother was out that night, of course, heading to the Breakers in Spring Lake down the shore to work with the nuns on the Ladder awards.

Matt Logan had to talk it out, wouldn't stop, according to Rizzo. He felt duty bound to educate them on the righteousness of his sister's acts. Was it his job to turn her in, he'd ask. His job to get her help? His job to just say no? Not before they were all dead. She was owed that, wasn't she? Didn't she deserve to get something out of life? Matt Logan thought so.

Rizzo stopped by the Honeypot one day to give me a copy of something from Maureen's death journal. The last two pages, he told me. It was a note. Written that last night, I thought. Probably when she flipped on that light. With me down below looking up at her. Maybe she wrote it looking down at me from the window.

At the top of the first page she had penned *To Ruane*. What she called me when she was serious. *From Mo*. And she had written out song lyrics. Dylan's.

> *May your hands always be busy*
> *May your feet always be swift*
> *May you have a strong foundation*
> *When the winds of changes shift*
> *May your heart always be joyful*
> *May your song always be sung*

May you stay forever young

A chilled wind went down my back. I still feel it. Just like she wished that one night on the street below long ago. When we both had a chance maybe to get out of here alive.

The second page was a Mac sketch, mostly in black and white. No writing. No lyrics. A rainy day at the beach, no sun, a ferociously angry black ocean. A man and a woman walking the beach some distance apart. No dog. The woman was tall and sharply thin, a dagger of a blood-red ponytail lunging down her back like a weapon. Isa.

Rizzo shrugged. "Not sure what to make of these. Figured they were for you. Given that beach house you shared with her and all."

I thanked him.

The more I think about it, the more I'm sure she saw me from the third floor that night I finally said goodbye. I may have been looking right back at her, but I simply didn't see.

Fifty-Four

Isa and I sit at our table at Surfer's Porch. We face the ocean. Large waves flex in the golden light dropping from a robust half moon that hangs low and big in the inky night sky.

We had joined Darby earlier for her award ceremony hosted by Rizzo down at the municipal building. She had received a special award for valor, with a representative from the Governor's office, Belmar's mayor, the newly anointed Chief of Police Mitchell Crombie from Edison, classmates from John Jay, colleagues from her last stint in Freehold, and Belmar's own men and women in blue all toasting her with cheap champagne in paper cups. Weed was responsible for the videotaping and Bosco paid a photographer for the occasion and was doing the front-page story himself.

It had been a good night. Isa and Darby even hugged out a long good-bye. I look across the table at Isa who's quiet, nursing a brandy, looking beautiful.

She leans over and takes my hand, and opens it palm up on the table. She traces the lines with a sharp fingernail painted blue for Darby's big night. "See this top line that crosses left to right across your hand? That's your heart line. It stops mid-palm and then, strangely, shoots up on a crooked angle to the top of your hand."

I look at it. "Meaning?"

"Who the fuck knows. I'm not a palm reader. But it shows me the direction of you heart. It looks like heart, interrupted."

"Isa ..."

"I am used to you not being there for me. I don't need you to be there."

"What ..."

"I need you to love me, if you're going to. That's all." She stands. "Come with me."

265

She walks out of the Porch, across Ocean Avenue and onto the sand. She walks to the waterline. I walk next to her.

She points out to the ocean. "See how the moon throws down a brightly lit path to the horizon?"

"I do."

"It's not a path, Bernie. It's an illusion. It's deep, deep water that will fill your throat and your lungs and drown you." She turns and puts her arms around my neck and pulls me into a slow dance. "That's no path from this shoreline, Bernie. It ends where it ends."

Our bodies touch and she whispers into my ear, "And hand in hand, on the edge of the sand, they danced by the light of the moon, the moon, the moon, ..."

"They danced by the light of the moon," I finish.

She unlocks her hands and stands back. She looks at me, looks out at the ocean, and then turns and walks back the way we came. "Make up your mind, Bernie, where you wanna go, if you wanna love. You've run out of room. And you're running out of time."

She walks away. The light of the moon reveals her footsteps over shifting sand leaving me at water's edge.

"Wait up," I call.

THE END

Look for Bernie Ruane's next Jersey Shore Noir Original – *Money Like Sand*

Made in the USA
Las Vegas, NV
03 November 2021